HIS SINS

Also published by Sylvia Behnish is "Roller Coaster Ride With Brain Injury (For Loved Ones)". This non-fiction book is the story of her partner's journey during the first year following his serious motorcycle accident. (Published by Trafford Publishing).

HIS SINS
Book I

Sylvia Behnish

Published by:

Trafford
1663 Liberty Drive, Suite 200
Bloomington, IN 47403, U.S.A.

Order this book online at www.trafford.com
or email orders@trafford.com

Most Trafford titles are also available at major online book retailers.

Cover design by Kerry Farrell
Edited by Maggie Taylor

ISBN: 978-1-4269-0680-0 (sc)
ISBN: 978-1-4269-0681-7 (dj)
ISBN: 978-1-4269-0682-4 (e-b)

*Our mission is to efficiently provide the world's finest, most comprehensive
book publishing service, enabling every author to experience success.
To find out how to publish your book, your way, and have it available
worldwide, visit us online at www.trafford.com*

Trafford rev. 02/04/2010

Trafford
PUBLISHING® www.trafford.com

North America & international
toll-free: 1 888 232 4444 (USA & Canada)
phone: 250 383 6864 ♦ fax: 812 355 4082

For my family – my love for them grows daily;
like flowers in a garden.

If you look deeply into the palm of your hand, you will see your parents and all generations of your ancestors. Each is present in your body. You are the continuation of each of these people.

-   Thich Nhat Hanh, Vietnamese Monk,

"His Sins" is a captivating novel about how some decisions have the capacity to withstand lifetimes and generations. We follow one man's decisions and see how the ripple effect lasts generations affecting not only his children, but his children's children, and their children also. It makes us think twice about the lives we lead, and the intentions we hold dear to our hearts. It warns us of our motivations and how they not only affect our own individual lives, but also the lives of those we love most, and even the lives of those we will never meet. *"His Sins"* makes us remember that what we do is important, and what we feel is even more so. - *Helen Edwards, M.Ed., Mental Health Therapist*

PART I   Alexander and Janet

Chapter I

Alexander sat, sullen and silent, a brooding scowl etched on the forehead of his young face, giving him the appearance of having aged prematurely. His icy hands circled the mug of steaming sweet tea while he watched from beneath hooded eyelids. Seething with anger, he saw his father double over in a bout of uncontrollable coughing, the phlegm heavy in the older man's congested chest. After the spasm had passed, his father sat up and wiping the beads of sweat from his face with the back of his coal-blackened hand, he reached for his own mug of the hot sweet black tea. Swallowing the tea in great, hurried gulps, fearful of being late for his shift in the pit, he began another bout of strangled coughing. Looking away, Alexander was no longer able to watch his father.

At only thirty-eight years of age, his father gave the appearance of being a much older man, as did most of the men who spent their lives in the mine. *'The mine will kill him,'* Alexander thought bitterly, unable to hide the anger he felt at his father's acceptance of what life had dealt him, *'but it'll not be getting me.'*

Turning to face his father, his thoughts focused, as they were every morning, on how much he hated going down into the pit. *'Why dinna he try to better himself and make life better for the family? He dinna care 'bout leaving the mine but I'll not stay a minute longer than I've got to,'* Alexander vowed under his breath while his father continued to gasp for air.

"Give over with you and help your Da," his mother cuffed him on the side of the head. Her shrill voice caused him to purse his lips tightly together knowing that whatever he would answer in response would only earn him another cuff for his effort.

"There's naught wrong with me, Elsa. We'd best be leaving now, lad." He picked up his meal bucket, the tally lamp and flask of pit oil. Alexander followed him with the 'ricketty' and the black powder.

"You help your Da now," his mother's harsh voice followed him into the cold morning air. "He don't need no lazy lump of a son when he's feelin' poorly."

By the time they reached the entrance to the mine, having pedalled on their bicycles in the freezing rain, Alexander's clothes were as damp as his spirits. *'No point in worrying none about it with water running in all of the seams too,'* he thought bitterly. Alexander was never dry enough, warm enough or full enough. It was five a.m. and the night was still as black as he knew the inside of the coal mine would be at the bottom of the shaft. No one spoke as the miners were lowered three thousand feet into the bowels of the earth. Each one silent, and each one dreading the thought of yet another gruelling day, knowing that this day could be their last.

Alexander worked with his father in their own area of the mine and today they were working in a coal seam that was only twenty inches in depth. Alexander crept along behind his father, holding the tally lamp as high as possible, it being the only means of lighting their way. He could hear one of the mine's ponies snorting in the distance in their underground stable. Alexander knew that the lives of the ponies were no better than his or his father's, or any of the other miners that worked each day in the mines.

"The ricketty, lad," his father reached behind him and Alexander handed the older man the small hand drill so he could drill holes in the coal seam which he would fill with explosives and a long fuse. "The black powder now, lad."

When the explosives were set, Alexander backed quickly out of the seam, closely followed by his father. Alexander always said a thankful prayer that his father always knew exactly how much black powder to put in each drilled hole. He didn't want his life shortened before he could get out of this black hell-hole. He had plans and, unlike his father, they didn't include spending the rest of his life under the ground breathing in coal dust until his skin turned gray and coughing up his insides by the time he was thirty-five. He was only eighteen and he'd already been down in the mine for four years. *'Four years too long,'* Alexander often thought as he worked silently beside his father beneath the unforgiving earth.

Each time they heard the series of explosions go off, they crawled back into the seams with their picks. It was Alexander's job to load the tubs with the coal and push it along the underground rail. By the time he had pushed it to the end of the haulage line and placed their identifying pin in the tub, the sweat was running down the inside of his already damp shirt. He retrieved an empty tub and brought it back to the opening of the seam. By the time he returned to where his father was chipping at the coal with his pick, Alexander had cooled off and was shivering again. He constantly alternated between freezing cold or dripping sweat. He wiped his runny nose with the back of his hand and renewed his deep hatred for the mine.

When the cage brought them to the surface at the end of their shift, it was dark again and Alexander often wondered if there had ever really been any daylight. As they bicycled home, Alexander's thoughts were of Janet. They were going to get married and leave Galston forever as soon as she had fulfilled her two year obligation as servant girl to her employers, the Cunninghams at the Manor House, and they had saved enough money to make the trip. He'd leave the damp pit and the coal dust and the constant poverty behind forever. He'd leave the miner's row of attached houses where every house looked like its neighbor with its stone walls and thatched roofs. Some said the row of buildings were eighty years old, most others didn't care. The roadways were unpaved and there was mud and pools of water during the winter in front of every doorstep. Almost fifty people lived in their row with only one earth closet and one ashpit. Human excrement littered the muddy yard and the stench was unbearable but the inhabitants of the row houses had long since become unaware of it. Only the visitors held their noses and wondered why anyone would want to live like this. But visitors weren't welcome so no one worried what they thought.

When they arrived home, Alexander's mother already had the old, dented zinc tub filled with warm water set before the open fire in their only room. Alexander knew that she would have spent most of the afternoon heating it on the old iron grate in the corner. Alexander's father bathed first, always omitting his back because he believed if he washed his back, he'd lose the strength in it. When it was Alexander's turn, he smiled to himself as he scrubbed his back vigorously. Refusing to look at his father, he knew the disapproval he would see there.

Alexander's mother bustled around the room as she finished her preparations for the evening meal. No privacy was required for the miners when they were bathing because everyone knew that they couldn't be seen when they were covered with the black coal dust. Dressing in his threadbare but clean clothing, Alexander sighed. This was the best part of the day when all the coal dust was washed from his body and he could almost believe that he wasn't a collier; that his pores weren't enlarged with imbedded coal dust, that it didn't cling in his nostrils and coat his tongue.

Alexander and his two brothers silently crowded around the small, worn and pitted old kitchen table eating tatties and veggies covered with the remaining drippings from last Sunday's meat. Knowing that they were hungry when they returned from the mine, his mother always had dinner ready for them by the time their baths were finished.

Alexander kept his eyes fastened onto his plate as he scooped the food hungrily into his open mouth, not wanting to meet the eyes of either of his parents. He realized with a shock that he rarely really looked into the faces of either of his parents and decided it was because he didn't want to see the passive acceptance on his father's sunken face or the bitterness that had etched deep lines on his mother's face.

Sopping up the last bit of gravy with a piece of heavy bread, Alexander shifted his chair back, the legs scraping loudly on the uneven stone floor. "I'll be goin' out now," he muttered.

"Our Alex is goin' over to see Janet," his younger brother John chanted.

Alexander's face turned a mottled red. Opening his mouth for a strong retort, his mother quickly intervened.

"Hush your mouth, our John," his mother cautioned while Alexander hurried out the door, anxious to be away from this house where words were rarely spoken except in ridicule or anger.

"Alexander," Janet, with a smile on her round face, rushed to him where they'd agreed to meet at the bottom of the brae. She reached up on tip toes, kissing him on the cheek before putting her small hand into his large one. "Tell me about your day, Alexander," Janet asked breathlessly. Janet always sounded breathless.

Alexander sighed in a rare moment of happiness. He liked the way Janet spoke and often thought it was probably her voice that had first made him notice her. It always made him think that something exciting was about to happen. Of course nothing ever changed but there was always the sound of hope in Janet's voice that enticed him.

"Same as it always is 'cepting everyday I hate the mine more than I did the day 'afore. It's goin' to kill my Da. He's coughin' almos' all the time now and my Mam don't give no one no peace."

"Less than two years now, Alexander and then we'll be able to leave. You'll see your dream, really you will. The time will go quickly. I just know it will happen." Her small hand squeezed his larger one in a quick show of affection.

"Two years! It'll seem more like two hundred years." Alexander put his face in his hands. "Sometimes I think that I'll never get away from this black hole. Look, at it. It's everywhere." He looked at his hands. "Do you think they'll ever be truly clean again?"

Janet put her arms around his hunched shoulders. "ALexander, listen to me. It's going to get better. We're going to be rich when we get to America. Everyone is rich there. Haven't they all said that?"

Alexander nodded his dark head. He knew Janet was right. They would be rich in America and they would work hard to get the money to go there. He managed to save a few pennies each week from his pay packet which he kept hidden away and the rest he turned over to the family. Janet had been saving as well and had done better than he had because she lived at the Manor House.

"Alexander," Janet broke excitedly into his thoughts, "the Missus Cunningham told me today that I am going to be given the task of upper house maid and that I will be earning a few pennies more each week. Isn't that grand?"

"Yes," Alexander answered, happy for her. "It is grand."

"The two years will pass and before we know it, we'll be on that ship and we'll never look back." Alexander's long narrow face lit up in one of his rare smiles. He became bonnier and his dark eyes looked brighter for a brief moment. He ran a rough hand through his dark, wiry hair making it stand up where so recently he had carefully brushed it down flat to his narrow head.

"I have to hurry back now Alexander but I'll meet you here on Sunday afternoon." She reached up and gave him a quick kiss on the cheek again before turning and running back across Oswald's Bridge.

He watched her slightly plump figure hurrying out of sight, her fair hair flying in the breeze she had created, and knew he was a lucky man. He felt she'd be the type of wife a man would want to come home to. She'd not be a carping one like his own Mam.

Chapter II

Alexander was glad of the rare moment he had to himself and would have savored it had it not been for the bad news he had just received. He had stood immobilized when he'd heard the words that had sent his world crashing to the ground where it lay in shattered pieces at his feet. He had only been able to stare at her, wide-eyed and open-mouthed, barely noticing the tears that slid down her face when she had told him. He'd had no words to explain how he had felt at that moment of realization. Finally, turning his back on her, he had left her standing on Oswald's Bridge, a lone figure with fears of her own.

"We almost made it," his fist slammed the rickety kitchen table. "Bloody hell," he muttered. "Bloody, bloody hell."

Another year down in that black hell hole! Leaning his elbows on the table, he covered his face with dirty, scarred hands. His mind desperately sought other options but none appeared to be available to him. He felt the tears prickle behind his eyelids as frustration welled up within him like bile in his throat. Glancing around he yelled to no one in particular, "Another year in this Gawd forsaken house and another year in Hell."

There was to be a wee bairn. They would be getting married in April, as they had planned, but leaving Galston would have to be delayed until after the bairn was born because, as Janet had patiently explained to him, she was already feeling poorly. "We can still leave by the next June," she had promised. "Then the bairn will be strong and it will be safe to make such a trip." In spite of her tears and the fear he saw in her eyes at his anger, she had been adamant when she had told him that they must wait.

Alexander had found it impossible to hide his disappointment and resentment.

"Alexander," Janet had tried to put her arms around him but he had turned his back to her. "It will work out. It's not much longer to wait. We'll be a real family when we have the bairn." But Alexander didn't want a bairn.

The following month, April of 1913, Janet and Alexander were married in the local church surrounded by all of Alexander's neighbors and his family. Janet's family had decided not to participate in the marriage of their middle daughter since they had been hoping for a better marriage for her than to that of a miner.

"Miner's," they told everyone they knew, "are little more than rodents, burrowing in the ground; only coming out at night. They're dirty creatures with coal dust instead of sweat coming out of their pores." Janet had smiled courageously in spite of their hurtful words but Mam Stewart saw the tears in her eyes.

Janet's pregnancy was not as yet obvious but the neighbors whispered that there was likely to be a seven month baby. "She has that look," they said.

"You ken tell by the eyes," another said. They shrugged. "There are a lot of nine pound seven month babies born but who counts anyway?"

After the simple wedding Janet moved into Alexander's parents' home sharing his narrow hurley bed. They hung a curtain around the bed for a modicum of privacy but he knew they could be heard as he had heard his parents' lovemaking these past many years.

The change had been difficult for Janet. At the Manor House, she had a room to herself and although it had been so cold in the winter that the water in her washing jug had frozen and so hot in the summer months that her prized cake of lavender-smelling soap had melted, it had been hers. Janet had once told Alexander that her room had been almost as large as their entire house.

To Alexander it was yet another reason to leave Galston. For as far back as he could remember, they had all lived and slept in one room. Privacy was not a word he was intimately familiar with but he yearned each day for that which he knew nothing about.

During the months immediately following their marriage, Janet changed slowly from the smiling, bubbly girl she had been to one who was always on the verge of tears. Her pregnancy was not an easy one.

Often ill, she retched into the bowl beside their bed. She became thin and drawn except for the large swell of her belly. Alexander thought that the huge mound of flesh, that was her distended belly, was obscene and refused to think of the bairn she carried.

He never spoke to his wife of the child and in fact, rarely spoke to his wife at all. "It's as if the bairn doesn't exist and I no longer seem to exist for Alexander either," Janet had once confided to Mam Stewart.

"Things will be different after the bairn is born," Mam Stewart had answered. But Alexander knew that would not be the case.

The child within Janet's growing belly became a major source of frustration and unhappiness for him. *'It be the fault of the bairn that we still be here crowded like rats into a single room instead of in America where we could be rich,'* Alexander thought as he stared at the floor while he listened to his wife retching in the far corner of the room. Large flies lit on Alexander's hand as he swatted impatiently at them, to no effect. Hearing their continual buzzing in the air around his head further angered him.

"Alexander," she called weakly. "I feel so poorly. My Mam weren't so poorly for this long. Could there be something wrong with the bairn, do you think?" Turning to face the wall when he gave no answer, he heard her crying softly.

"I'm goin' out," he told her as anger boiled over him like water on a hot stove. "I'll be back in a wee while."

He walked down to Oswald's Bridge, glad to be away from the sickness for awhile. It wasn't just Janet. It seemed to be everywhere. His father coughed all the time now but it was still necessary for him to go into the mine because the family needed the money he made. "The house smells evil—sickness and rot are everywhere," he grumbled, kicking a lump of filing with the toe of his worn-out boot. He prayed for deliverance from the mine, from the constant poverty and a chance to go to America.

"Alexander, Alexander," a young lad from the village called from the top of the brae. "Your Mam said to come home straight away. Somethin' terrible has happened."

'The child,' Alexander thought as he ran up the hill. Alexander didn't care about the child but he did, in his own way, still care about Janet.

When he reached the top of the hill, he paused to catch his breath holding his side to ease the stitch he felt there. Raising his head, he saw his mother running towards him in a queer lurching gait on the rutted road.

"Alexander," she moaned, collapsing at his feet while tears cascaded down her crumpled face. "It happened," she whimpered grasping his hand, "I knowed it would." Sobbing with loud sucking gasps, her shoulders shook uncontrollably.

"What happened?" he demanded angrily, impatient with both her tears and her grasping hand. "Answer me now!" He pulled her roughly to her feet and started dragging her back towards the row houses. "Is it Janet?"

She shook her gray streaked head. "Jack—he was there. He said it were ever so quick like." A fresh flood of tears overflowed her red-rimmed eyes. Pulling free from him, she turned, running in the queer gait towards Jack's house.

Jack was standing outside his open doorway, his capless head inclined towards John while his arm circled the shoulders of Richard, Alexander's youngest brother. Jack raised his head as mother and son approached.

"I'm sorry, Alexander. There was naught that could be done."

Alexander saw the tears on the young faces of John and Richard. "Where's my Da?"

Jack jerked his thumb towards the open doorway. "We tried but there weren't nothin' we could do. He was gone ever so quick like. We sent for the Doc but there's naught he ken do neither."

"What happened?" Alexander remained dry-eyed, his voice steady.

"We were playin' them cards your Da loved so much and he started that coughin' of his and it was like he was chokin'. I pounded him on his back but I swear there was no more breath left in him. His coughin' turned to a gurgle and he kept gasping until his face started to turn blue and he fell onto the floor. I lifted him onto one of them beds then sent one of my boys over to your place and your Mam came over with your two young brothers. She took one look at your Da and ran screamin' outa here lookin' for you. There was no stoppin' her."

Alexander nodded and moved slowly towards the open doorway. He stepped carefully over the mudhole in front of the door. Inside he saw his father lying on a hurley bed and with a distant part of his mind was thankful that someone had thought to close his eyes. He looked relaxed and serene like he'd not looked in years. In recent months, his face had become permanently contorted with the effort of coughing. Alexander stood silently looking down at the man who'd been his father and the full implication of what his death meant hit him like a hammer blow between the eyes and he almost staggered backwards with the force of it.

He would now be the head of the family and they would all be depending on him. *'I won't ever be going to America,'* he thought miserably. *'Not now. Maybe never.'* His fist slammed into the palm of his hand. Turning abruptly , he almost knocked over his mother who had been standing behind him staring at the man who had been her husband for almost twenty-one years.

Alexander returned to Oswald's Bridge. *'The bairn! We'd be in America by now if it weren't for the bairn.'* He angrily brushed aside the tears that threatened to fall. He thought of his brother John who at fourteen would now have to go down into the pit. John would take his place and he would have to do the work of his Da. Richard was only nine years old so couldn't legally work in the mine yet.

Walking slowly back up the hill, his hands shoved deeply into his pockets, Alexander looked to neither the right nor to the left. He paused briefly when he reached Jack's house, undecided, before knocking hesitantly on the door.

Jack answered immediately. "The missus is with your Mam and the boys. Me and some of the men will see to your Da and then we'll bring him over and lay him out for you. You go on home to your family, Alexander, they need you now." He laid his coal-stained hand awkwardly on Alexander's hunched shoulder.

Before Alexander opened the door to his own house, he could hear his mother's high-pitched wailing. Janet sat on the edge of the set-in bed, her thin arms wrapped around his Mam's shaking shoulders. In a moment of clarity, he suddenly realized how thin Janet was. He'd not touched her for some time and didn't realize that her once bonny body was now just sharp, jutting bones except for her extended belly. His eyes slid to his mother and the feeling of compassion left him almost as soon as it had come.

She looked up when Alexander closed the door, her eyes enormous in her waxen face. John and Richard sat at the old table watching their mother, tears spilling from their reddened eyes. As Alexander took in the scene before him, all the bitterness he'd been feeling welled up in a lump in his stomach. They would all lean on him, sucking him dry and he would become like his father. The dreams would be squeezed out of him with the hard work and the heavy load of responsibility. Alexander saw his life slip away from him like a puddle of water into the crack of a sidewalk.

"Alexander, I'm truly sorry about your Da. It's so sudden. I knew he was feeling poorly but I never thought he would go so quick-like," Jack's missus said.

Alexander nodded his head. "Your Jack and some of the other men are bringing Da over and laying him out. I'll have to go and make arrangements with the Minister for the funeral."

"Your Da was a good man, Alexander. He was well liked and a lot of folks will want to come and pay their last respects to him. I'll get some of the women folk to help with the food preparation what with Janet being sick and all and now your Mam having this great sorrow to bear."

"We appreciate all your help, Missus Buchanan. I hate to put you out further but would you be kind enough to stay with them for a while longer. I'm away to make arrangements with the Minister."

"You go along, lad and I'll look after things here."

Alexander left the house abruptly without speaking further to anyone else. So deep in his own thoughts was he that he would have been of little comfort to anyone had he stayed.

Alexander realized that unless his father was to be buried in a pauper's grave, without even a proper coffin, he would have to use a large portion of the money he and Janet had been saving for their trip to America; his anger and frustrations intensified.

"My Da will not be buried in a pauper's grave. He'll have a decent send off and a proper resting place," Alexander had told the Minister through clenched teeth.

As he walked home, Alexander was unaware of the heavy drizzle which had started to fall while he had been making the necessary arrangements. He thought of America—where the streets were lined with gold; where there was a job for every man willing to work; where there was music and laughter and meat on every dinner table and now he would never see it. *'I'll end up dying in the mine like my Da,'* he thought miserably.

Returning to the house, he found his mother sleeping fitfully, having exhausted herself with grief. Jack and the men had laid his father out in the corner of the room. A single candle flickered beside him, casting eerie shadows onto his gaunt, gray face.

John and Richard sat motionless at the kitchen table, not appearing to have moved since he'd left them, their eyes fastened vacantly on their father's face. Janet was lying on their bed in a fetal position, her back turned to the room. "Best get to bed now," he told his brothers gruffly.

Alexander chucked his clothes into a damp pile on the floor beside his bed. Not looking at his father again, he climbed into bed. When he lay down beside Janet, she turned to him, putting her thin arm across his chest. "I thought of your Da as if he were my own, Alexander," she whispered. "I'm very sorry he's gone."

"So am I. And our dreams of America are gone now too like a wisp of smoke up the chimney, they are."

"We'll get there. It'll just take us a little while longer. We can't give up on our dreams, Alexander but your Mam needs us here right now."

He turned his back to her without answering, watching the light of the candle create flickering shadows on the opposite wall. Sometime later he saw the shadows of his brothers climbing into the hurley bed they shared. He listened to them whispering quietly to each other and their occasional muffled sobs before they finally fell into a restless sleep.

He could hear Janet's irregular breathing and knew she wasn't asleep yet either. *'But what does she know about dead dreams?'* he asked himself angrily. *'She hasn't been planning this for half of her lifetime.'*

*   *   *   *   *

His Da's burial had been well attended and even the Messrs. Johnlittle, the Coalmasters, had been there to offer their condolences. Each and every one of the miners and their families had come to pay their respect to the gentle, quiet man who had been loved by all of them.

When the shovels of dirt had been thrown onto his coffin, they had to drag his mother away from the gaping hole for fear that she would throw herself down upon him. Closing his ears to her screams of anguish, he had concentrated on the anger he felt at life's injustices, allowing it to grow and fester within him.

When later in the evening Janet had collapsed, the miner's wives had attended to her, murmuring their sympathies. "She looks peaked," one well-meaning soul had told him.

Another said, "She's pitiful thin, poor lass. Poor wee thing, her belly be swollen so big, it looks near to goin' pop and her being only five months gone and all." He heard the gossip and his anger grew.

"She never complains, such a quiet one, I've never seen." He had walked angrily away from the chattering women.

'No,' he had to admit to himself, *'there never are any complaints from Janet, but Mam never quits,'* Alexander thought later when he remembered their gossip. His mother's disposition hadn't improved any and he was the one who mainly bore the brunt of it, as he had always done. *'She surely has it in for me,'* he thought angrily as he lay in a small pool of dirty water chipping away at the coal in the cramped seam.

The day following his father's burial, John went down into the pit with his brother. Alexander gathered up the mining tools that had belonged to his Da and would now belong to him. Climbing onto his Da's old bicycle, he cycled towards the mine with John following so closely behind him that he could hear his brother's teeth chattering in the frosty air.

Alexander showed John how to fill the tubs and place their identifying pin so they would get credit for the coal they dug each day. He showed him where to push the hutch and often, during those first few days, had to lend his back as well because of John's slender build and lack of physical strength. He clamped his mouth tightly shut when he saw tears glistening in John's eyes knowing that if he berrated him, there would be even less work done that day.

Each time Alexander set the explosives, as he had seen his Da do, he said a silent little prayer. If he lacked his father's talent and made an error, they could both be dead or worse than dead. Every miner knew that being a cripple was far worse than being dead. At least a corpse didn't have to be fed and wouldn't become a burden to his family.

*   *   *   *   *

"John, I need more light at this end," he called angrily to his young brother. "John?" He continued chipping, straining his eyes in the dim light. "Where be that tally lamp, John?"

"Alexander?" John crawled into the seam behind him.

"Where you bin? I can't see without that tally lamp. Give it over here."

"Alexander," John looked ready to cry. "Timmy just tol' me to get you. He said that you're wanted up top, Alexander." The tears were bright on his fair eyelashes. "What do you think has happened? Do you think somethin' has happened to Mam?"

"Won't know 'til I get there, is my guess," Alexander replied irritably. "Did he say if you were to come up top too?"

John shook his head. "He just said you were to get to the top quick like."

"Finish loading this coal into the tub and pick more to make a full load and then push it to the end of the haulage. I'll either be back down or send someone for you if you're needed up top."

The tears spilled down John's cheeks and he dashed them away with the back of his coal-stained hand leaving dirty black streaks across his young face.

At the entrance of the pit, Richard ran to his older brother, catching his hand. "Mam said you're to come home real quick, our Alex." Dropping Alexander's hand abruptly, he raced off in the opposite direction from the row houses.

Arriving home out of breath, Alexander's mother met him at the door. "The bairn is going to be born, our Alex. Our Richard has gone for the midwife."

Janet's hair lay in damp strings on her sodden pillow, and her thin face streamed with perspiration as she lay exhausted from the heavy labour. With her eyes closed, her dark eyelashes created long shadows on her waxen face. She seemed not to be aware of his presence as she focused on the bairn within her body.

"How long has she been like this?" he demanded.

"Since shortly after you left. She didn't want to worry you none but I thought you would want to know. This birthing is not an easy one."

Suddenly Janet's swollen body went rigid and a scream was forced from between her clenched lips, the sound filling the room of the small row house.

"Hush," Mam Stewart murmured as she bathed Janet's sweat-drenched face.

Pulling Alexander aside, she lowered her voice, "The pains are five minutes apart and strong but I haven't felt no life from the bairn since they began. I've got water on to boil but to my way of thinking, we've got a long wait for this one."

"Is she going to live?" He felt beads of perspiration begin to form along his upper lip.

His mother shrugged. "Janet's strong and determined but the bairn will only be a wee mite of a thing when he gets here. If it's alive," she muttered turning her back on her son.

"I don't care about the bairn," he spat at her.

She nodded her head knowingly. "That be the reason for all of this," she said, waving her hand to where Janet lay. "God is punishing you. He's punishing you for having so much hate in you. Your Da was content with his lot in life but you never have been. And now to hate this wee, helpless bairn. I warned you." She wagged her finger angrily under his nose. "God will keep on punishing you for the hate you carry but your family will be made to suffer along with you."

His mother's tirade was broken off when Janet screamed again. After the pain had subsided, she breathed in short shallow gasps. "Stop," she whispered, "I... ... can't... ... I don't....Please... ."

"See our Alexander, you mind your mouth now. There's no call to go upsetting her. Now fetch me some towels and then go and see if our Richard has found ol' Missus McCallum. She'll know what to do. I am thinking that this wee bairn is turned wrong end 'round."

16

Alexander left to do as he was bid, glad to be away from his mother's scoldings and the screams of his wife. Returning later, without finding either Richard or the midwife, he opened the door to hear another unearthly scream coming from Janet. The midwife, bent over Janet, was attempting to pull the child from her swollen body.

"Push now dearie," she crooned. "Ah here you be, lad. This wee bairn of yor'n don't want to make it easy for his Mam." She wiped the sweat from her forehead with the dirty sleeve of her dress and resumed trying to free the bairn.

"Ah, here he comes, and not surprised I am that he be bottom first." Janet screamed again as she strained further to push the child from within; her face contorted with the effort of the difficult labour.

"That's right, dearie. Keep pushing now. It won't be much longer now," she coaxed Janet.

"Dear God in heaven," his mother gasped as the baby was finally freed. "God is punishing us," she wailed. "I knew he would."

"The bairn... what's ... the matter?" Janet's voice was weak and almost unheard in the din being made by Mam Stewart.

The midwife looked to where Alexander stood. "Poor wee mite, he didn't have no chance. The cord were wrapped 'round his neck." She held the tiny infant in her hands, its body limp and blue, its face a dark mottled purple stain. Alexander looked at the dark hair covering the top of its doll-sized head before turning his attention to Janet.

Janet stared silently at her first-born child with tears sliding slowly down her cheeks before turning her face to the wall.

*   *   *   *   *

Naming the bairn William Neil, they had laid him to rest next to Alexander's Da and more of their precious savings had been used for his burial. In spite of her weakness after the birth of their child, Janet had fiercely demanded that he be buried in a proper coffin, in a proper grave. Alexander gave the child naught a thought other than to resent the cost of the wee coffin.

After the child had been buried, Janet slowly began to recover her physical strength but emotionally she had withdrawn, spending long hours each day at his graveside. The neighbours noticed how thin and pale she remain. "She has lost her spirit," they said, "and I've not heard her laugh since the wee bairn died."

"And have you noticed that she only enters into a conversation when she has been spoken to directly? She is a mere shell of who she once was. Since she is not communicating with those of us here on earth, perhaps she is talking to the wee one."

"Look at how long she will sit staring straight ahead with that faraway look on her face. The poor girl!"

"She appears to be in her own world, seeming not to hear others. She used to be such a bubbling one." If Janet was interrupted when she was in 'her mood' as it became known by the neighbors, she would turn with a startled and puzzled expression on her sad face. "Do you think she's gone daft?" one asked another.

Mam Stewart, in an effort to help her daughter-in-law, felt that if Janet returned to her position as upper house maid at the Manor House, she would have something else to think about besides the loss of her bairn.

"I would be delighted to have Janet back," Missus Cunningham assured Mam Stewart when they had spoken. "She is such a hardworking girl. What a sad thing to have happen to her. She was so excited about the bairn."

Returning to the Manor House four months after her son's burial, Janet thought often about William Neil as she walked the two miles there and back each day. She remembered his tiny face, blue from lack of air, each time seeing the soft black hair on his doll-sized head. She had loved him fiercely while she had been carrying him, and knowing that his father didn't, she had felt even more for him than she otherwise might have realizing that she would have had to love him enough for both of them.

Life seemed to return to a semblance of normality for the Stewart family but Janet continued to remain withdrawn and unhappy. She found it difficult to smile and almost impossible to laugh. There seemed to be so little to be happy about. She knew that the village gossips placed much of the blame for the change in her on her dour and moody husband. She knew that Alexander had also changed. He had been disappointed at not being able to leave the mine as he had hoped to do before his father had died and before little William had been lost to them. But when she thought about it, she knew that she must bear much of the responsibility as well. Before everything had happened, she had been the one to boost Alexander's spirits but she no longer made any attempt to do so. She had been greatly disappointed in Alexander's feelings towards their baby and his obvious lack of feelings for her since the trip to America had been postponed. The only attention he ever paid her now was when he wanted her as his partner in bed.

Janet had a lot of time to think on her walks back and forth to work. 'That has changed as well,' she often thought. 'There is only anger when he wants me. There's no love between us now when we come together.' Many tears were hastily brushed aside before the Manor House came into view. Trying not to show how she felt, she knew Missus Cunningham often looked sadly into her face when she saw the hint of tears dried upon her cheeks.

Chapter III

A little more than a year after the bairn had died, Mam Stewart took her eldest son aside, "I believe our Janet is with another child, Alex."

"No," Alexander argued, "look at the thinness of herself. She can't be," he argued vehemently.

"The eyes show it first and I never have been wrong 'bout that. I want you to promise that you will be good to her; that you will treat her well." Alexander turned his back, walking angrily away. His mother saw the stiffness of his shoulders and knew he was upset that there was yet another stumbling block in his effort to leave the mine. She also knew that since Janet had returned to her position at the Manor House, they were slowly beginning to replenish the savings that had been used for the two burials.

Shortly after Mam Stewart had confided in her son, Alexander approached Janet, "Do you want to walk down to Oswald's Bridge?"

"Yes, that would be nice, Alexander," she smiled briefly at her husband, surprised at the rare invitation while hope fluttered momentarily in her heart.

"Mam says you're with another child," he said without preamble, when they had reached the bridge. He made no attempt to hide his bitterness and disappointment when he uttered the words.

Janet looked away unhappily. "I haven't told you yet because I know it's not what you want."

"Not telling me doesn't alter the fact of its existence, does it?"

"Well you can hope that this one won't live either then," her eyes filled with tears and quickly turning her head, she gazed down into the rushing water as it tumbled heedlessly over moss-covered boulders far below the bridge.

Alexander didn't touch her and she hadn't expected it. "I've had this dream of going to America since Jack's brother went. He's a rich man now and will never have to want for a thing. It's not that I don't want a bairn, it's just … .just that my dream is more important to me right now."

"I know." Janet's voice was muffled. "It's more important than anything else is to you. Even me. I used to think there was love between us." She searched his face looking for what she hoped she'd find. Not finding it, she lowered her eyes, searching the ground at her feet for a clue that would help to make her existence happier.

"That's right! Gawd damn it, that's right," his fist slammed the wooden railing. "Nothin' is more important to me."

Janet looked at him for a long moment before she brushed angrily past him and slowly made her way up the steep incline.

Alexander watched until she was out of sight and knew that he resented the new child she carried in her womb even more than he had the last one.

$*$ $*$ $*$ $*$ $*$

Janet's second pregnancy went well and she didn't experience the terrible sickness and fatigue that she had previously. Without the terrible sickness, she realized she had discovered the clue she had been looking for to make her life happier.

"Janet's lookin' real bonnie of late," Jack's missus confided to Mam Stewart one day. "She almos' seems like her old self an' she's got a spring to her step."

"The bairn will be here mos' any day now and she still walks to the Manor House mos' times for at least part of the day."

"This one should come out right. This one's mos' likely meant to be."

"If things don't go right this time 'round, I think it would likely kill her, she grieved so last time," Mam Stewart confided to her neighbor.

Jack's missus nodded sympathetically. "There be your Alexander and John now, home from their shift."

Alexander passed the women, acknowledging their presence with only a nod of his head. The old tub was set up before the fire, already filled with the soothing warm water. He shed his filthy pit clothes and climbed into it with a sigh. His thoughts now were almost constantly of America and what it would be like when he finally arrived in the land across the ocean. It was an obsession and he gave in to it. Leaning his head on the stool where his clean clothes were neatly piled, he pictured himself in a tall top hat wearing a fancy weskit with a gold chain looping to his watch pocket. He would be a right toff and no one would ever look down on him again.

In the mirror of his mind he saw himself riding down the street high on a beautiful chestnut horse. He could almost feel the sun warm on his back, smell the fresh, clean air and hear leaves rustling in the trees that lined the cobblestone streets. In the distance he could see snow-capped mountains and fluffy clouds floating by in the pale blue sky overhead.

At the sound of the door slamming, his eyes flew open, effectively killing his dream images. "Alexander, the stable boy from the Manor House has just come with the news. There weren't time, he says for nothin', it came that quick. Our Janet, Alexander….. the bairn… .," his mother babbled excitedly. "Hurry now, he'll take us over in the carriage. Missus Cunningham sent him over to collect us. That be right nice of her."

Alexander angrily grabbed the rough worn towel and stepped dripping out of the tub. "We'll not need to be treated like charity cases," he told her, "and I'll be beholden to no one. So you ken be tellin' the stable boy that we'll take no favors from no one."

*   *   *   *   *

"Congratulations, Mister Alexander," Missus Cunningham greeted him when he finally arrived on foot at the Manor House. "You have a fine, healthy son there. He bellowed a great loud yell the minute he saw the daylight. Janet is tired but the labour went very quickly."

"Where is my wife?" Alexander ignored the woman's jabberings.

"Come this way. You'll be anxious to see your son and wife. He's a fine looking lad, Mr. Stewart. You'll be most proud of him. Listen, he's already making himself heard."

Alexander could hear the bairn's gusty complaints and Janet's gentle crooning as he neared the door at the end of the narrow passageway.

Missus Cunningham quietly opened the door but Janet was so engrossed in her newborn bairn that she failed to notice the entrance of her husband. Alexander's guts became a lump of rock in the pit of his stomach when he saw the look on Janet's face as she gazed lovingly at the babe in her arms.

When she became aware of his presence, she looked up with a beatific smile at her husband. "Alexander, he's so lovely and look at how big he is!"

Alexander nodded, barely glancing at the child in her arms. "Were the midwife here?"

"No. Our son was in such a rush to be born, he didn't wait for the midwife. Mrs. Cook, the housekeeper helped the Missus Cunningham and Alexander, it was so much easier than last time." Her eyes misted over at the remembrance.

"So we won't be having to pay the midwife then."

"Alexander! We have a lovely healthy son and all you're worried about is having to pay the midwife. Forget America for just this once. There are other things in life that are important besides going to America. You have a lovely son. I should think you would be proud of that fact. Come and take a look at your son, Alexander."

"Going to America is what's important to me," he answered angrily and turning to leave, he bumped into his mother. Mam Stewart was standing inside the door with a disapproving look on her long narrow face. Her dark deep-set eyes were cold and in her anger, her face looked hard. "You ungrateful lump. You should be down on your knees thanking the good Lord that he didn't see fit to punish you again for the anger you carry within you," she hissed as he brushed past her. The scowl on his face deepened as he left the room.

"It has nothing to do with you," he muttered and was gone without another word to his wife or much more than a brief glance at his new son.

Missus Cunningham bounced around nervously fussing with Janet's pillows. "Oh dear, oh dear. Don't you worry now. Your Alexander just has the new-papa fears. It happens to a lot of new papas."

"Thank you, Missus Cunningham. There's more to it than that but it doesn't matter now," Janet said as the tears spilled down her face. She lightly kissed the top of the baby's downy head and smiled. "This wee bairn has me to love him as much as any two parents could ever love their child."

Janet stayed at the Manor House until Missus Cunningham felt she was strong enough to go back home and in that time she only received one terse note from Alexander inquiring as to when she planned to return to her own home.

Janet had decided to name the child Alexander William, partly in an attempt to appease Alexander and partly in memory of her first born son. Mam Stewart had made the walk several times to see Janet and her first grandchild. Alexander had never been mentioned although Janet was aware of his mother's strong disapproval of her son.

When Alexander William was two weeks old, Missus Cunningham had the stable boy drive Janet back to her own home. Entering the house, she shivered in the dampness and although it was spring, beads of moisture still clung to the inside walls and her nostrils filled with the cloying musty smell. Holding the babe protectively close to her breast, she felt like a stranger in her own home.

Looking around, Janet realized that Alexander and John had not yet returned home from the pit. Mam Stewart was already getting their water heated on the old grate in readiness for their bath. Richard sat at the table with a school tablet open in front of him. Smiling shyly at Janet, he glanced with curiosity at the bairn in her arms.

The older woman turned at the sound of Janet entering the room and her lips stretched across her blackened teeth when she saw her daughter-in-law. Her old tired eyes quickly darted to the babe in Janet's arms. "He be a strong, healthy one?"

"He's already grown since last you saw him. See?" Janet held the tiny bundle up, proudly displaying her newborn son.

Mam Stewart nodded. "Yourself is looking fit as well. Got some color in your cheeks, you have."

"I feel quite well and Missus Cunningham said I was to come and work for her again as soon as I am back on my feet an' the babe don't need so much of my milk."

"Alexander will be glad to hear of that. He's my son but he's not the man his Da were. Your load will be a heavy one, I'm thinking," she said bitterly knowing full well what her moody and taciturn son was like.

"I will manage, Mam. Alexander doesn't realize that I have my own dreams too. I am his wife and I will help him all that I am able to but my son is my life now. He is where my dreams will take me."

"You will be able to handle our Alexander, is what I'm thinking."

When Alexander returned home from the mine at the end of his shift, he paid no attention to the bairn lying quietly in the wooden crate that Janet had salvaged from the Manor House.

"Finally decided you had a home and husband to come back to, I see," he grumbled.

"Alexander, I don't want to fight with you. We're a family. We have a child now. Doesn't that mean anything to you?"

"Going to America means something to me. You don't know anything about it, Janet. You don't know what it's like to have to go down into that pit every day, not knowing if this day will be your last or not. Not knowing if the explosives will blow you to pieces or if the shaft will collapse or if you'll drown if the pumps stop working. And every miner knows for sure that in the end the mine is going to kill him one way or the other like it did to my Da."

Young Richard cowered at the table, his eyes bright with unshed tears. Alexander's voice grew louder as his anger rose to the surface. The bairn began to whimper in his makeshift cot and Janet hurried to pick him up, cuddling him to her as if to protect him from his father's violent outburst. She rocked him, humming softly until his whimpering stopped.

Alexander watched her, a ferocious scowl darkening his brow. The frown lines between his heavy eyebrows, at twenty-two years, were already deeply etched and gave his eyes the appearance of being hooded like those of a hawk. The deep crevices on each side of his mouth pulled his lips down into an already habitual grimace giving testimony to his growing discontentment. There was a strong likeness in appearance between mother and son but neither would have been happy to hear it nor willing to admit the fact.

"Put the child back in his cot. I'll not have you mollycoddling him. Your husband needs lookin' after now," he growled.

Janet kissed the infant's velvety cheek before returning him to his cot and made a resolve to return to her position at the Manor House as soon as possible. She'd not give Alexander any cause for complaint.

*   *   *   *   *

Alexander William was a happy and contented child, loved by all except his father. He appeared not to be aware of his father's singular lack of attention because with the exception of his father he quickly became the one that all love was centered upon.

"Alexander William show me your letters," his uncle Richard was fond of asking him as he grew older.

"Me do. Me show you, unka Rich," the child would answer, a large smile transforming his chubby face.

"Alexander William, sing me a song," John would ask the child when Alexander had left the house.

"Me do. Me ting 'Tinkle Tars'," Alexander William would smile shyly at his mother before beginning his favorite tune.

"Alexander William, tell Mammy the verse you learnt today," Mam Stewart would whisper in his ear.

Standing proudly, smiling at his loving audience, Alexander William repeated his verses well, learning them quickly from his Uncle Richard.

Janet was proud of her son. He was so unlike his father in both temperament and appearance, tending to be more like mother than like father. While Alexander was dark with a forbidding appearance, becoming more so in recent years, Alexander William had blonde curls, an open look and a constant smile, only becoming quiet when his father was around; as was the whole family.

Working at the Manor House, Janet had been able to save some money to add to their meager savings for their move to America. But as she saved, Alexander drank, going each evening after his shift to the local pub, the Rose and Thorne, for a pint of ale. Before long one pint became two pints until Alexander would finally stagger home drunk, becoming more angry with every step nearer home he got. By the time he pushed the door open and lurched inside, he was ready for a fight. The family began to dread his homecomings, often feigning sleep in order to avoid a confrontation with him. And as he drank, the less he talked about going to America, becoming instead more bitter as each day passed.

One evening, when young Alexander was four years old, Alexander came home more inebriated than was usual and bumping into the table, sent the dishes clattering to the floor.

"John," he yelled yanking his young brother up from his sleep. "Get up with you. We have to talk."

John looked up bleary-eyed. "Aw, Alexander, can't it wait 'til the 'morrow?"

"It ken't. I bin thinkin' that it's 'bout time for you to be head of this family now that you're almost nineteen. An' Mam ken quit making a sissy out of Richard. It be time for him to go down into the pit. Me and Janet is goin' to be leavin' this Hell-hole of a place."

"Mam won't be lettin' you send our Richard down. She says he's got book learning so's he won't have to go down now."

"An' I'm sayin' he'll be goin' down."

"We'll talk 'bout it in the 'morrow our Alexander."

"Nuthin' to talk 'bout. It's decided," he lurched over to the table in the corner knocking another plate onto the stone floor with a loud crash.

Janet glanced over to where Mam Stewart lay and knew she was no longer sleeping either. They had all learned that there was no point discussing anything with Alexander when he had the ale in him. "Dear God," she prayed silently, "please let him go to sleep quickly before anything else happens."

She hadn't told Alexander of her suspicions yet but knew that she couldn't put off telling him of her pregnancy much longer. She had thus far avoided raising the subject because she knew Alexander's anger would know no bounds. Janet shivered nervously, feigning sleep while she watched her husband stumble drunkenly around the cramped area bumping into things and swearing angrily to himself.

This child had been conceived a month previously when Alexander had come home drunk one evening, and in a vicious temper had pinned her beneath his great weight, taking her roughly with no care for the pain he was causing her. When he was finished with her and had fallen into a drunken sleep, snoring loudly, she had lain there and hated him with every breath that she took. She resented also the baby she now carried within her that had been conceived in such pain and bitterness.

Alexander didn't love her or his son and she knew this baby would be no different to him. It would be an additional burden that she would have to carry on her own.

Thinking of Alexander William she permitted herself a small smile in the darkness. He was so boisterous and full of life but with an instinctiveness that gave him the ability to be virtually invisible when the situation required it. He had the ability to simulate and become two entirely different people. When forced to interact with his father, he became quiet and restrained; a much different child than he was with the rest of the family. Janet couldn't understand this awareness and ability in a child so young.

At the evening meal the following day, Mam Stewart said, "Alexander, our Richard will nae be goin' into the pit!"

Richard looked fearfully at Alexander and Janet put her arm protectively around Alexander William's warm shoulders as he leaned against her, watching his father anxiously with huge brown eyes. "One more year and he ken train for the Ministry."

"The Ministry!" Alexander roared, his face becoming red with anger. "One more year, you say? There isn't goin' to be one more year. You've made him into a sissy. He'll go into the pit like the rest of us." He threw his fork onto the table and slamming out the door, headed to the Rose and Thorne.

"Do I have to go, Mam?" Richard asked, his voice quavering.

"I'll be thinking on it, our Richard. Have you told Alexander that you're with child again, Janet?"

Janet shook her head. "There hasn't been a good time to tell him."

"There won't ever be a good time Janet. Tell him soon before he knows about our Richard, else it'll be worse for you, I'm thinking," Mam Stewart said not unkindly.

"Mam," Alexander's small voice interrupted, "what does Grandma mean, 'with child'?"

"Nothin', my sweet," she answered tousling his blonde curls. "Nothin' that you have to worry 'bout."

"But Mam," young Alexander persisted, "why do you got wet things in your eyes?"

"Don't ask so many questions child. Now run and get your book and I'll read you a story."

Alexander William ran to get his dog-eared book from beneath his pillow where he kept it hidden away from his father's disapproving eyes.

"I'll tell him tomorrow, for sure," Janet whispered to her mother-in-law unhappily.

"I'll be seeing 'bout our Richard very soon now an' when Alexander finds out.... .." she didn't finish, it wasn't necessary. They all knew what Alexander's temper would be like when he heard the news.

"Mam," young Alexander was back with his beloved book, "will you read me this one?" he asked pointing to his favorite story. Janet enjoyed this time of the day when she and her son could enjoy a closeness they weren't able to have when Alexander was around. As he climbed upon her knee, his head burrowed in the hollow of her neck, her heart swelled with love for her son. Thinking of the love she felt for Alexander William, her mind refused to think about the other child growing within her womb.

After a silent meal the following evening, Janet suggested to Alexander that they walk down to Oswald's Bridge before he left for the Rose and Thorne. He looked at her with surprise but agreed to her unusual request. They walked in silence while Janet considered how she would tell him the news.

When they reached the bridge, he turned to her, "I know there's somethin' on your mind. If you're goin' to talk to me 'bout Richard, there's naught to talk 'bout."

"It's not 'bout Richard, Alexander. It's 'bout us," she hesitated, afraid to continue. She took a deep breath in an attempt to calm her inner trembling. "There's goin' to be another bairn." Her heart was pounding so loudly she thought it nearly likely would jump from her breast.

He stared at her for a full minute before finally speaking. "I ken only hope it goes like the last one," he said referring to her miscarriage of the previous year.

Janet dashed the tears from her eyes as she watched him stride angrily in the direction of the Rose and Thorne. She feared what his mood would be like upon his return.

Chapter IV

One evening, almost two weeks later, upon Janet's return from the Manor House, she was surprised when Richard didn't appear at the table for the evening meal. Mam Stewart and Richard had been absent during the day on several occasions but Janet had asked no questions. Surprisingly Alexander had not mentioned Richard going into the mine lately but she knew the matter had not been dropped.

"I've talked to Mister Johnlittle and they've agreed to take Richard on beginning the first of next week," Alexander told his mother as he was getting into clean clothes after his bath that evening. He looked around suddenly. "Where's our Richard? He's usually here by now."

"Our Richard has left," Mam Stewart's voice was quiet but firm.

"Left? What do you mean? Left where?"

"The Minister McLean has taken him to study the ministry under a colleague of his, he said he were."

"Where?" he yelled. "I'll drag him back to his rightful place." He turned to his wife and grabbing her arm in a vise-like grip, "You knew about this, didn't you? You've turned against your husband. What kind of a wife are you?" Raising his hand, Janet cringed with fear when she saw the loathing in her husband's eyes.

"Leave her be," Mam Stewart pulled at his shirt. "Leave her be, I said. She didn't know nothin'. I told no one what I had planned."

Janet saw the hatred registered on her husband's face before he swung towards his mother, his face contorted with rage.

"Don't you lay a hand on our Mam," John's voice was a low growl in the back of his throat. "Richard has a chance of somethin' better, give him that chance, Alexander."

"You be lookin' for somethin' better too our Alexander. America is your dream and the Ministry is Richard's dream," Mam Stewart spat angrily at him.

"But he's got his and I'm still waitin' for mine," Alexander kicked at the chair leg, sending it crashing to the floor before stomping angrily out of the house. His footsteps led him towards the Rose and Thorne.

"I'll talk to Alexander in the mine tomorrow. It should make no mind to him that our Richard is gone. It's one less mouth to be feeding," John said.

*   *   *   *   *

The months passed and Janet's belly became large as the baby within her grew but she never thought of the child or wondered about it as she had done when she'd been pregnant with Alexander William. It was as if the baby didn't exist. As Janet's pregnancy advanced, Alexander became more morose as the wished-for miscarriage didn't materialize and the reality of what Richard's absence meant to his plans became a blight on every thought he had while he struggled below the earth.

Janet continued on at the Manor House during her entire pregnancy refusing the Missus Cunningham's advise to take time off. On a cold and rainy Sunday in November of 1920, on her day off, Janet's contractions began like a vise gripping her innards. "Mam, I think the bairn will be here soon."

"It be too early for the bairn," Mam Stewart worried when Janet told her that it was time. "How far apart are the pains?"

"I'm not sure, Mam," Janet suddenly doubled over, gasping as a huge pain seared through her body.

Helping Janet to bed, Mam Stewart said, "John, you be taking Alexander William with you and you might try lookin' for your brother whilst you're at it. But don't be hurrying back with him 'cause we've no need of any trouble at the moment, I'm thinking."

As Janet lay panting between the contractions, she was finally forced to think about this child that she had carried for almost eight and a half months. A child that was conceived, not in love, but in violence and she shed a tear for one that was wanted by neither father nor mother.

"Dear God," she prayed, "I will try to love this poor wee bairn," she whispered praying that it might be true.

Five hours later the child lay in the crook of her arm and Janet, seeing that her daughter was the image of Alexander, knew she would have difficulty in keeping her promise. "Poor wee thing," she murmured, "it's a hard life you'll be having." The thin, wizened face with the narrow eyes peered up at her seeming to ask for love and acceptance. Turning her gaze from her daughter, she watched her son Alexander with his blonde curls, dark eyes and mischievous smile and her heart constricted with her love for him. Stealing a glance at her daughter again, she said, "We'll call her Elsa Mary, after you Mam," Janet smiled briefly at her mother-in-law.

"Is it going to stay here?" Alexander William pouted while he looked unhappily at the intruder.

"Yes, my sweet. What do you think of your little sister?"

Young Alexander studied the infant for a few minutes and then shrugging said, "Did I look like her do when I were borned?"

"No you didn't and you were much louder. She has barely made a sound but you were heard almost from the minute you were born. You made such loud noises that the sheep in the field heard your cries."

Young Alexander giggled at his mother. "The sheep did?"

"Yes, and they all wanted to see what you looked like. They wanted to be your friend."

Alexander looked again at his sister. "She's all wrinkly. Maybe I won't like her."

"I'm sure you will, Alexander. She'll be a little playmate for you. Won't that be nice?" Janet said with a confidence she didn't feel.

"Do you got to hold her always?" Alexander William asked, his small mouth puckering. "I want you to read me a story."

Suddenly the door crashed open and Alexander staggered into the room, "Wha's sis I hear?" he slurred his words. "I no' fit to tell the news to?"

"Our John has been out lookin' for you for hours, our Alexander," Mam Stewart said.

"Don' tell me lies. You're all liars," he sneered and then tripping over the corner of the hurley bed, collapsed onto young Alexander's bed. Alexander William ran and stood beside his mother, his face white with fear.

"You have a daug… … .," Janet began but her husband had already begun to snore loudly. "Son, you can sleep with John this night. He won't be minding your company."

"Here's the old crate we had for young Alexander. We ken be usin' it for this wee bairn as well," Mam Stewart said, taking the infant from Janet and placing her gently inside. "She sure be a quiet one, don't she now?"

"So different from Alexander William," Janet mused.

Mam Stewart studied the child in the crate. "Poor little lass," she murmured gently caressing its tiny pink fist with her old brown gnarled finger. It's tiny fingers grasped the elderly woman's larger finger and a bond was instantly formed.

Janet lay awake thinking for a long while after the others were asleep. Alexander's dream of going to America was not her dream. The only family she had were here and she knew in America she and the children would be at the mercy of Alexander's violent outbursts. Here they at least had the protection of John and Mam Stewart.

She no longer believed, as Alexander did, that everyone in America was rich. She had heard tales. Stories that told of poor people, much like the miners in Scotland. Alexander had said it was all 'vicious lies' when she had told him what she had heard. "I don't want to leave our homeland," she whispered to the darkness. She finally fell exhausted into a dreamless sleep hearing neither John when he returned home or the new bairn when she awoke with a small squeak of a cry.

During the following few months, Elsa made few demands on the adults in her life with Mam Stewart assuming most of the responsibility for her care. Her cry was little more than a whimper when she did cry as if she instinctively knew that she hadn't been wanted and was determined not to cause any extra trouble to anyone. It seemed as if she was quietly waiting, hoping that love would eventually come her way.

Janet returned to the Manor House, at the Missus Cunningham's request, at the beginning of February and the few pennies she made were carefully tucked away in the tin box under the bed. Alexander never asked if there was other money than what she gave him.

*   *   *   *   *

In February of 1921, life changed drastically for the miners of their small town. All who belonged to the Miner's Union, which had recently been formed, went on strike. The family rarely saw Alexander during this time as he spent most of his time either on the picket line or at the Rose and Thorne. But there was none that missed his presence in the crowded little row house.

The strike of February slowly dragged into March and still the miners struck. The coalmasters steadfastly refused to meet the demands of the colliers who asked for higher wages and better working conditions; only what they considered was their due.

The coalmasters, who owned the row houses, threatened to throw the miners out of their homes in retaliation. In anger the women got involved, joining the men on their picket lines. As the strike continued the fight heated up and the coalmasters brought in the police in an attempt to force the miners back to work. The miners knew the coalmasters threats were idle ones. Banding together, they refused to be intimidated by either the coalmasters or the police.

"We've got right on our side," the miners chanted into the faces of the coalmasters, their bravery enhanced by their large numbers.

Janet didn't join the men and women on the picket line because she still had her job at the Manor House and as she walked past the striking miners and their wives, she knew there were some that resented the fact that she had a job.

Soon it was April and still nothing had been settled for the miners. The Stewart family were a little better off than most because they still had some of the money they have been saving for their trip to America.

"We have to use it," Janet pleaded with Alexander. "You've used some of it for drink but there's food to be got now, Alexander." He ignored her pleadings and on the day she realized she was again pregnant, she sat down and wept huge bitter tears of self-pity.

"And Elsa barely five months old," she confided tearfully to Mam Stewart. "How will we make it? There's barely enough food as it is."

Glancing over guiltily at her daughter lying quietly in the middle of Alexander William's bed, she knew she didn't want another bairn.

"Poor thing," she said half to herself. "She's so serious for a child so young," Janet murmured to her mother-in-law. Rarely smiling, the child quietly watched her mother and grandmother with knowing eyes and often Janet felt as if wee Elsa could see the thoughts that ran through her head. The feeling made her even more uncomfortable when she looked into the face of her young daughter.

The child had not become any bonnier as she grew older. Her thin face and dark deep-set eyes gave her the appearance of a child much older than she was, especially when her seemingly all-seeing, all-knowing eyes looked into the eyes of the adults in her life. She had a small amount of dark patchy hair that grew in tufts standing straight up from her head like dark spikes. She was long and thin without the natural chubbiness of an infant her age.

Janet looked worriedly at her mother-in-law. "If this strike continues on much longer, things will only get worse," Janet sighed.

"The Minister McLean said that the coalmasters can't hold out much longer now."

"But neither can the miners. By June end, most of our savings will be gone. I don't know how the other families are managing. It would be better for us if Alexander stayed away from the Rose and Thorne instead of spending money on drink. He won't even listen to our John. I don't know how the other miners manage because they're at the Rose and Thorne also. They must be going into debt."

"I thank God that Alexander is nae goin' into debt for his ale. Alexander listens to no one about anything an' he nae would 'bout that either. He's a man who hears only his own drummer and marches always to the wrong beat." Reaching into her pocket, she said, "Minister McLean gave me this letter from our Richard." Mam Stewart pulled the crumpled paper from the pocket of her apron. "I don't want Alexander to know about the letter. Would you read me what he says, our Janet?"

"He says, 'Dear Mam and Family. I've been learnin' so many things that my head feels fit to be burstin' but everyone is so kind to me and I have a room all to myself and near to twenty books that I ken call my own. I hope you are well and I miss you all, Love Richard'."

Mam dabbed at the corners of her eyes with her apron. Shoving the letter back into her pocket, she quietly went about her preparations for the evening meal.

The strike continued until the end of August when a settlement was finally reached; one that could have been reached months earlier and which satisfied neither side. But by this time, both sides were desperate. The money Janet earned at the Manor House helped stretch the meager savings that were left and they were able to keep their heads above water. Many of the others had not been so lucky and were heavily indebted to the company stores which were owned by the coalmasters. In the end, for most of the miners, the win was overwhelmingly ultimately the coalmasters.

When Alexander and John finally returned to their work in the pit, the family slowly began to put away a few pennies in an effort to replenish their savings. To have to begin again was a major blow to Alexander and for a while he stopped going to the Rose and Thorne.

A bleak fall turned into a blustery winter and Elsa was now walking. She was the apple of her grandmother's eye but virtually ignored by the rest of her family. She was still pathetically thin and exceedingly tall for her age. Her hair had grown in although it was fine and hung limply beside her narrow face. Her face remained long and thin and her worried expression seemed habitual, unusual in a child so young. When she smiled, it was fleeting and only if coaxed. She seemed aloof and watchful but it was obvious that she returned her grandmother's deep affection.

Janet had been surprised that her next pregnancy had not been an issue with Alexander and for the most part was neither acknowledged nor spoken of. Janet's feelings about this pregnancy were mixed, in part brought about by her feelings of guilt for wee Elsa. By the time she learned of her new pregnancy, she realized that Alexander was not the husband she had expected him to be and nor would he ever be. Her old dreams of what their life together would be like were buried in the cold ground with William Neil. With this realization confronting her, she decided that her children would be where the love she had to give was placed. When she thought of her children, she cringed with shame about the difficulty she still had with her feelings for Elsa. She hoped in time that what she felt for the child would change.

Before Elizabeth Ann was born in January of 1922, Alexander had resumed his daily jaunts to the Rose and Thorne and the family saw very little of him. Elizabeth was born easily when she was due and was as pretty as her brother was handsome. She demanded attention and received it. Even Alexander took notice of his second daughter and it wasn't long before she had even her father wrapped around her chubby little finger. She smiled and laughed early and little Elsa took it upon herself to follow Elizabeth around to keep her out of the mischief that she was forever getting into.

Elsa seemed not to mind the attention her pretty younger sister attracted and loved her as much as everyone else did. Elizabeth looked up to her older sister and when the two played together, Elsa seemed to have more confidence in herself than she normally did.

"Me not do naughty tings," Elizabeth constantly promised her older sister, promptly forgetting her promise as soon as the words were out of her mouth. But no one seemed to mind the problems she caused. With a coy smile and a blink of her huge, blue eyes, the naughty deed was quickly forgotten.

In late August Alexander came home early from the Rose and Thorne. "I just had a pint of ale with this foreigner chap from America and he says we've almos' got enough saved to go abroad. He says the next ship leaves in October an' if we pay part of our passage, there's farmers that live in Canada that will pay the rest if you work on their farm for at least two years. By October we'll have enough saved," he excitedly told Janet.

"Canada? There are Indians everywhere and I've heard that Canada is nothing but wild country. We'll all be scalped in our sleep." Janet's face had become ashen with Alexander's startling announcement.

"Where did you hear them stories? T'aint true. They be as civilized as Scotland. This chap says they need people to work the farms and that's why they'll pay most of our way over. They have hundreds of acres, more than one family can look after."

"But Elizabeth is too young to go so far right now."

"She be almos' two years old when we leave in October and look at how healthy she is. Never once sick a day."

"But it's so sudden, Alexander! How can we be ready by October?"

"Sudden? I been planning and thinking 'bout this for fifteen years now. I'm meeting with this chap tomorrow. We'll be goin', Janet. We'll not be letting this chance go by." His cold, unloving eyes never left Janet's face. "And I'll be goin' with or without you."

Janet glanced at Mam Stewart and saw the unshed tears glittering in her mother-in-law's eyes as she gazed lovingly at Elsa. The child's worried expression creased her small face as she looked at her grandmother for confirmation that her life was not going to tumble around her. *'But she couldn't know what we're talkin' 'bout, could she?'* Janet wondered.

Alexander came back from the Rose and Thorne the following day excitedly waving a piece of paper with the name of the farmer who was going to sponsor their trip. "An' Henry says that this Canada is full of trees and lakes and rivers and mountains and there's work for everyone and that workin' on a farm is the best life there is. He says that there be dairy farms and pig farms and farms that grow wheat and oats. He said that wherever you go in Canada, there are different things – and besides the farms, there's lots of industry in the small towns and the cities so no one ever has to worry about havin' a job."

"Do we write to this farmer in Canada?"

"Henry said he would look after all of that an' all we have to do is get our papers in order. He'll even book our passage for us on the ship."

"What will this Henry get out of doing all of this for us, Alexander?"

"Nothin'! He's a friend an' he knows how bad I want to get out of the mine."

"Alexander, he's never met you before. He's not a friend, he's a foreigner. And he won't be doing it for nothin' either. No one does anything for nothing, Alexander."

"He didn't ask for nothin'; only said he'd need our money for our share to book passage for us."

"How do you know that's what he'll do with our money" How do you know he won't just disappear with it?"

"Ol' Robert, the bartender at the Rose and Thorne says he's done this 'afore for families going to America and nothin's gone amiss."

Janet shook her head doubtfully. "When does he want our money and when is he goin' to book the passage?"

"Henry said he'd have to book the passage no later than two weeks from now and he says that's leavin' it tight being as there's five of us."

"If we give him all of our money for the passage, we won't have any when we get there. How will we live?"

"Henry says it's not necessary because that's part of the deal—the farmer gives us lodging and food from the farm."

"I don't like the sound of it, Alexander. No one gives anyone somethin' for nothin'."

"It's not for nothin'. We'll be working for them until we pay the passage back."

"If it's so good, why are there not men in Canada to work on the farms?"

Alexander shrugged. "It'll be good! I know it will. Hasn't everyone said that the streets are paved with gold?"

Long after Alexander had gone to sleep, Janet lay tossing and turning, unable to sleep. *'Alexander's eyes are set so firmly on America, he can't see anythin' else,'* she fretted. *'I don't trust this Henry at all.'* When she had finally made the decision that either Alexander or herself would have to go with Henry to get their tickets, she relaxed slightly, eventually falling into a restless, dream-filled sleep.

She dreamed that when they got to Canada, there was no one there to meet them and having no money and no place to sleep, they had all slept curled up on a stoop in a doorway in a stinking rat-infested, rubbish-strewn alley. She had waken with tears streaming down her face and a deep feeling of dread for what was to come.

Alexander, grunting in his sleep, rolled over onto his back and snoring loudly had flung his arm across Janet's chest. Unable to move, she had lain wide awake until the first light of morning.

The month of September was busy as they made the necessary arrangements to get their papers in order for the sailing. Janet had made her first ever trip to Kilmarnock to get this done and had also gone with Henry to get the tickets for their passage. She had waited while he had stood patiently in the long line up. Returning to where she stood, he handed her the tickets with a flourish. "Ma'am, your tickets. And a safe trip to you, I might add."

'He seems most pleasant and full of good humor,' she thought. Softening slightly towards him, she felt guilty for distrusting him.

Mam Stewart spent long tedious hours sewing warm coats for the children; the candle burning until late into each night. Henry had told Alexander that northern Canada was very cold and had many long months of winter. Young Alexander danced around the crowded room when he heard that there would be a lot of snow and he would be able to build snowmen and snow forts to hide in while he kept the Indians away. Janet shuddered to think what the family was getting themselves into.

On Janet's last day at the Manor House, the staff got together and gave Janet small gifts that they thought the family might need on their long journey to Canada. Then the Missus Cunningham took Janet aside and pressing an envelope into her hand said, "I've become very fond of you, lass. Almos' as if you were my very own daughter. I would like you to take this in case of an emergency. I shouldna say this, but keep it hidden 'til the time comes that you really need it." Putting her arms around Janet's thin shoulders, she hugged her against her ample bosom.

The tears slid unchecked down Janet's cheeks. "I don't know what to say. You've done so much for me already and I can't ever repay you."

"You already have, my dear," Missus Cunningham smiled, "by just being yourself."

The tears continued to fall in spite of Janet's effort to stop them. "I wish that I never had to leave all of you. Or Mam Stewart. She has treated me like a daughter, better than my own mother. I don't know what she will do when we've left. She will miss Elsa. She's been like her own child and Elsa will grieve for her grandmam." Looking at the floor, Janet hesitated before speaking again, "But I know it's a wife's duty to go with her husband. I could make no other decision."

"This is a hard road for you, Janet," Missus Cunningham's eyes were bright with unshed tears. "But it's a road I know you will travel well."

The last few days before their departure were difficult ones for Janet and she was painfully aware, they were also for Mam Stewart. *'I'm leaving Scotland, which I love, and a family and friends for a country I know nothing about with a man I no longer love or respect. I must be daft,'* she thought. A cloud of depression hung heavily over her head as she packed their few meager possessions; blankets, pots and dishes, a few staples, clothing, personal possessions and a few odds and ends of things that they would require in their new home. Most of it was contained in a pathetically few cardboard cartons which she tied with twine, labeling clearly, vaguely proud of her neat printing.

Janet glanced often at Mam Stewart who was constantly at Elsa's side. The older woman talked to the child and played their favorite games for hours on end. Janet felt the loneliness the older woman would feel when they had all departed and the row house was empty except for Mam Stewart and John. Five less people in the crowded house would make it feel like a tomb. The family had been a reason for her to live since Alexander's father had died, giving some joy to the old woman against the loneliness and constant poverty. Now there would only be John as it had been many months since any word had been received from Richard.

Janet hesitated before asking, "Mam, what will you do when we're gone? It will be difficult for you."

Mam Stewart cast an unhappy glance in Elsa's direction. "I'll miss the wee lass." A tear trickled down her cheek. Hastily wiping it away, she said, "I've spoken with the coalmaster's wife and I'll be doing laundry up there for a wee while."

Mam Stewart again looked at Elsa who sat quietly on the bed in the opposite corner of the room. *'What will happen to the poor wee lass now?'* she wondered sadly as she looked at the silent, withdrawn child.

Janet herself was aware that Elsa had become even quieter and more withdrawn during the recent weeks of activity. She would be leaving her main provider of comfort and love. Janet herself wasn't sure how the child would handle the separation.

Near the end of September, an incident happened in the pit that caused Alexander to be even more convinced of his decision to leave the mines and Scotland behind forever. Late of an afternoon, near the end of a shift when workers are tired and often careless, a friend of Alexander's, from the Rose and Thorne, slipped beneath a loaded tub of coal. Alexander had heard the commotion at the end of the haulage line and backing out of his seam had hurried toward the sounds. John was already there with their own tub of coal. "What's the matter, our John?"

"It be Sam McCulloch who got it. Slipped under the wheels, he did."

"Sam?" Alexander pushed through the group of men gathered around his friend. The man lay across the haulage tracks, his body twisted and his legs mangled. *'He'll not be walking again,'* Alexander thought and feeling his stomach heave, he turned from the sight of his friend.

"Help's comin' ," someone yelled.

One of the miners had laid his jacket across the injured man's chest. *'It's God's mercy, he be unconscious,'* thought Alexander and turning towards his friend again, he removed his own jacket and placed it beneath Sam's head. Alexander saw that the face of the injured man was ashen beneath the gray film of coal dust. As he watched, he realized that he could barely see the rise and fall of Sam's chest.

Two men and a stretcher finally arrived and lifting Sam gently, they placed him on the makeshift stretcher, wrapping blankets around his still form. Alexander followed the stretcher to the cage and waited until his friend was lifted to the surface before following up with some of the other miners. In the back of every miner's mind was the silent thought that it could easily have been any one of them.

When Alexander arrived at the top, Sam had already been taken to the hospital by the local make-shift ambulance. Instead of going home, Alexander went to the Rose and Thorne to await the news of his friend. Others followed and although they sat clustered around the tables there was none of the usual chatter as they drank their pints of ale. Whenever someone in their midst was killed or injured, it brought home to each man the dangers of the mine. Each day that they climbed into the cage to be lowered into the bowels of the earth, they were aware of the danger. And each man lived with the knowledge that this day could be his last day. *'There but for the Grace of God, goes I,'* thought Alexander.

Few words were exchanged as the evening progressed and when word was received, most unabashedly wiped away a tear or two from their eyes. When Alexander heard the news, he put his tankard of ale, unfinished on the table and without a word to his companions, left the bar. Walking down to Oswald's Bridge, he thought, *'This be where everything important has ever happened. When I have forgotten other things, I will always remember Oswald's Bridge.'*

He thought about Sam and his young family. Sam had a dream, much like Alexander's. Sam had wanted to get out of the pit and become a blacksmith but his dream had died with him, at the bottom of the mine. *'It's too late for Sam now but it's not too late for me. My life is just beginning.'* And with that last hazy drunken thought, he staggered home.

On the day of their departure, Elsa clung unhappily to her grandmother, her dark eyes brimming with tears, her small mouth trembling. Young Alexander danced around with boyish enthusiasm and some of that enthusiasm transferred itself to Elizabeth. Many of their neighbors from the row houses came to see them off, wishing them well, each bringing a small farewell gift of food.

Finally they were on their way, on the first lap of their long journey to their new home in Canada. Janet turned, watching unhappily as the village receded and the waving miners and their families became small dots on the cloudy horizon.

The train ride to Glasgow improved Janet's spirits. Never having been on a train, it was an adventure for the whole family. With faces pressed against the windows, they watched the passing landscape, comparing it to the row houses in Galston. As the steam engine chugged along in a gray puff of smoke, young Alexander was mesmerized and fearful of missing a single thing. He had refused to be anywhere except with his nose pressed firmly against the cold glass of the window. Elsa sat mutely in the corner of the cushioned seat, a frightened expression on her small thin face while Elizabeth bounced happily around their enclosed space. She was soon the darling of their compartment.

Upon arriving in Glasgow, they hired a cab to take them to the dock with their few parcels and cartons. Alexander William carried the squirming Elizabeth when she refused to hang firmly onto his hand, and Janet helped Alexander with their possessions. Elsa lagged unhappily behind the family group.

Standing on the dock, waiting to board the ship that was to be their home for more than a week, Janet felt her innards begin to constrict with a new fear. "It looks to be such an old ship," she muttered. "Are you sure the ship is safe, Alexander?"

Alexander turned impatiently to his wife. "Of course it be. We have no need to worry. They wouldna be selling tickets for a sinking ship."

"Is this it?" Alexander William's handsome young face glowed with excitement. "Is this the ship we're to be sleeping on?"

"That," Alexander pointed a coal-stained finger at the huge vessel, "is our way to freedom, to riches young man," his voice boomed.

Many turned to look at Alexander, tired expressions on their weary faces. Others created more space between themselves and the gray-faced man with the booming voice.

Janet realized with a surprised shock that there was a smile, such as she had never seen before, on Alexander's narrow face. *'Maybe everything will right itself,'* she fervently hoped.

"If we're to be rich, can I have a bicycle when we get to Canada?" Alexander William asked, a smile wreathing his round face.

"If we are to be rich, I'm sure you'll get your bicycle," his mother answered absent-mindedly while she watched the other passengers and, not for the first time, noticed that those standing on the wharf all looked as poor or poorer than themselves.

"What do you think is the hold-up about boarding, Alexander? Some of the other passengers seem to be allowed on board, even when they have come later than us." She began to feel uneasy. "Do you think there is somethin' wrong, Alexander?" she whispered to her husband, not wanting to alarm the children.

Alexander turned angrily to her. "Wrong? Whad'ya mean? What could possibly be wrong, woman?"

"They're not allowing us to board and we were here long before some of them that are being allowed to board."

"We just have to wait our turn like all the rest of these here people. Look, we're starting to move now. You worry too much."

The ragged, vacant-eyed people herded together with them began to shuffle slowly forward like sheep being led to slaughter instead of like the happy group Alexander seemed to think he was part of. They carried, what Janet suspected was all of their worldly possessions in their arms or strapped onto their backs in much the same way that the Stewart family was carrying their luggage.

"Down below, down below," a sailor yelled to them as they reached the top of the gang plank.

"Down below? What does he mean, Alexander?"

"How be I know?" he asked irritably. "Quit nagging woman. Mister?" Alexander caught the sailor's attention. "We be lookin' for our cabin."

The sailor's hostile eyes travelled insolently over Alexander not missing the fact of his threadbare clothing and the coal dust ingrained in his enlarged pores. His lips curled in a contemptuous sneer. "Down below, I said. Don't be putting on airs with me. You're riff-raff like the rest of these here …… Down below, I say."

"There be a mistake, I'm thinking," Alexander persevered.

"There ain't no mistake, mister. I'm tellin' you, down below," the sailor roared.

"But we was to have a cabin. It's what was paid for." Alexander's face was red with ill-controlled fury.

"Give me a look at that ticket," the sailor grabbed it from Alexander's outstretched hand. "Nope! No cabin on this ticket. Like I says, you're on that deck," he jerked his thumb below. "Now don't give me no more trouble," he gave Alexander a shove before turning to the other passengers who were patiently waiting in a line-up behind them. Janet grabbed her husband's arm pulling him in the direction the sailor had indicated before he could retaliate further in anger.

They were carried along by the other passengers making their way uncomplainingly down below. "We'll speak to the Captain later, Alexander."

Down below they found three hammocks in a somewhat private alcove. Walking carefully on the oil-smeared rough plank flooring Janet took Elsa's cold hand firmly in her own. "Careful Alexander William, the floor is slippery."

Young Alexander lay the sleeping Elizabeth in one of the filthy hammocks and rubbed his aching arms. "Is this where we're staying?" He wrinkled his nose as he watched others settle into their own areas of the ship's steerage.

When the cartons were stacked beside their make-shift beds, Elsa dropped to the floor and clasping her thin arms tightly around her bony legs, leaned her head against their possessions watching the noisy passengers with wide frightened eyes.

"The bastard," Alexander hissed from between his clenched teeth when later he returned from speaking with the Captain about the mix-up. "He stole our money."

"Sh-h, the children will hear you, Alexander. What are you talking about? Who stole our money?" Janet whispered.

"Henry is the one that did this. Our passage, to include a cabin, was paid for by the farmer Murphy; money which were given to Henry. He kept the extra money for the cabin, and the money we placed into his hands all went into his own deep pocket. I'll be choking his scrawny neck with my own bare hands if ever I be seeing him again."

"Oh Alexander," Janet felt the tears spring to her eyes. "Do you think he lied about all the rest of it?"

"The rest? Whad'ya mean, the rest?" A look of fear lay in the dark pools of Alexander's eyes.

"Is our rail fare paid from Halifax to Alberta or will we have to be paying for that ourselves now too?"

"The Captain said that our rail fare tickets are being held by the immigration officials in Halifax. He says that we will have to be checked by some medical people in Halifax when we get there. He said there are many scoundrels waiting to take our money and we must be very careful who we trust. We were not the first to be robbed and we won't be the last, he says. He said that the people who steal from people like us get a bounty for each passenger and that be how they make their livin'. Plus the money he got from us. It's a nice living he makes cheating poor folks."

Janet looked around the ship's hold at the hundreds of people tightly packed together with barely a foot between family groups. She wondered if it was possible to make it as far as Canada, with so many people, in a ship that looked ready to fall apart in the first strong wind.

Chapter V

Disembarking from the train, the freezing wind sweeping across the wide open spaces quickly penetrated their unsuitable clothing. "I'm cold Mam," Elizabeth whimpered.

"Hush now child. I'm sure Mr. Murphy will be here before long," Janet put her arm around her youngest although she herself felt as if she was standing naked on the railway platform. Raising her head, as if to confirm her promise to Elizabeth, she saw their new employer pull up in a sleigh drawn by two large farm horses.

"Hello, hello," he beamed down at them. "My apologies for not being here when your train pulled in. You've arrived on one of our worst days yet. But you'll get used to it." Smiling he lifted the children into the sleigh and covered them tightly with warm fur wraps.

Alexander sat up front with Mr. Murphy while Janet sat with the children in the rear seat of the sleigh. Warm beneath their fur wraps, they watched their new surroundings as they bounced along the rutted tracks.

"The wife has your new home all fixed up for you. We're mighty happy that you decided to make your home with us."

Janet vaguely heard Alexander's responses but as the numbness slowly left her limbs, she watched this new world that now surrounded them. The fluffy flakes swirled around their heads turning their hair and eyelashes white like those of the old people they had seen sitting with heads bowed on the train that had carried them to Glasgow.

Young Alexander stuck his tongue out to catch the snow in his mouth and Elizabeth giggling, tried to imitate her older brother. Elsa burrowed further beneath the cozy fur wraps to keep the fluffy flakes from landing on her face which, when it happened, caused her small features to crinkle up with displeasure.

Janet smiled proudly at the antics of Alexander and Elizabeth and then glancing quickly at Elsa thought, *'Such a timid little creature,'* she sighed inwardly. *'So different from the other two. However will she manage in her new home?'*

It had been a long and difficult trip from Halifax and the family did not reach the Peace River District in northern Alberta until late November of 1924. With the exception of Alexander, they had all been seasick and had barely been aware, nor cared, about their living conditions for their first four days at sea. For the balance of the trip, they had eaten sparingly of the poor quality food they had been given, subsidizing it with the gifts of food they had received from their neighbors and friends before leaving Scotland.

When they arrived in Halifax, they'd all had to go through the rigors of immigration where their meager possessions had been poked through and snickered at. They had then been placed in quarantine and checked by medical officials. Janet had resented the way they had been treated, as if they were dirty and contaminated, and in some way untouchables. The experience had left her with a deep anger, not only at those who had put them through the grilling, but was also directed towards Alexander for his insistence about them coming to this strange and foreign country.

After the quarantine and medical check, Janet had been thankful when they were safely on board the train to Alberta. But the rail trip had proven to be a disappointment as well because of the biting cold and the dirt, which was everywhere. They had been forced to spend their nights sleeping sitting up in the crowded, noisy compartments with ill-behaved children and frightened animals.

Now, riding in the sleigh towards their new home, Janet turned her attention to Mr. Murphy who chatted almost non-stop, seemingly unaware of Alexander's abbreviated answers. Alexander's dream, she knew, was not turning out to be quite like he had expected it to be either. So far they had seen no riches, only poor people much like themselves who looked no happier than most of those in Galston.

"I've lived on this land my whole life," Mr. Murphy was saying. "We've three hundred and twenty acres, a half section it's called. We're about eight miles from Spirit River and about two hundred and fifty miles northwest of Edmonton. My folks came from the Old Country too. They've passed away now and there's just me and the wife. We'ren't blessed with little 'uns though. My wife has missed that. Must be a joy having young 'uns, Mr. Stewart?"

Alexander grunted noncommittedly in reply.

Mr. Murphy continued, undeterred, "There's lots of work on a farm. Keeps us busy most of the time. In the winter months, there's the animals to look after and the roadways to keep clear of snow and trips to town for supplies. In the spring and summer is when we're the busiest though. In the spring the ground has to be prepared for the crops and then the planting done and in the summer, we have to harvest and get our wood supplies in so we're warm and toasty for the long winter. Winter here seems to last forever and most days the temperature never goes above freezing but it's still a good life. Lots of fresh air and open space and it'll be good for your young 'uns. It'll take a while to feel right with yourselves coming all this way to a new country but you will and before you know it, Canada will be home to you like it is to us and you won't be able to imagine home as being anywhere else."

Janet knew Alexander well enough to know that his feelings wouldn't exactly coincide with Mr. Murphy's. Alexander would be looking for the gold. He wouldn't care about fresh air and open space, and although that may be what he would like, nothing would really count but the gold. She suspected that for his whole life, he would be searching for the gold. Sitting snug and cozy on the back seat of the sleigh, she sensed unhappily that this wouldn't be the end of their traveling.

The horses trotted along while little puffs of vapor formed around their mouths with each breath they took in the freezing night air. Janet liked the muffled sound their hooves made in the snow and the slap of leather against their flanks.

"Lookee folks, there's your new home." Mr. Murphy pointed happily to a tar paper cabin set back from the main track. Smoke drifted lazily from its chimney and bright spears of light shone in the windows beaconing to them, giving the young family a warm sense of welcome. Trees surrounded the cabin, "to break the wind," their new employer told them. "It helps to keep the cabin warmer in the winter too."

Pulling on the reins, the horses stopped in front of the doorway and jumping out, Mr. Murphy reached up to help Janet and the children down.

Once inside the cabin, Janet breathed in sharply. *'It may not be heaven,'* she thought with a sudden feeling of happiness, *'but it surely will do.'*

There were three rooms with two small bedrooms and a combination kitchen and living area. A wood stove stood in the corner of the front room radiating its welcoming warmth. The floors were of rough hewn wood with colorful woven mats covering them. The rooms were sparsely but warmly furnished with one bedroom having a large bed, a wardrobe, a dresser, a large overstuffed chair and a chamber pot. The second bedroom had three small beds, a wardrobe, a chamber pot and mats covering the floor. Janet sighed happily. It was much better than she had ever expected that it might be.

"The outhouse is in the backyard," Mr. Murphy told them, "but those are for your night time use," he said pointing to the chamber pots.

On closer inspection, Janet realized that the shelves in the main room were stacked with home-made preserves of vegetables, fruit and poultry and there were bins filled with all the staples they would need. *'I was wrong, this is heaven for sure,'* she sighed as she spun around to get a better look at their new home.

"Now you all must be tired from your long trip so I'll leave you be for now. Both me and the Missus hope you will be happy here." Turning to Janet he said, "The Missus will be 'round to see you tomorrow, Mrs. Stewart."

"We're up at five a.m. for the animals, Mr. Stewart. I'll be seeing you then," and touching his hat in a formal gesture, he let himself out into the below freezing temperatures.

Even Alexander permitted himself a small smile. "It'll do, I'll be thinking."

"Alexander, three rooms! And all to ourselves. And it's so—so—so," Janet shrugged, "wonderful. Maybe we will be rich after all."

"Of course we'll be rich. And no more coal dust ever again."

Young Alexander let out a loud whoop of joy as he threw himself onto one of the beds in the smaller of the two rooms while Elizabeth toddled along behind him giggling. Elsa remained in the living area, quietly studying her surroundings in an effort to make sense out of the collapse of her world as she had known it.

*   *   *   *   *

When the snow had finally melted in early April, they had been left with deep gumbo mud which had sucked the boots off the children's feet when they played outside. Both young Alexander and Elizabeth had laughed in delight, shaking their bare feet so their mother could see. Elsa, not liking the dirt and mud, preferred to stay inside the cabin.

Alexander began to help Mr. Murphy prepare the fields for seeding as soon as the frost was out of the ground. When spring turned into summer and the buds on the trees became full leaf, Janet marveled at the brilliant green of the plants surrounding her; plants that were not gray with a layer of coal dust. She watched the new sprouts poke their bright green tips through the freshly turned black earth and was happy for the changes in Alexander and for the fresh air but most of all for the friendship of the Murphys.

Young Alexander helped in the fields when he was allowed and loving every minute of his self-proclaimed importance, he followed Mr. Murphy around with a constant stream of chatter. Even Elsa eventually came out of herself a little and helped by keeping Elizabeth amused and out of trouble while her mother, under the expert tuteledge of Mrs. Murphy, learned the art of preserving the fruit and vegetables they grew in the huge backyard garden. They also separated the milk, which Alexander brought in each morning from the barn after he had done the milking, and in a hand-turned separator they made cottage cheese and butter that would last them through the long winter months. The butter took hours and everyone had to take a turn with the churn. The children thought it was fun at first but quickly grew tired of it. When the ball of butter in the churn grew as large as it was going to get, they took large wooden spoons and squeezed the excess moisture out of it. The children helped to collect eggs from the clucking chickens in the henhouse, laughing when a possessive hen decided to chase them. They made jam from the sweet strawberries that grew in the garden and jelly from the wild blackberries that grew beside their cabin. As the coal dust slowly seeped from their bodies, they began to taste the food as they had never been able to do before.

When the men killed some of the chickens, Elsa cried heartbrokenly at the discovery that they were going to be eaten. "Where you be thinkin' the meat on your plate comes from, young lady?" her father had harshly asked his daughter when he'd seen her tears.

Janet had been of little help when Mrs. Murphy first began to teach her the way to pluck the feathers and clean the gizzards of the newly killed chickens. Gagging and covering her mouth with her hand, she had run outside where she was sick over the railing into the morning glory vines below.

Mrs. Murphy had laughed kindly at her. "You'll get used to it quick enough 'round here, dearie," she told her. "You'll find there will be little winter meat if the chickens aren't killed and canned."

Janet enjoyed the daily companionship of the older woman and for the first time in her life, felt she had a good and true friend. The Murphy household was a happy one with Mrs. Murphy's constant chatter and Mr. Murphy's unusual but funny sense of humor; a humor that was usually aimed at himself.

Janet occasionally felt twinges of envy for the closeness that the two older people so obviously shared and thought of her own marriage where there was little communication and no love shared with her husband. However, she didn't begrudge the happiness of the Murphys. There were times, as the two women worked together, when Janet was even able to share some of her feelings with the older woman.

During their first summer on the farm, the children became brown and healthy and even Alexander had sweated most of the coal dust out of his pores by the end of that first year. He worked hard scything the tall hay and raking it into high stooks to dry in the hot summer sun.

"If we're lucky," Mr. Murphy said each time, "and the rains hold off, we'll get several cuttings off the hay field. Every year that is our prayer so that we have enough food for the animals for the whole winter through. If the animals have enough to eat, we'll have enough to eat."

After the crops were in and the food gathered for the winter, the men cut wood before the first snow flurries could make the task more difficult. It was the women's job to load it into the wagon and stack it under cover, adjacent to each home. They were careful not to pile it in front of the previous year's wood pile which had already been seasoned and would make roaring hot fires in the winter to come.

In September, the question of young Alexander's schooling arose. "Eight miles to school, in our winter weather, is too far for a young lad," Mrs. Murphy said. "I've got plenty of books here so you come along over here each morning, Alexander and I'll teach you your numbers and letters." And so Alexander's schooling became a daily and much looked-forward to ritual. The classes, much to young Alexander's disappointment were not held on Saturdays and Sundays. Besides the lessons, he enjoyed the warmth he found in the Murphy's home and the attention they showed him.

One day Mrs. Murphy, watching Elsa mother Elizabeth said, "She's such a quiet one, isn't she? I've rarely heard her say anything except when she's with her young sister," she said in an undertone to Janet. "Has she always been like that or was it the move that did it to her?"

"She has always been rather timid and aloof, even as a baby. She had formed a very special attachment to her grandmother and found it very difficult to leave her."

"Elsa dear, come here child," Mrs. Murphy held out her plump hand, her motherly face wreathed in a kindly smile.

Elsa obediently came to her side but didn't take the offer of the older woman's hand.

"Would you like to help me make some gingerbread cookies tomorrow, dear? If your mama agrees?" she added glancing at Janet.

Elsa looked tentatively at her mother and Janet nodded her head. "That would be fine. I'm sure Elsa would enjoy doing that."

Mrs. Murphy stroked Elsa's straight brown hair, smiling gently at the tiny person studying her with so much intensity. At her first opportunity, Elsa moved back to Elizabeth's side although she glanced over often at Mrs. Murphy's kind face, with her sad brown eyes.

*   *   *   *   *

At the end of the Stewart family's second year in Canada, Elsa turned six. Being tall for her age, she was still painfully thin and no prettier in spite of Mrs. Murphy's vain attempts to do something with her wiry, straight hair. She tried tying the child's hair in rag curls each evening but the following morning the curls immediately fell out within the hour. The braids that Janet did the child's hair in did nothing to enhance her long thin face. Elsa seemed to be the happiest when she was either with Elizabeth or alone with Mrs. Murphy and it was only then did something of the child she could be become evident. But it was always fleeting and later Mrs. Murphy was never sure if that little spark she thought she had glimpsed had really been there or if she had imagined it in her eagerness for Elsa's happiness.

'Poor little soul,' Mrs. Murphy often thought, 'she needs love so badly that she's starving.' Mrs. Murphy spent more and more time with the child because it was obvious that Janet doted on her son and everyone doted on Elizabeth and for the Stewart family Elsa hardly seemed to exist.

At the end of the second year, the family's obligation to the Murphys was over as their passage had been repaid. It was now up to them whether they wished to stay and remain working on the farm or look for another type of employment.

Alexander, Janet knew, was beginning to feel restless. He was enjoying their life but he still had a vision of himself as a man of riches, and not some little importance, and that image would never be fulfilled if he remained forever working on another man's farm. His dream was to own land of his own and not work someone else's land. For Janet, the past two years had been the happiest of her life.

"We'll stay another year so we ken save a wee bit o' money 'afore we leave for Vancouver," Alexander had finally conceded to Janet. "Vancouver is where we'll find riches. It's the cities that you have to go to get the well-paid jobs."

During their third year on the farm, Elsa's attachment to Mrs. Murphy became almost obsessive. She had slowly let down her guard when she was alone with Mrs. Murphy offering her a few glimpses of the child she really was. One day when the two were busily mixing bread dough, a chore Elsa loved to help with because she was allowed to make a 'little person' out of the dough to be baked, she had asked, "If you were my mother, would you love me?"

Mrs. Murphy felt the tears fill her eyes. "I love you now, Elsa. And so does your mother," she hoped she was right about the latter but had serious doubts.

"No, " she shook her small head emphatically, "she don't love me. And my father don't neither."

"I'm sure they do, dear. Different people have different ways of showing love. You're such a sweet girl, how could they not love you? And Mr. Murphy loves you also. He has often said, 'What a nice little girl that Elsa is'."

Elsa didn't argue further but shyly placed her small dough-covered hand inside Mrs. Murphy's larger hand and offered her a small, fleeting smile. Mrs. Murphy hugged the child to her and wondered how such a young child could have built such a high wall around herself. *What could have happened in one so young? Life will be hard for one without confidence or happiness. My dear,'* she thought, *'I wish there was something I could do for you to ease this heavy burden you carry.'* Hugging her again before releasing her, she gave her more of the bread dough so she could make bread figures for her brother and sister.

Alexander decided to wait until after the crops had been planted in the spring before leaving for Vancouver. Hearing the discussions between her parents, Elsa was determined that she didn't want to leave the farm. Gathering her courage, she approached Mrs. Murphy with tears streaming down her face, "I want to stay with you. I don't want to leave here."

Lifting Elsa onto her lap, Mrs. Murphy's plump arm circled the thin child. "Elsa dear, Mr. Murphy and I would love to have you stay with us and be our own little girl but I'm sure your parents would never allow it. They will want you to go with them but I will speak to your mother about it, if you want me to."

Elsa nodded her head. "Please, Mrs. Murphy. I don't want to go away. I want to stay with you for ever and ever and ever."

The lump in Mrs. Murphy's throat tightened but she smiled at the small child, her round face dimpling. "For ever and ever and ever is a very long time Elsa but we shall see what your parents say about the matter."

A little later when Mrs. Murphy and Janet were plucking chickens on the back porch, she had tentatively broached the subject of Elsa staying with them. Racing into the house Janet had turned on her daughter in a rage, "You terrible little girl. How could you do that? You have a family and that is where you belong. You have embarrassed our family by not wanting to come with us. What would people think when a child would rather stay with strangers than go with her family?" She raised her hand as if to strike the terrified child.

"Janet," Mrs. Murphy's warning voice forced her to drop her hand to her side. "Elsa and I get along well. We have a feeling for each other and it was a natural question to be asked when she knew she was leaving. She meant no harm. You can't mean harm when you ask from the heart. Elsa has a good heart and a kind soul; please don't be so hard on the child, Janet. You may say that I have no call to be getting involved and you may be right but I had to ask for Mr. Murphy and myself as well as for Elsa. We were never blessed with children and we would've been very happy to have raised Elsa as our own. But it's only natural that you don't want to give her up. Had she been mine, I wouldn't want to either." Smiling affectionately at Elsa, she dried the tears from the young girl's cheeks.

"Perhaps she'll be able to come and visit. We are so fond of her that we would hate to lose contact with her," Mrs. Murphy turned to Janet.

"Perhaps. We shall see," she answered grudgingly but the anger still showing on Janet's face when she glanced at her daughter did not give Mrs. Murphy much hope for the future.

The matter had not been mentioned again and in June of 1927, the family gathered up their few possessions and saying goodbye to the Murphy's, set off for the city of Vancouver in British Columbia.

Mrs. Murphy had fretted and worried about Elsa since the discussion with Janet, aware that the small changes that had so recently been evident in the child would quickly disappear, possibly forever, without the love she so desperately needed. She knew as she watched the family ride off in the farm buggy to catch the train in Edmonton that she would never forget the last glimpse she had of Elsa. Tears had run silently down the child's thin face, her eyes never leaving Mrs. Murphy's plump face. Elsa's small hand had waved until Mrs. Murphy could no longer see her. It was a picture of total and abject misery and Mrs. Murphy knew that the image would stay with her for the rest of her life.

Chapter VI

When the family first arrived in Vancouver, they had stayed in a three-storey clap-board lodging house near the heart of the downtown area. Sleeping in two cramped bedrooms, they had taken their meals with the rest of the boarders. Elsa had taken an instant aversion to the traffic, the noise and the smells and everywhere she looked, there were fearful stern-faced strangers. Everything frightened her and for the first few weeks they were there, she remained in the room she shared with her brother and sister, preferring to be by herself. She missed Mrs. Murphy desperately and at six and one-half years old had never felt so alone, unloved and unwanted.

In the first few months of living in the boarding house, Elsa refused to join her family in the parlour in the evening. "Elsa, you can't stay up here forever," her mother often chastised her. "Why don't you go out and play with the other children?" But finally shaking her head in frustration, she'd leave her daughter to her own devices. Eventually however, on a day that was her mother's birthday, Elsa agreed to join the family in the parlour.

After Elsa began to join her family during the dinner hour, one of the lodgers, a man named Frank Wilson, began to take a special interest in both Elsa and Elizabeth, often reading them stories or playing funny little tunes on the piano for them. He showed Elsa how to play chopsticks one day and how to read the notes of music. "E-G-B-D-F," he told her. "Every Good Boy Deserves Fudge and these are your F-A-C-E," he said, picking the notes out on the yellowed keyboard. He took her hand, moving her fingers over the keys. "See, you're playing a song. Here's another one and if you're a very good girl, I'll teach you how to play it all on your own."

With his fingers loudly striking the notes, he sang off-key in a loud voice, "Tom Lettie's goat was feeling fine. Grabbed three old shirts from off the line. Tom got a rope and tied him to the slippery slope."

Elizabeth went into fits of giggles and said, "Sing some more Mr. Man, please."

"How's this wee Elizabeth? The Owl and the Pussycat went to sea in a beautiful pea green boat," Frank Wilson sang out of tune as he turned to smile at the happy child.

"Play some more Mr. Man," Elizabeth sang as she ran around the room in time to the music.

"Your little sister likes my music. Do you like it too, Elsa?" His gray eyes held Elsa's in an almost physical grip. She nodded her head timidly. "If you would like me to show you how to play songs on the piano, you come down to the parlour tomorrow morning and I'll show you some more notes." He lowered his voice almost to a whisper, "And it'll be a surprise for your Mama and Pappa. It'll be our little secret, okay Elsa? Do you like secrets?" Elsa didn't know what to say to this strange man. "Okay, young lady, we'll see you tomorrow." Lifting her off the piano bench, he patted her bottom as she turned to go back upstairs to her room.

Each morning Frank Wilson would call to Elsa for her piano lesson and often in the afternoon would take her and Elizabeth for long walks in the small neighborhood park. Elizabeth would run excitedly on ahead while Elsa walked sedately by his side.

Sometimes he would take her small hand in his own large one, talking to her in a quiet, soothing voice. Elsa began to feel more comfortable with this large man and enjoyed their visits to the park. On the way home he would often stop at the neighborhood corner store, buying them each a sweet, hard candy. Elizabeth would thank him enthusiastically, hopping up and down, before running ahead again. Elsa always quietly thanked him, offering him one of her rare smiles as a special thank you for his kindness before popping the candy into her mouth where she would let it slowly melt while she savored the sticky treat. She also felt a slight twinge of embarrassment at her sister's lack of appreciation and manners.

"I'm so glad that you're finally getting outside, Elsa. A big girl like you shouldn't stay in her room all day long." Janet spoke to her daughter in a half-caring way as she casually leafed through a magazine.

As the weeks slowly passed, often only Elsa went for walks with Mr. Wilson and he told her stories of his wanderings and of his life as a drifter. He didn't seem to require any conversation from her and, in fact, seemed to be quite happy just to have a listener, however young that listener may be. And he always stopped and bought her a candy and sometimes even two sweets at the same time, one of which she always saved for her sister. Elsa enjoyed the attention she received from the kind man after her traumatic separation from Mrs. Murphy.

When the weather got colder, and sunny days turned to freezing rain and icy sleet, he'd often invite Elsa into his room to tell her stories or read her sections from a large book that he kept on a table beside his bed which she didn't understand. He'd tug at his dark shaggy beard as he did so and stare at her with his winter gray eyes burning into hers with an intensity that made her feel uncomfortable. At those times Elsa wanted to jump down off the bed and leave and then suddenly he would smile his lopsided crooked-toothed smile and the thing Elsa didn't understand would be gone as quickly as it had been there. Each day when she left his room, he would stroke her hair or hold her to him in a brief hug before releasing her with the offer of another candy.

Over the winter she continued to go to Mr. Wilson's room after the piano lessons, not because she wanted to but because he asked her and she didn't want to be rude by saying no. She knew that it was polite to be nice to him because he was teaching her notes on the piano. He continued to tell her stories, some from the big book which she didn't understand and didn't much like. And sometimes he would hold her small body close to his. At those times she could feel his breath warm on her cheek and sometimes he'd breathe loudly in her ear whispering things she didn't understand.

On those occasions, she would try to move away but he would hold her more tightly to him, only releasing her when he felt inclined to do so, patting her lightly on the bottom when he did so. She was uncomfortable with this attention but when his face became transformed into a grin, the feelings of uneasiness would pass. He was nice to her and she felt guilty for being unhappy that he touched her in ways that she did not like. She tried to avoid going to his room after those occasions but he would seek her out and tell her how lonely he was and that he needed a little girl just like her to listen to his stories.

One day when he took Elsa into his room, he had patted the bed beside him saying, "Come and sit beside me, dear." Elsa remained where she was standing not wanting to sit on the bed beside this strange man.

"Elsa dear," he smiled his peculiar grin, "please do as you're told," and taking her hand, he firmly pulled her to sit on the bed beside him. Picking up the large book that Elsa didn't like, he leafed through it until he came to a page of pictures. Elsa didn't understand the pictures and didn't want to look at them.

She tried to slide off the bed. "No Elsa," he grabbed her thin wrist tightly and the lopsided grin quickly disappeared from his face. "I haven't said you can leave yet and besides I have a candy for you. Don't you want your candy?" Mr. Wilson looked quite different from the man who had taught her the notes on the piano.

She shook her head and tried to pull away but he held her tightly with one strong hand while his other hand slid down inside her panties touching her, fondling her, his fingers probing, hurting her.

The tears slid silently down her face as she struggled to get out of his grasp. His face was inches from hers and he grinned, "You're not going to tell your mama or papa about this, are you dear? Because if you do, somethin' terrible might happen to that pretty little sister of yours. And you wouldn't want that to happen, would you? Would you?" he repeated squeezing her wrist again.

Elsa shook her head in terror while the tears continued to stream down her stricken face. 'Leave me alone,' a tiny voice screamed inside her head but there was no one to hear the frantic words she was too frightened to utter.

"You'll have to come and visit me often, Elsa dear," he grinned at her, "and this will be our little secret. I know you like secrets because the piano lessons were a secret too, weren't they?"

Finally releasing her, he put a candy into her pocket. "Remember what I said about that pretty little sister of yours, Elsa," he reminded her before letting her out the door. "And come back and visit me tomorrow afternoon," he grinned again into her frightened face. "Now stop the tears. We don't want that mama and papa of yours asking any stupid questions, do we?"

Elsa ran down the hallway and locking herself in the bathroom she sobbed, afraid to come out. *'I can't tell Mam,'* she cried to herself, *'she'll say it was my fault and that I was a bad girl.'* She saw the sticky red blood on her panties and sobbing harder, she took them off. She flushed them down the toilet afraid that her mother might find them and spank her for being so bad.

Elsa stayed in the bathroom for what seemed like a very long time, overwhelmed by her feelings of guilt and shame and unhappiness until she heard her mother calling for her. Slipping into her bedroom she got a clean pair of underwear before creeping downstairs, tear-stained and untidy.

"Where have you been, young lady? See the look of yourself, Elsa. And what have you been doing?" Janet peered closely at her eldest daughter. "Have you been crying? Now what's the matter with you?" she demanded loudly, her hands on her hips. "I've naught ever seen a child who spills the tears as much as the likes of you."

"Nothing," Elsa answered in a tiny voice. "Nothing is the matter, Mam." Elsa kept her eyes on the floor.

"I want you to look at me when you're speaking, young lady. Is there something that you should be telling me? Have you done something you shouldn't have been doing?"

Elsa shook her head, fearful that her mother would guess the truth about the terrible thing she had done. "No-no," she stuttered.

Janet turned to gather up an armload of laundry. "Well then, come along now, young lady and you ken lend a hand with this. You've naught helped me with a single thing all day. You're a selfish girl with naught a thought for anyone else but yourself; just doing what you want to do all the time. You're almost seven years old now; it's time you learned that everyone has to work in this life and you're no exception. Everyone has to help 'round here. Look at how much your brother Alexander does. He's always helping. He's a son to be proud of. And where is Elizabeth? I bet you don't know where she is either. Well, young lady, things are going to change 'round here. Now you ken help fold these clothes. I don't want to hear any arguments and you can quit your blubbering too.

You've had it too easy." Keeping her head lowered, Elsa silently began to fold the laundry and when she next looked up, Janet was gone.

Elsa managed to avoid Frank Wilson the following day and avoided her mother's wrath by making herself useful. She had also stayed very close to Elizabeth. In the evening, Elsa had said she was feeling sick, not wishing to go down to the dinner table with the rest of the boarders.

"It don't matter how sick you be, young lady; 'tis manners to attend dinner with the family. An' I won't hear another word 'bout it. You look just fine to me. If you stay up here, in an hour you'll be whining that you're hungry and then everyone will be inconvenienced," her father's angry voice admonished her.

Sitting at her place at the dining table, she had kept her eyes fastened to her plate, refusing to look to where Mr. Wilson sat even when she felt his gaze upon her.

Later she overheard him talking to her father. "That young daughter of yours, Elsa, she must be hard of hearing. I tried talking to her the other day and it was like she was stone deaf."

Elsa didn't wait to hear her father's reply but slipped away to the room that she shared with Elizabeth and young Alexander.

Much later, when Elsa was almost asleep, her father came to their room, tipsy and ill-tempered, "Wha's sis I hear, young lady? You been rude ta Mr. Wilson, he says." He lurched and then pointing his finger at her, said, "Tomorrow, young lady, you ken go to him and 'pologize for your rudeness."

"Yes Pa," Elsa had shrunk inside of herself at the tone of his voice.

Later that night, after Elizabeth and Alexander William had fallen into deep sleeps, Elsa had lain wide-eyed, tossing and turning. Unable to sleep, she worried about the apology she would have to make to Mr. Wilson the following day. She could think of no way of getting out of the situation. Whatever she did, she'd have to face either her father or Mr. Wilson and neither alternative was a pleasant prospect to think about. As she was finally beginning to doze off, she heard a sudden loud pounding on the front door of the boarding house.

"Open up, in the name of the law." The shouts were loud through the partly opened window and the pounding continued.

"Just a minute, just a minute." Elsa could hear Mr. Brown's sleepy voice floating up the stairwell as he hurried to the door. "What do you want at this hour of the night, gentlemen?"

"We've been led to believe that a Frank Wilson is a resident of your establishment, Sir and we have a warrant here for his arrest."

"Mr. Wilson? Yes, he lives here. He's never caused us no trouble. Are you sure you have the right person? Why are you arresting him, gentlemen? Heh, you can't just barge in here like this. This is private property you're on."

"The charges are serious, Sir. We do have a search warrant at our disposal so if you would be so kind as to show us which room is his, you will be able to return to the comfort of your bed without having missed too much sleep for the night."

"He's on the third floor at the back of the house. But with all of the noise you have made, he's very likely left by the back way."

"It won't have done him any good. We have the back entrance covered as well. We have foreseen all eventualities, I believe, Sir."

Elsa heard the heavy footsteps as they came up to the second floor landing and then pass by her door as they continued on their way up to the third floor. She heard the pounding on Mr. Wilson's door and then his deep angry voice, "What's the meaning of this?"

"Is your name Frank Wilson? Yes? Mr. Wilson, I regret to inform you that we must place you under arrest."

As Elsa listened, everything became a jumble of various sounds. Voices became louder and angrier but Mr. Wilson's voice was the loudest of them all. She then heard the scuffing and dragging sounds on the two flights of stairs before the front door finally banged shut and there was silence in the boarding house once again.

Elsa crept out of bed and pulled the curtain back slightly. Looking down into the almost deserted street, Elsa was in time to see Mr. Wilson struggling, his hands behind his back, being pushed into the back of a large black police van. She shivered in the cold room as she watched it drive out of sight, hoping that Mr. Wilson would never return again to the lodging house.

The following morning everyone was talking excitedly about what had happened to Mr. Wilson and why the police had taken him away in the middle of the night. Elsa listened while each of the lodgers gave their own theory. Elsa didn't care why he was gone only that he would never come back and she would not have to apologize to him.

"Very strange," Alexander muttered to Janet. "I saw naught wrong with him. He treated the girls as if they were his own."

"The police very possibly were wrong an' he'll be walking through the door in time for dinner," Janet answered. "He always had a candy for the children; I'm sure there's been a terrible mistake."

Days turned into weeks and Mr. Wilson never did return to the lodging house. However, Elsa continued to carry the fear and guilt with her and each time she thought of that terrible day, tears came readily to her eyes.

The Stewart family were in Vancouver for almost five months before Alexander finally found work in a factory that killed chickens and cleaned and plucked them in preparation for selling them to the meat markets.

Alexander hated his job, each day returning home crusted with dried blood and in a fouler mood than the day before. He adamantly refused to admit that it had been a terrible mistake to leave the Murphy's quiet farm where the air was fresh and the sounds of birds in the trees brought happiness to everyone. In his new job, Alexander's days were long and filled with the sounds of loud machinery, grating noises, yelling people and frightened, clucking chickens.

"But we were so happy there," Janet reminded him one morning as she stirred the porridge on the old wood stove. Elsa stared at the box containing the Quaker Oats her mother had just put into the boiling water and the Quaker man stared sympathetically back at her.

She looked around the kitchen of the two bedroom furnished apartment her family had moved into after her father had got his job at the chicken factory. The yellowed linoleum was cracked and broken. The dirt collected in the spaces in the linoleum and it was Elsa's job to keep the floors clean and free of the dirt. The paint was peeling above the stove and the counter top was old worn wood in need of being repainted. But she had been happy to leave the boarding house so she didn't mind this apartment.

"Somethin' better will come along." Alexander remained steadfast in this belief but continued to take his bad temper out on those around him, Elsa and Janet particularly. "And I don't want to hear 'bout the

Murphy's from you," he glared angrily at his wife, "or you," he said, pointing his finger warningly at the frightened child.

Janet glanced toward Elsa, where she sat hunched on the battered kitchen chair, and for a brief instance there was understanding between mother and daughter.

Young Alexander, at twelve, ignored his father, preferring to leave the house completely when he became too unbearable. Elsa was left to take the brunt of her father's verbal abusiveness. At seven Elsa didn't have the same opportunity to leave and so withdrew further in order to avoid the unpleasantness caused by her father's attacks on both her mother and herself.

Not long after his frustrations began with his job, Alexander began drinking again and becoming physically abusive, he often struck Janet leaving her with blackened eyes and bruised bones. Becoming thinner and more nervous and high-strung than she had previously been, she cried more easily often yelling at the children for no real reason other than as a result of her own frustrations. Elsa was the main target of her mother's unhappiness.

Watching her husband stumble around after one such incident while in his drunken state, Janet tried to remember why she had come to Canada with him. She also no longer knew why she had ever thought she loved him; it had all been so long ago. Suddenly remembering the money the Missus Cunningham had given her, miraculously still hidden away, she tried to think of ways of returning to the Murphy's farm or of returning to their home in Scotland.

'Mam Stewart,' Janet thought on one such day, "*has never written to us, not a word. But how could she; she who couldn't write a word? She loved each of us in her way, even her son, Alexander. What has happened to her? And to John and young Richard? Is young Richard a clergyman now? Mam Stewart would be so proud.*' Janet sighed as she wondered about her family so far away.

Turning to look at her daughter, she felt another pang of guilt, as she sometimes did, where Elsa was concerned. The sharp words seemed to jump out of her mouth without thought or reason where the child was concerned. Seeing the child now hunched up in the battered kitchen chair, shrinking from her father's words, she felt a fleeting moment of affection for her.

School life for Elsa was no better than her home life. Beginning on the first day of school when Janet had left her with Mrs. Smith, a stern-faced woman who taught the primary grades in the small school house, Elsa had been unhappy. Elsa had backed instinctively away from the austere woman with the rimrod straight back and the unsmiling stare. Her gray hair was pulled tightly back giving her a skeletal appearance. The woman had taken Elsa's small hand firmly in hers, pulling her stiff, small figure into the classroom. "Children," she said authoritatively, "this is our newest pupil, Elsa."

It was a nightmare come true for Elsa when she saw thirty strange faces staring back at her. "Elsa, say hello to your new little friends," Mrs. Smith commanded.

Elsa pulled her small hand from Mrs. Smith's grasp and running from the classroom, through the cloakroom, into the schoolyard, had found refuge behind the trunk of a large old oak tree. Clinging desperately to the tree, she wept as if her heart would break.

"Elsa, you naughty girl! Come here this instant," Mrs. Smith was getting closer to Elsa's hiding spot. "Oh, there you are. That was very naughty of you, Elsa. I shall have to speak with your mother about your behavior. This is not a good beginning to your education or your school life." Taking Elsa's hand, she squeezed her fingers pressing the bones of her knuckles tightly as she did so. In the classroom she forced Elsa to sit at a small desk directly in front of her own larger one. Elsa felt as if Mrs. Smith's angry eyes never left her.

"Now children, we'll get on with our lessons. I'm sure Elsa is ashamed of what she has done."

Elsa could hear the children behind her giggling and saw the ones sitting beside her, pointing their fingers in her direction. Wiping the tears from her face, she left dirty smudges on her thin cheeks. Staring defiantly at the blackboard, she tried to ignore the taunts of her classmates. But at lunchtime, when the children made a circle around her chanting, "Elsa is a crybaby, Elsa is a crybaby," she found it difficult to pretend that their taunts didn't hurt.

At the end of the day, Mrs. Smith gave Elsa a note. "You are to give this to your mother when you get home, young lady. She will want to know how you behaved in class on your first day. I can see that I will have to keep my eyes on you."

"Elsa," her mother called when she arrived home, "how was your first day at school?"

"Okay." Elsa tried to hurry to her room.

"Did nothing of interest happen?"

"No. It was okay."

"Well, when you get cleaned up, you can come and help me get dinner ready."

As the days turned into weeks the children, for the most part, lost interest in taunting Elsa. And because of her excessive shyness, she made no effort to join in their games during lunch hour or recess. Her free time at school were lonely times for her as she had yet to find a friend.

Class times were not any better. If she failed to understand something, Elsa rarely asked for fear of being embarrassed by Mrs. Smith or teased by the other children. And unable to ask either her father, who only came home when he was drunk, or her mother, who was becoming increasingly unhappy, for help with her school work, she found it difficult to keep up with her studies. She discovered that there was no help either from her brother Alexander since he stayed away from home as much as was possible.

Before long the children in her classroom had another chant to make her life miserable, "Elsa is a dumb bunny." Elsa's school life very quickly became as solitary and lonely as her home life had always been.

"What is this, young lady?" Janet glanced sideways at Elsa. "This is not a good report card. Your father expects far better from you than this. Mrs. Smith also says here that you don't get along well with the other children. Is that so?" Janet sighed. "Elsa, we have many problems. Need you bring us more?"

Elsa shrugged and having no answer for her mother, said nothing.

"What are we going to do with you, Elsa? You behave poorly at home and so it would seem at school also. See how you would have embarrassed us had you stayed with the Murphys. Mrs. Murphy wrote again asking about you but since I have nothing good to say of you to her, I will not answer her letter. Now are you satisfied? That's right, cry like you do over everything. Go to your room now. I do not wish to have to look at such a poorly behaved girl."

In her room Elsa cried softly for the loss of Mrs. Murphy. She had looked forward to those letters, often with a special note tucked inside for her. When she ran her fingers over the writing she imagined that she could feel Mrs. Murphy's love through the ink on the paper. Now she would never hear from her again.

*   *   *   *   *

In Elsa's second year of school, a new girl joined the class who was almost as shy as Elsa. The two girls quickly became good friends and life at school finally became enjoyable for Elsa. With her new-found friendship came an improved self-confidence and her grades gradually improved.

Melissa, Elsa's new friend was a foster child who had to work around her home to "earn my keep, my Pa says," Melissa told Elsa. "If I don't do what he tells me as good as he wants, he takes me out back and whips me with his leather belt. An' he always makes sure that the buckle gets me, but never where it shows. See, this is what he did to me last night."

"Doesn't anyone make him stop? Can't you tell the Police?" Elsa looked at the red welt on her friend's skinny shoulder. "Why did he do it?" she asked with tears in her eyes.

Melissa shrugged. "He said that I didn't look at him with enough respect. But I can't say anything because then they might put me someplace where it's even worse. I've been where it's worse and I don't want to go there again," she said in a small grown-up voice.

"My father doesn't whip me 'cause he hardly ever sees me an' he almost never talks to me neither except when he's mad or drunk. Elizabeth talks to me and sometimes my brother Alexander, 'cept he's hardly ever home either."

"What about your mother?" Melissa asked.

"She talks when she has to but most of the time she just lies on her bed and cries. My father is almost as mean to her as he is to me. The only one he isn't mean to is Elizabeth. Most times I just stay in my room and read or play with the doll that Mrs. Murphy sent to me. I love Mrs. Murphy. I wish I could go and live with her. She wanted me to live with them but my parents wouldn't let me."

"Who is Mrs. Murphy?"

Elsa smiled sadly. "She's a really, really nice lady and she loves me. A lot. She told me so. I don't know why my parents wouldn't let me stay with them when we moved here because they act like I'm not here anyway and I know they don't love me."

"I like you, Elsa. You're my very best friend. I've never had a best friend before."

Elsa smiled shyly at her new best friend and taking her hand, they ran over to the swings.

*   *   *   *   *

In 1929, when Elsa was almost nine years old, the country sank into a severe depression and Elsa's father joined the ranks of thousands of unemployed workers. Spending his days tramping the streets of Vancouver in search of work, he'd return home each evening ready to pick a fight with anyone who looked at him in the 'wrong' way. But there was never a 'right' way to look at her father, Elsa had long ago decided.

"Alexander, why don't we ask the Murphy's if we can come back and work on their farm?" Janet again begged her husband, while tears cascaded down her cheeks.

"No! We'll not be crawling back to them begging for hand-outs," he roared. "And you'll nae be whining to them either," he warned her angrily.

Janet could not understand Alexander. He was a stranger—someone she no longer knew. "They wouldn't think it was hand-outs, Alexander. They thought of us as family." She said the words quietly but her eyes were bright with tears that were impossible to control.

"We'll nae be goin'. Not now or any time," he yelled. Leaving the house, he angrily slammed the door shut behind him.

As weeks passed and Alexander had still found no work, young Alexander got a job selling newspapers. Janet, in an effort to help the family make it through the tough times, went into the rich ladies' homes and did their washing and ironing and dreamed of living as they did. The family managed to eek by a meager existence but occasionally Janet had to reluctantly dip into her small secret nest egg that Missus Cunningham had given her. Each time she did so, she sent a thankful prayer to the kindness of her former employer. She had never told Alexander of its existence or it would have been long gone for the drink he consumed daily.

Elsa and Melissa were inseparable during their elementary school days but never saw each other outside of school hours. The distance they lived from each other and the amount of work Melissa was required to do left them with little time for playing.

Elsa spent her summer holidays between the sixth and seventh grades doing household chores and minding Elizabeth while her mother was away at other people's homes. By the end of August, she was anxious to begin school again so she could get away from the constant criticism of her father. Having given up on job hunting, he hung around the house all day, waiting for other unemployed buddies to show up so he could go drinking again.

She was also anxiously looking forward to seeing her friend again. Melissa's companionship at school had made the last few years bearable and because of their friendship, her whole life seemed to have improved. She enjoyed being able to share her secrets with Melissa although she had never confided her biggest secret and the shame she still felt about it.

Elsa hurried happily to school on that first sunny day in September only to discover that Melissa wasn't there. She tried to hide the deep disappointment that she felt at her best friend's absence and looked forward to seeing her the following day.

However, she did not show up on the second or the third day either and by the end of the week, Elsa realized forlornly that Melissa was never going to come back. She mourned the lost friendship as loneliness again engulfed her. She had no one that she could confide her feelings to and no one to help her with her loss. And worst of all, there was no one to ask what had happened to her best friend.

With Elsa's grudging acceptance of Melissa's departure, she pretended that she was more interested in reading than in playing and that she wasn't as lonely and miserable as she felt. She wished it wasn't so difficult to make friends and that she wasn't so shy or so plain. She didn't feel comfortable with the other children's loud and boisterous ways and again withdrew into herself. But when she watched them from the corner of her eye, she envied them their confidence and exuberance.

Near the end of her seventh grade, a new girl came to the school and Elsa discovered she had finally found another new friend. Katrin was an immigrant, like herself, whose parents were Polish, speaking almost no English. Katrin, an only child, felt almost as insecure as Elsa did and it wasn't long before a bond quickly formed between the two lonely girls.

Elsa spent most of her free time at Katrin's home because her father had finally gotten a job as a janitor working the graveyard shift and while he slept during the day, he demanded absolute quiet within the house.

"Elsa," Katrin asked one day, "why don't you let my mother do your hair for you? She knows how to do hair." Elsa eyed herself critically in the mirror. Looking like Little Orphan Annie would be preferable to the way she now looked, she decided. *'My head looks like a square block,'* she thought as she looked at her brown hair cut just below her ears with the bangs hanging in a straight line across her high forehead. No effort whatsoever had been made with her appearance. When she had asked her mother for help, she had been told that she had no talent for doing hair and it was best that she learn how to do it herself. Her eyebrows were thick and dark, like her father's, and she hated the resemblance to him. "My face is so skinny," she complained puffing up her cheeks to make them appear fuller.

Katrin laughed at her friend when she next sucked in her cheeks giving her face a skeletal appearance. "I like the way you look," Katrin smiled.

"I don't. Do you think your mother could make me look pretty like Elizabeth?"

"Let's go ask her. She does everybody's hair."

Chapter VII

By 1937 when the girls were almost seventeen years old, Elsa, though still not pretty, had filled out a little and Katrin's mother had worked wonders with her hair. It now lay in soft waves around her face and swung freely against her shoulders. The rinses Katrin's mother used gave highlights to her mouse-colored brown hair. And because Elizabeth had now grown taller than Elsa, she was able to wear her sister's better cast-off clothes. Although her face was still too long and thin to be considered attractive, her appearance had improved so much that she felt more confident when she walked down the street.

*   *   *   *   *

The country had been in a terrible economic situation for eight years and few families hadn't felt the effects of it. The New York Stock Market had crashed in October of 1929 marking the beginning of the most severe depression the world had yet to see. To the people of Canada, it was worsened by the drought in the prairie provinces. Farmers walked away from their parched farms because the wind had blown away all of the topsoil. Wheat was scarce and their animals starved to death. Then the grasshoppers had come out of the skies devouring their crops and leaving them with nothing. With no jobs, the people had stopped buying and banks refused to loan them money. The poor were treated like criminals and people worked under the most terrible conditions because anything was better than nothing. A woman could work sixty hours a week in a textile factory for the total sum of five dollars. It was a time when hundreds of thousands of people were on public relief, factories and mines were closed, municipalities went bankrupt and people did anything they could to make some money just to be able to survive. Men travelled back and forth across the country riding the rails in search of jobs and when none could be found, they were sent to relief camps on make-work programs doing no-mind jobs earning twenty cents per day. There were hobo jungles beneath the bridges of Vancouver and across the country where hungry men gathered to share what little they had with a fellow human. There were bread lines and soup kitchens, the Salvation Army Old Clothes Depot and the 1935 Regina Riot which ended in the death of a police constable. The wounds of lost pride left deep and lasting scars in the hearts and minds of many of these people.

Elsa and Katrin had felt the effects of the depression as well. They felt it every day when they went looking for work, having joined the lines of the unemployed. They looked for anything; work as clerks, in a factory or as waitresses but each place they went, there were long line-ups queing for the few jobs available. Everyone was willing to work for mere pennies because a job was a job and if you had one, you were glad of it.

Alexander worked only sporadically and as the Depression years passed, he became even more discontented and bitter with his life and what he felt he had missed. His dream of being rich had died and at forty-four years of age, he looked like a man at least ten years his senior.

Over the years, the man he had become was evident in the cruelty that could be seen in his deeply lined face. He was slightly stooped and thin, with a slight concave chest, and although he did not appear to be strong, even strangers could sense the brutality just beneath the surface of his demeanor. He had no friends and even his family avoided his company whenever possible.

The years of the Depression, and her difficult life with Alexander, had not been kind to Janet either. She had aged greatly since their arrival in Vancouver. Rarely smiling and obviously unhappy, she had few friends. If Missus Cunningham could see her again, she would not recognize her as the same cheerful, bubbly girl who had first come to work at the Manor House those many years ago.

Elsa saw the unhappiness on her mother's face increase as the years passed. Janet became especially depressed when her only son, who she loved dearly, had left three years previously to join the thousands of young men riding back and forth across the country looking for work. They had heard nothing from him since and knew not whether he was alive or dead.

Elsa felt strangely unmoved by her mother's unhappiness and felt even less so for her father. She viewed both of them as little more than strangers. There had been a semblance of a family but never a real family and there had been a house but never a home. The fire in the fireplace, although real, had warmed neither family nor house and the coldness was there whether it was summer or winter.

During her growing up years, Elsa had successfully built a strong barrier against hurt and felt that the only one who could truly hurt her now would be Katrin and possibly, but less so, Elizabeth.

Finally in the Fall of 1937 Elsa found employment as a helper for a young mother living in a remote logging camp on Vancouver Island.

Elsa was torn between happiness at finally finding a position and the unhappy prospect of having to leave Katrin, her only friend. She knew that she would have to suffer the effects of loneliness again. Initially the thought of living with strangers had terrified her until she realized that she had been doing that all of her life. But all who searched tirelessly for work knew that a job was a job and you didn't turn one down no matter how unappealing it may be to you. "I'm going to miss you Katrin but I have to go."

"I know." Katrin hugged her friend. "I just wish that you weren't going to be there, among strangers, on your seventeenth birthday."

"I will think of you on my birthday and then I won't feel so alone. I used to think of Mrs. Murphy when I felt very alone. Sometimes it helped."

PART II ELSA

Chapter I

Walking aboard the C.P.R. Ferry from the downtown Vancouver wharf, Elsa clutched her battered old cardboard suitcase tightly. She had the beginnings of a hard lump in the pit of her stomach. Waving at Katrin, she leaned on the railing of the outer deck, letting the icy wind whip at her hair. As the vessel moved further out into the water, she watched the deep troughs of waves following behind as it made a wide arc, gradually leaving the wharf, and Katrin, far behind. She might have been crossing the ocean back to Scotland, so lonely did she feel.

Seagulls screeched overhead, occasionally landing on the railing nearby. Wrapping her coat more tightly around her body for warmth, she remain on the deck, not wanting to go into the interior of the crowded ship. She preferred instead to be alone with her misery.

Her parting from Katrin had been difficult with each girl promising to write every day. Elsa and Elizabeth had parted with hugs and promises of letters but Elsa knew that Elizabeth, with her active social life, would have little time for writing. Her father had made no comment when she had told him about the job she had secured for herself and had barely acknowledged her farewell. Her mother had awkwardly kissed her eldest daughter on the cheek and Elsa had smiled wryly when she realized it was the first kiss she ever remembered receiving from her mother. Even Katrin's parents' farewell had been more affectionate than her own family's had been when they had said goodbye. This fact did not bother Elsa and nor was it a surprise.

She was to be met at the Ferry in Nanaimo and then would be driven to the inland logging camp further up the island. Mrs. Clarkson, the lady she would be working for, had said that it was a two hour drive from the Ferry and to be prepared for the rough ride. "For the most part," she said, "the logging roads are barely cleared enough for the large trucks that travel back and forth constantly. I only go when I have to and now with another baby coming, it's not worth the trip".

Elsa had never travelled toVancouver Island before and in spite of the biting cold and her extreme nervousness about the task before her, she discovered that she was beginning to enjoy the ferry ride. She was even vaguely excited about the new life before her. She knew she would be responsible for the care of three small children, as well as household duties. The care of a small baby would be exciting too, she expected. "The meals will not be your responsibility," Mrs. Clarkson had written, "but all of the other duties of running the household will be expected. My husband is very particular about his meals so I will be preparing them myself." Her duties did not overly concern her because she was used to work but she wondered what her employers would be like.

'Would Mrs. Clarkson be a difficult mistress? And Mr. Clarkson? Would he be friendly? Maybe even too friendly?' Elsa was particularly shy and uncomfortable around men and for that reason was more concerned about her meeting with Mr. Clarkson than she was about meeting his wife. As the ferry ploughed its way through the water to Nanaimo, Elsa had many questions running through her head.

After the Ferry had docked, she walked out to the passenger loading area and saw a bright red pick-up truck with "Anmore Logging Inc." stencilled onto the side with bold black lettering. A man of perhaps fifty stood beside the truck, a haze of purple smoke circling his head. He had black curly hair, streaked with gray and what appeared to be a two or three day growth of whiskers on his weathered face. His eyes were alert and intelligent as he watched a group of small children playing, a paternal and good-natured smile hovering on his lips. Elsa walked timidly towards him. "Mr. Morrison?"

"Ah, you must be the new girl, Elsa Stewart. Am I right?" his friendly face was wreathed in a huge smile.

Elsa nodded her head causing her hat to bob vigorously on her head. She grabbed it before it could fall to the ground, feeling her face grow warm with embarrassment.

"It's very nice to meet you, Miss. The Clarkson children have been bouncing around for the last few days, plenty excited about meeting you." Elsa decided she liked this tall man. Grabbing her suitcase, he threw it into the back of the truck before turning to open the door of the cab for her.

"By the way, the name's Cye Morrison," he said extending a weathered hand in Elsa's direction. "Must be pretty scary for a young girl like yourself comin' all this way to live with complete strangers." Elsa swallowed with difficulty as she struggled to hold back her tears.

"Yup. I 'member when I first left my parents' home. Left when I was but fifteen and never went back. Don't regret it none though. Done a lot of things. Seen a lot of things but it ain't the same for a girl. A man likes to travel around and see the world but a woman needs roots; needs to know where she belongs. Ain't never had no daughter but imagine how your folks must feel havin' you leave home and all. Hard times we've got now but most folks are pleased to have any job, wherever we have to go. Your Pa working?"

"He gets work sometimes and my mother works sometimes too. They get by," Elsa answered as she watched the green forest pass by her window.

"Well, they're the lucky ones then. Before I lucked into this here job, I traveled 'round a lot. Weren't much work. Rode the rods, collected some pogey. Hated collectin' that pogey though. No man should have to get so low that he's forced to take hand-outs. Makes a man feel like he's a nothin' and that's hard for any man to take.

"Mrs. Clarkson here," he continued, "you'll have to get used to her. She's a bit on the moody side, they say, but okay from what I hear. The kids are real cute but a handful. I see them once in a while; more lately since the last girl left. Mrs. Clarkson doesn't have any control over them. Ain't had no discipline. Their Pa's in the woods all day long and the wife has been sick of late but you look like you can handle them.

"A quiet one, aren't you?" Cye laughed, not unkindly. "Ain't that just like me. I've done all the talking and haven't let you get a word in edge-wise."

Pausing for a brief moment, he continued, "Hear you're from Scotland. Do you remember much about it? Pretty young when you left, I guess?"

"I only remember my Grand Mam and that I didn't want to leave her," Elsa answered shyly.

"Must have been hard alright. Then you were in the Peace River District, Mrs. Clarkson tells me. Now there's a pretty piece of country."

"I liked the farm but my father's dream since we left Scotland was to come to Vancouver."

"Well farming ain't for everyone. There's some that like the cities. Myself, I prefer the country where there's birds and trees and some quiet time so a man can hear his thoughts. We're almost there. You'll feel a little overwhelmed at first but those kids will make you forget that in no time." Elsa smiled briefly and felt thankful that this friendly man would be nearby.

"Now if you have any questions or problems while you're here, you just come and find me and I'll be pleased to help you," he told her as he carried her suitcase up to the front door of her new home. "You may find it hard to make friends in a place like this. There's not too many women around; mostly just the loggers. So if you're ever feeling lonely, you come and talk to me. You and me will get along just fine, I think. You're a good listener. That'll come in handy with Mrs. Clarkson too."

With a nod of his head, he left her when the door was opened by a tall thin woman with piercing blue eyes. Mrs. Clarkson, looking severe and unfriendly, vaguely reminded Elsa of her old grade one teacher, Mrs. Smith.

"You must be the new girl, Elsa. Come on in. I've had a wretched headache all day and these children have been making my life miserable." She put her hand to her forehead. "They're going to drive me to the looney bin one of these days, I keep telling them. Now that you're here, I think I'll just lie down and then maybe I'll feel better," she sighed.

"That will be your room over there. Children," she called, "the new girl is here.

"This is Allan," she pointed to a boy of about four and a half with flaming red hair and the same piercing blue eyes as his mother. "And this one is Eloise," a slightly smaller child smiled shyly at Elsa from behind her mother's skirt, her blonde hair hanging in a tangled mess down her back. "And this one is Richard," she bent to pick up a young bald-headed child of about one and a half years old with a soggy diaper and a dirty face. "I want all of you children to be good for Elsa." She wagged her finger at them.

"Mommy is going to lie down. Allan will tell you where everything is." Leaving Elsa standing in the middle of the room with her suitcase still clutched in her hand, she shut her bedroom door firmly behind her, disappearing from sight.

Elsa looked around helplessly. The house was a disaster. Dirty laundry was piled high on the floor in one corner of the kitchen and soiled diapers sat in an uncovered white enamel diaper pail, permeating the air with its pungent odor, while large flies circled lazily above it.

The counter was littered with greasy dishes all stuck with dried food and disgusting congealed leftovers. Elsa didn't want to look any further. Nothing, it appeared, had been done for some time.

The three small faces watched her silently with wide-eyed curiosity. Elsa smiled nervously at them. "Allan, do you know where your mother keeps the diapers?"

Allan rushed off, returning with a fresh, unfolded diaper and handed it to Elsa. Elsa had never folded a diaper before and after several false attempts, the small boy took it from her awkward hands. "See," he showed her, "this is how to do it. I didn't know ladies couldn't do that."

After the baby had been changed, Elsa decided to begin with the dishes. The task seemed overwhelming but preferable to washing the dirty diapers since no wringer washer seemed to be available. Rolling up her sleeves, she filled the basin with the hot water that was already heating on the back of the sawdust-burning stove and turned to the task at hand.

"Elsa, Elsa, come. See what Richard has done," Eloise grabbed her hand and pulling her towards the parlour she self-righteously pointed her chubby finger at her baby brother. "See, he pulled Mommy's plant over and it's all over the sofa—and the floor," she added for emphasis. "He's going to be in trouble. You're a very, very naughty boy Richard." She shook her finger at her young brother in imitation of an angry mother.

"It's all right, Eloise," Allan chimed in. "He's only a baby. It wasn't his fault. He just wanted to get up here with us. Isn't that right, Elsa?"

"Yes. Now can you help me clean this up, both of you?"

After the mess was cleaned up, Elsa returned to the stack of dishes. "You can't do that," Eloise shrieked from the parlour.

"Yes, I can. I'm bigger than you are so I can do anything I want. Mommy says so."

"She did not."

"She did so. Ask Elsa."

"Elsa doesn't know."

"Children, children, you'll wake up your mother. How will she get rid of her headache if you're going to shout like that? What happened to Richard?" Elsa turned to the sobbing child, cradling him to her.

"Eloise stepped on his finger. You're always hurting him," Allan yelled punching her in the back.

"I am not. You're telling a lie and I'm going to tell Mommy." Walking towards her mother's bedroom, Elsa could see jam in the child's hair.

"Tattle-tale, tattle-tale, stick your nose in gingerale," Allan chanted at her retreating figure.

"Elsa," tears had started down Eloise's bright pink cheeks. "Make him stop. I am not a tattle-tale."

"Let's do some coloring at the kitchen table. Why don't you get some crayons and paper. You can draw some pretty pictures for your mother for when she wakes up." Elsa again returned to the dishes.

"Elsa," Eloise was screaming a few minutes later, "Richard is eating a crayon. He's going to die. He's going to die," she sobbed.

"It was your crayon. Why did you let him have it?" Allan demanded.

"I didn't let him have it," Eloise screamed.

"Shush, Eloise. Your brother is not going to die." Elsa cleaned the bits of crayon out of the baby's puckered mouth while Allan and Eloise watched. When Elsa had finished, Allan carried his young brother back into the parlour and Elsa hurried to finish the dishes before calamity struck again.

Elsa had fallen exhausted into bed on that first night after tidying the house and finishing the mountain of dishes. Her plan was to tackle the laundry first thing the following morning.

Unfortunately the rest of the week did not go any better than her first day had. The children were constantly getting into things and undoing what was done. And Elsa had quickly discovered that Mrs. Clarkson was not an easy mistress to work for quickly realizing there was no room for individuality, at least not Elsa's. Although the lady spent most of her time in her room resting or reading, she was very particular about how things should be done; her demands were specific and very much to the point. Elsa soon learned that her mistress' way was the only way to do things and a task wasn't worth doing otherwise.

Mr. Clarkson was not around very much, leaving at six each morning, he didn't return home for dinner until about six each evening. He made the hours between seven and eight on weekday evenings available for the loggers to meet with him in his office to discuss any problems they had. They also came to the house to collect their pay packets each week. Elsa paid little attention to their comings and goings, being too busy and too tired by the end of each day to care or to notice.

Allowed only one-half day off each Sunday when the family worshipped at a small nearby chapel, Elsa took advantage of the time to spend on her own. In the many years she had spent feeling lonely, she hadn't realized how wonderful being on her own could be as she enjoyed the few hours of peace and quiet away from the children and the Clarksons.

On one such Sunday, after Elsa had been with the family for almost three months, she was enjoying a quiet, solitary walk with last years fallen leaves crisp with unmelted frost crackling beneath her feet. Her face tingling in the brisk winter air, thinking she was alone, she stopped suddenly, sensing that another person was enjoying nature much as she was.

"Heh, aren't you the girl that's helping out at the Clarksons' place?"

Turning in the direction of the booming voice, she saw a man she had vaguely noticed once at the house, bundled up against the cold. He was wearing a heavy beige jacket with a red scarf wound around his neck. From beneath the woollen cap on his head, she could see a fringe of brown wavy hair. She noticed that the end of his rather prominent nose was bright red from the cold. He scrutinized her with eyes of the bluest steel. She looked away, feeling suddenly uncomfortable with the intense way he studied her.

Elsa remembered now that he had been talking with Mr. Clarkson at the house one evening, having come earlier than the men usually did. She had only noticed because he had a booming voice and was louder than any of the other men who came to visit.

"Yes. I'm the Mother's helper."

"The name's Peter Hall, Peter John Hall," he extended his callused hand in her direction. Elsa reluctantly shook his large hand, shying subconsciously away from his loud voice.

"Don't think I've heard your name yet."

"Elsa Stewart," she answered timidly.

"Ah, a quiet one," he boomed. "Always said, you gotta watch out for them quiet ones. Yep, they're the ones you gotta watch," he laughed loudly at his own joke. "Where are you from?"

"Vancouver."

"I lived in Vancouver for a coupla years. Was born in Ottawa though, down Ontario way. Came to British Columbia awhile back lookin' for work. Finally found this job. Lucky too. Not much else around. Not a bad place to work. Tough times these. You don't talk much, do you?"

"I say what I have to say." Elsa tried to move away. She couldn't think of anything she wanted to say to this loud, overbearing stranger. Her brain seemed to have suddenly shrunk up into a hard, tight little ball.

"You like walking, heh?" He fell into step beside her and without waiting for a reply continued, "We work the woods here six days a week, most weeks. Been here for 'most a year now. A bit boring 'less we go into Nanaimo for a bit of fun. Some of the guys do that on Saturday nights. I usually go too but didn't last night. If I had, I'd still be in my bed nursing a mighty bad hangover. But the truck had a flat so that killed our plans and we had no booze in the bunkhouse. What a miserable way to spend a Saturday night!"

Elsa smiled politely. Her fingers freezing in spite of her woollen gloves, she quickened her pace. She was anxious to toast her hands and feet in front of the warm stove in the kitchen before the family returned from church.

"Seem in a mighty hurry there, Elsa."

"I have to get back," she answered quietly. "The family will be back soon."

"Well, I'll just walk along with you. I'm headed back that way myself. Mr. Clarkson said for me to drop by later for a drink after they get back from church."

Elsa's heart sank when she realized that she wouldn't be able to enjoy a few precious moments to herself before the others returned.

"Those children are a handful from what I hear. The girl before you just up and left with no notice or anything. Just couldn't handle it, she said. She liked the night life. There's not much here 'though she'd come to Nanaimo most Saturday nights with the fellas. But it wasn't enough, I guess. Went back home to her folks. Funny girl, she was. Pretty enough but never stopped chattering and a little on the wild side too. Wanted to party all the time. I like to party myself but I think girls should be more the homebody type."

Elsa glanced sideways at him and wondered how anyone, male or female, could chatter away in his presence since he had talked continuously from the moment they met. He hadn't yet run out of conversation and did not appear to notice whether she answered him or not. It was a bit of a relief though, she had to admit, that nothing was expected of her in the way of conversation. All she had to do was listen and she suspected that may not even have been important. They were within sight of the house now and Elsa saw the bluish-gray smoke curling out of the chimney.

"They were without anyone for 'bout a month," Peter continued. "That's why things were the way they were. She don't do too much." He nodded toward the Clarkson home. "I wouldn't put up with it myself if I were her husband but to each his own, I guess. I think if a woman can't look after her husband and her children... .. That's her job! What else does a woman have to do?"

Elsa was beginning to feel extremely annoyed with Peter Hall. Opening her mouth to say something to him, the front door swung open and Allan's small face appeared in the doorway. "Elsa, Elsa, we've been looking everywhere for you," he smiled happily at her. "We thought you had gone away." Eloise appeared at his side. Elsa waved to her small welcoming committee while Mr. Hall followed her up the path.

"It's been nice talkin' to you," he said with a wink in her direction, "and I'll be seein' you around soon, I'm sure." Elsa could feel herself blush a deep crimson red.

During the next few months, Elsa occasionally saw Mr. Hall at the Clarkson home and would nod in recognition, smiling shyly.

Then not seeing him again for some time, suddenly one Sunday early in June when she had been there almost eight months, she ran into him when she had taken the children down to the creek. "Ah, Elsa Stewart! It's been awhile since we last met and how has life been treating you?" His booming voice greeted her with friendliness.

Elsa opened her mouth to speak but he continued. "I've been meaning to call on you and ask if you'd join me in going to Nanaimo one Saturday evening. Next Saturday night there is a concert at the Hall and I wondered if you might like to come along." He smiled, his thin lips stretching across even white teeth.

"W..., well," Elsa began, stammering slightly. "I'd have to check with Mrs......"

"Can you get away by 6:30, else we'll be late. The Concert begins at 8:30."

"I'll have to speak to the... ... "

"I'm sure there won't be no problem with that. Like I told you before, Margaret, the girl that worked for the Clarkson's before you came along always went into Nanaimo on Saturday nights. Well, gotta run now. I'll come by in the pick-up at 6:30 next Saturday. See you then."

Elsa watched him strut away, oozing with self-confidence. She smiled to herself when she realized that she was going on her first date without having had to say one complete sentence.

As Saturday approached, Elsa began to feel very nervous and wondering why she had agreed, realized that she hadn't. Her stomach was a tangle of knots and she was unable to eat for fear that she would be sick if she did. The Clarkson's had been surprised when she had told them that she would like to go to Nanaimo for the evening.

"I hadn't thought he'd be your type," Mr. Clarkson had muttered. "Best be careful young lady. He can talk anyone into doing anything and by the time he's finished with you, he'll have you thinking it was your own idea and you'll be the one with the problem. Margaret, the girl that… "

"George," Mrs. Clarkson interrupted, "I think Elsa is a sensible girl. She's not a wild one like that Margaret was and I'm sure you're worrying needlessly."

Mr. Clarkson sighed deeply, "I suppose you're right, dear."

When Elsa heard the truck in front of the house, she nervously pulled on her jacket, wiping her sticky palms on her handkerchief as she did so. He knocked loudly on the door and without waiting for anyone to answer, stuck his head inside.

"All ready, I see. Good, I hate to be kept waiting. Women seem to think it makes them more desirable but it isn't so in my mind. I admire punctuality."

On the ride to Nanaimo, she sat sandwiched between Peter and another logger named Earle. They talked across her, passing a bottle of cheap wine back and forth between them. Elsa was glad that they didn't ask her any questions and soon stopped listening to their conversation until Peter asked, "Isn't that right, Elsa?"

Elsa suddenly felt overly warm in the enclosed cab, "Pardon? I didn't hear what you said," she stammered.

Peter laughed loudly. "Isn't that just like a woman? Her mind is already trailing off somewhere else."

"Peter said that you're from Vancouver. Have you lived there long?"

"Oh Earle," Peter interrupted, "here we are. Look at that line-up, will you? Mighty good luck that your brother can let us in the back door, eh?"

*   *   *   *   *   *

When Elsa had climbed into her narrow bed later that night, she thought that the evening hadn't gone too badly. The conversation had buzzed around her and almost no conversation had been required of her. The concert had been good and later they had gone to the home of a friend of Earle's brother. She had felt out of place and ill-at-ease at first until she realized that everyone had forgotten she was in the room. Sitting quietly in a corner, she had watched and listened to the young people around her. It was all a new experience for her.

Peter had been the loudest and most talkative, standing in the center of the room entertaining the large group gathered around him with one joke after the other. He never seemed to be without a beer in his hand she had noticed and as the evening wore on, his words had become more slurred. "Oh Peter, you're so funny," one girl had called to him, giggling hysterically and Peter had grinned happily, saluting her with his bottle of Old Style.

As weeks followed months Peter continued to escort Elsa on Saturday evenings to Nanaimo and sometimes spent Sunday afternoons with her as well if he wasn't too hung-over. They developed a relationship of sorts and Elsa began to feel comfortable with him because she wasn't expected to talk or to be witty. The effort would have been useless in any event so the situation suited Elsa's shy nature. Nothing was required of her. Decisions were made for her and nothing was asked of her. In groups he took over and did all the talking so she was not very different than anyone else so gradually she began to feel part of them.

The onus was off herself because he talked enough for both of them. So when Peter asked her to marry him, she said 'yes'. It wasn't love like she had imagined love might have been, she acknowledged secretly, but it was what she needed and maybe, she decided, she was unrealistic in her expectations of what love might be. Maybe love wasn't bells and whistles like the books she had read said it was.

And for his part, Peter was confident that Elsa would not say no to his proposal. There wouldn't be a lot of proposals for a mouse such as her, he thought feeling quite proud of the fact that he was doing her a huge favour. That would keep her in line if she decided to get out of hand and he would have no problem reminding her of that fact. He did not want to marry any of the wild girls he had kept company with in the past. He knew when he had met Elsa for the first time that he'd met the perfect girl to become his wife. She would be quiet and easily controlled and she would never question what he did or interfere in his life. It would, he had decided early on, be a perfect match.

Peter John Hall had been born in 1917 of English parentage, an only child, doted on by aging parents who had been nearly forty when he had arrived unexpectedly in their quiet, well laid-out lives. As a young child, he had been allowed to behave in an abrasive manner because his parents had found it easier to allow than to control.

As a teenager, he had carried his cocky self-confidence over into being the leader of any group he had been in. He had worn the flashiest clothes, dated the wildest girls, gone to all the parties, whether he had been invited or not; and because he always had a mickey of rye in his hip pocket, had been popular at any party he attended.

He had cursed more than the rest of his friends and had a loyal following which encouraged him to more of the excesses. It wasn't that he was particularly well liked but everyone knew that wherever Peter went, things were happening and life wouldn't be dull or boring.

When the Depression hit Canada Peter had left his home in Ottawa, like many other young men his age. He had taken with him his already well established personality of arrogance. Wherever he went, he became the acknowledged leader whether it was in a boxcar or in a hobo jungle.

As a child, he had liked to be the centre of attention and he hadn't changed as the years passed. There were times when he went too far and only managed to get out of town minutes before the police got to him. When this happened, he'd be gone without a backward glance or a thought for the trouble he had left behind.

Peter and Elsa were married in August of 1939, shortly before Elsa's nineteenth birthday, with Katrin standing up for her in the minister's cramped vestibule. After the short ceremony, the small wedding party had gone to a dingy hole-in-the-wall restaurant in Nanaimo that Peter claimed had the best food in town.

It had been dark, smokey and loud and the waiter attending their table had looked dirty with a greasy apron tied around his ample belly.

Elsa's parents and Elizabeth had made the effort to take the trip across on the C.P.R. Ferry for the occasion, much to Elsa's surprise. During the dinner of roast beef and mashed potatoes, Peter had been so talkative and so loud that the entire restaurant had been entertained and even Alexander, Elsa had been amused to notice, had been at a loss for words when confronted with his new overbearing son-in-law.

Only Elizabeth had the audacity to persevere, causing Peter to frown at her continued attempts at bubbling chatter. Elsa had finally relaxed when she realized that her miserable attempts at conversation were not required. She'd have had to shout to be heard and since that was hardly in her nature, none expected otherwise. The only thing that marred the occasion for Elsa was her friend's obvious dislike of her new husband. It was so unlike Katrin to be so obviously critical. As Katrin was getting ready to leave, when they were finally alone, she said, "I will pray every night that you will be happy, my friend." Elsa wondered what lay behind the softly spoken words. She was aware of Peter's obvious faults but wondered if Katrin saw more than she saw.

When they had returned to the logging camp, after having spent the night in a run-down cockroach-infested hotel on the outskirts of Nanaimo, they gathered up Elsa's belongings from the Clarkson home and moved into one of the camp houses. It was little more than a cabin with two rooms and an outdoor privy. Peter did not wish her to return to her position in the Clarkson household because her hours had been long and she would not have been home to make his own life comfortable.

Reluctantly giving up her job, she began to realize in the early months of her marriage that what little independence she had managed to achieve for herself was now gone.

"Could I not work part-time for the Clarksons?" Elsa had asked Peter. "It doesn't take me very long to tidy and clean here and if I'm home to cook dinner, it should work out well."

"No, Elsa. I told you that I didn't want you to work for them. Find something to do if you're bored. Knit, or something," he had finally flung at her impatiently. With no one to visit, she spent long, lonely hours going for walks and thinking; trying to make sense out of a life that didn't make sense. There were too many things that she didn't understand and wished she could.

'If I could discover the problem,' she often thought, *'maybe I could do something to right it.'* She often thought of her parents and how things were with them and wondered what she had done to make them dislike her. Why did her father never look her directly in the face? Why did her mother never show her any affection as she did with Alexander William and Elizabeth? And Peter, she realized very quickly was too involved with Peter to care about anyone else. Why did no one seem to care whether she laughed or cried? How she felt seemed of little importance to anyone other than Katrin but Katrin was so far away. On those days when she was particularly sad and lonely, she felt that her life, her very existence seemed to be of no consequence. So why was she here? Why did she exist? What was her purpose in life? Was there one; she felt there must be a reason for her existence. There were always more questions than there ever were answers.

There was none who had ever cared except Mam Stewart, who was a faint memory and Mrs. Murphy who she remembered with a loving feeling. What terrible thing had she done to deserve this treatment? She searched her memory for a clue but could never find one. And why had Mr. Wilson done what he did to her? Had she encouraged him? Had she let him think that she wanted him to touch her? She couldn't discard the feelings of guilt, the embarrassment when she thought about it; the sick feeling she'd get in the pit of her stomach when she thought of anyone finding out about her deep, dark secret.

On their wedding night in the grubby hotel Peter had whispered drunkenly, "It's been a long time since I've had me a virgin." She didn't know what that long-ago experience meant with regards to her being a virgin. Was she still one? If not, would Peter be angry if he found out?

Grabbing her roughly, he had pulled her towards him, quickly fondling her breasts as he did so. When he took her as his wife, she fought to control the threatening tears. *'I thought our wedding night would be beautiful, like it always is in books,'* Elsa had thought later, feeling confused and disappointed. She found it difficult to think that what had just transpired between them was 'making love'. There had been no special words of endearment and the word 'love' had not been said once. Grunting, he had rolled onto his back, falling asleep almost immediately.

Waking in the early morning after their wedding night, he had looked at her out of narrowed, and bleery eyes, "You were a virgin, Elsa? I would have thought you were.

"You looked untouched by any other man but now I wonder." The stale smell of liquor came out in little puffs as he spoke.

"I was….until you." she lowered her eyes, not daring to look at him.

"Umm. It was different somehow."

"I fell and hurt myself when I was a child." She couldn't discern his mood and felt nervous under his piercing gaze. He was too contained and too quiet. "On my brother's bicycle. On the bar," she finally answered, her voice a mere whisper.

"On the bar, eh? Can I believe you, dear wife of mine?" He took her wrist and squeezed tightly causing her to gasp with the pain. "Because I don't like to be made a fool." He smiled a thin smile that didn't reach his eyes. "Well?"

"It's… . the truth. I was a… … virgin….until you….until last night. You're hurting me Peter."

"It had better be the truth because if I ever find out different, you will wish… … well never mind. Come here." He reached for her again. "I guess you didn't know what a sexy, horny husband you had, eh?"

Chapter II

It wasn't long before the world had turned topsy-turvey and Elsa had little time to think about her own problems. Hitler had marched on Europe and Canada entered the War in September. Going down to the recruiting office to join up with the army, Peter had returned home angrier than Elsa had ever seen him.

"They've rejected me," he told her disbelievingly. "Said my eyesight wasn't good enough. And something about a fallen arch. Capitalist pigs!" he ranted. "I know it's because they think I'm a Communist and they don't want any Communists in the army. They think we're nothing but troublemakers and agitators."

Elsa blinked uncomprehendingly not knowing anything about Communism. "Why would they think you're a Communist?" she asked timidly, fearful that his anger would be turned against her.

Peter glared at his dim-witted wife. "The world is eventually going to become communist, my dear little mouse," the words grated from between his clenched teeth. "Soon, through my efforts and people like me, there won't be any capitalism and there won't be Fascists like Hitler either. It will all be like Russia where the workers, the proletariat, are the ones who will be in power. There will no longer be a rich ruling class and all men will be equal. Leninism and Marxism will be taught in the schools instead of this garbage they teach now."

He paused for a moment. Elsa didn't know what to make of this sudden outburst. *'No,'* she thought frantically, *'Peter's a communist.'* "Will they put us in jail?" she asked nervously.

"You know," he continued, "when we marched from Vancouver to Regina in 1935, they called it the Regina Riot but that's a laugh. It could've been the start of a revolution if we'd had the proper leader. They called us 'commie agitators'. And some people called the C.C.F.

party communists—ha! They're pussycats compared to us! When we find a real leader, we'll have a strong party and when people see what communism stands for, they'll be begging to join our party. See," he pulled out his wallet, "I'm a card-carrying member," he told her proudly.

Elsa felt momentarily dizzy. "A communist? Why didn't you tell me?" she whispered, her heart pounding loudly within her breast.

"Why? What difference would it have made? I'm your husband and as my wife, you will accept my beliefs. In fact, I have some books I'll give you to read. You should try to understand my ideology. Do you know anything at all about Leninism or Marxism? I thought not," he said derisively when she shook her head.

"Matter of fact, I've been thinking that we should move back to Vancouver; I've been thinking about it a lot lately. Not much doing 'round here. Certainly no political action." He stood up. "I gotta go talk to Earle." He left her then and went down to the bunkhouse where most of the loggers stayed when they were in camp.

Elsa was glad to see him go so she could think about this new development. *'Everyone knows that Communists are terrible people,'* she thought. *'My own husband! How could I not have known?'* She felt ill when she realized that there was nothing she could do about the situation. *'I can't leave him,'* she thought. Her parents had made it plain when she married that she had made her bed and now must lie in it and that any decisions made by herself must be lived with, whatever the results. She struggled to keep from crying, not wanting him to see her tear-stained face when he returned. *'He'll know why and he'll be angry,'* she knew instinctively.

In the short time they had been married, she had discovered that he was neither patient nor tolerant and she didn't want to give him any cause for an argument. He loved nothing better than an argument. She had seen him with others and none had ever bested him in a verbal altercation. The words tumbled out of his mouth, seemingly without thought, all apparently just waiting on the edge of his tongue for an opportunity to be spoken.

Elsa had never found conversation easy, having to dredge each reluctant thought from the depths of her soul and then examine each one thoroughly before deciding whether it was worthy of verbalizing.

Often when the decision had finally been reached to speak the words, the moment had passed beyond when the thought could reasonably be said. So often when others thought she had nothing to say, they were wrong. It was only that the effort to say them had not been made or had been made too late.

While she sat there pondering this new dilemma in her life, the cabin had grown dark without her being aware of the approach of evening. "What are you doing sitting here in the dark?"

Peter had returned and she knew from the sound of his voice that he had been drinking. "Sulking, are you?" He lit the coal oil lamp on the kitchen table and then approached her on slightly unsteady legs.

"Heh! I want to get something clear right now dear wife. I hate to hear a woman nagging. It drove me crazy when I'd hear my mother go on to my father all the time so I never want to hear anything about me being a communist. It's my business and no one tells me how to run my business. Have you got that?" He grabbed her chin, pulling her face up until she was looking directly at him.

Elsa nodded her head slowly. Reaching down, he put his hand inside the front of her blouse and squeezed her nipple roughly, his eyes glazed from drink and lust. "If you want to be in the dark, come to bed. You've got yourself a horny husband, woman."

He pulled her up from the chair and pushing her in front of him into the bedroom, he shed his clothes into a heap on the floor. Elsa slowly stepped out of hers, carefully folding them and placing them on a nearby chair. "Hurry up! What's taking you so long. I told you I was horny and when I'm horny, I want a woman right now! You're lucky that I come home to eat even though I don't get my appetite around here."

Elsa climbed into bed beside him still thinking with shock of what Peter being a communist might mean to their life together. He pulled her towards him and began stroking her expertly.

Their times together, since their wedding night, had improved. Peter, Elsa conceded reluctantly, was an experienced lover and technically adept at making love. In spite of his abrasiveness on the other side of the bedroom door, he was usually patient and tireless once he had climbed between the sheets in his efforts to arouse her sexually.

$$*\qquad*\qquad*\qquad*\qquad*$$

At the end of January 1940, Elsa and Peter moved back to Vancouver. Elsa was happy with the move because she'd be able to really talk to Katrin again and tell her everything that had been happening. Her letters to her friend had been stilted and evasive fearing that Peter might read them. Now she could open up her heart to her friend.

Elsa had been suspecting for the last few weeks that she was pregnant and planned to see a doctor when they got to Vancouver. She hadn't mentioned her suspicions to Peter yet as she wasn't sure what his reaction to the news would be. On the rare occasions when things were going well, she didn't want to rock the boat and when things were bad, she didn't want to make them worse.

They had found a furnished one bedroom apartment above a Deli in the Italian section of the city and Peter had found a job in a meat processing plant. He loved it because conditions were so terrible that he was sure he would have many converts to his beliefs before too long.

Elsa had seen an old Italian doctor in the neighborhood who spoke poor English but who had confirmed her pregnancy. She waited for the right moment to tell Peter the news.

Several days after Elsa had been to see the doctor, Peter returned home from work in exceptionally good spirits. He had been agitating secretly for a union in his plant and was finding more support than he'd originally anticipated without being required to take heavy-handed measures. He had spoken separately with each of the employees to get their views about joining and several of them were now willing to meet with the union leader. A meeting was being set up for the following Friday evening. Peter was jubilant.

"Peter?" Elsa began timidly. "Can we talk? I have something to tell you." She smiled but couldn't quite control the slight tremor at the corners of her mouth.

"Can you make it quick? I have a couple of people that I have to meet with tonight that want to get involved in the meeting on Friday."

Elsa sat down, feeling the need of support. She hated it when he put her on the spot, making her feel inadequate and unimportant.

"Okay, what is it?" He looked anxiously at his watch.

"Well... .I went... . to the doctor, and... . he said... . that we were going to... . have a baby."

"A baby? Now?" He pursed his lips for a moment. "Haven't thought much about having any kids before but I guess it'll give you something to do while I'm busy with union matters. Then you won't be whining at me all the time." He looked again at his watch. "I don't have time to talk right now. I have to meet them at eight o'clock."

Elsa didn't know exactly what she expected. She thought he might have been furious but she hadn't expected this total indifference either. The union and his communist activities were all he seemed to be interested in. She patted her still flat stomach. 'Don't worry Baby,' she whispered, "I'll love you enough for both of us."

Over the next few months, the baby brought a new purpose to Elsa's life. When she first felt the baby move within her womb, she experienced a joy such as she never expected to feel. While sewing and knitting tiny little garments for the baby, she marvelled at the wonder of this new life growing within her. The baby would be truly hers. She would love it and she knew it would love her in return.

She shared her excitement about the baby with Katrin. Her friend was, as yet, unmarried although she was keeping the company of a very pleasant young man whom Elsa liked enormously. Katrin would occasionally show up with some small gift for the baby and Elsa would lovingly place it with the rest of the things that she had made.

"Have you seen your mother or father lately?" Katrin asked on one of her visits.

"No. My father never comes to visit and my mother has been only once since she heard about the baby. She looks so old now. I couldn't get over it when I saw her last. Elizabeth has been a few times though and she told me that they had heard that Alexander has joined the army. Peter is green with jealousy that Alexander got into the army and he couldn't. Why has Michael not gone to fight Katrin? I thought every able-bodied man was planning to join up."

Katrin shrugged. "Michael feels it will be over soon but the main reason is he doesn't believe in wars. He says the only reason there are wars is because there are fools willing to fight and that if the heads of government want to have wars, they should fight it themselves."

"Peter says Hitler is a Fascist and has to be stopped. He said Hitler will take over Europe if he's not stopped and then maybe North America will be next. I don't see how one man can be that powerful, do you?"

"I don't know. I'm just glad that Michael isn't going to fight. Every day that you hear the news, more soldiers have been killed. No matter who you talk to, they know someone who has been killed. I hate war." Katrin smiled suddenly. "It's not too long now before Baby will be here. I can hardly wait." She patted her friend's enlarged belly.

"I can hardly wait either although I love the feeling of the baby moving." The sadness had lifted from Elsa's face when she thought of her baby. She had become bonnier during her pregnancy since her face had filled out into a rounder, softer shape and her eyes had a shine that had not been there previously. Anxiously awaiting the moment of the birth of her first born child, she said, "I'm all ready. I even have the baby's coming home clothes packed."

$$* \qquad * \qquad * \qquad * \qquad *$$

Elsa went into labour three days after their first wedding anniversary. When the water had broken and the pains were five minutes apart, Peter had reluctantly postponed a meeting and taken her to the hospital. Elsa knew that in some way she would have to eventually pay for this inconvenience to him. "This kid," Peter complained, " is coming at a very bad time. I'm in the middle of negotiations between labour leaders, union representatives and the employees of the plant."

Elsa panted between contractions. "I'm sorry Peter but it couldn't be planned. It's almost two weeks late as it is. You're so busy that no time would really be convenient."

"I will remember that. I have gone to the effort of taking you to the hospital and this is the appreciation I get."

At the hospital, the doctor had explained in his poor English, after examining Elsa, that the baby would be some time yet in arriving, perhaps not until the following morning. "Then there's no point in me hanging around," Peter said upon hearing this news. Leaving, he had half-heartedly promised to return as soon as he had sorted the problem out between the various groups.

"And," he told Elsa before he left, "I expect that you understand and appreciate the importance of my attendance at these meetings. I've brought it this far and I have no intention of dropping it like a hot potato. They count on me and they need me. I am their leader. Do you understand?"

Elsa had nodded when suddenly a fierce pain had gripped her. When the pain had subsided, she opened her eyes and with her face glistening with perspiration, she realized that her husband had already left. She didn't really mind. *'This is my baby and I will do anything for him, even die for him if necessary,'* she thought.

At three a.m., William Peter James made his entrance into the world much earlier than the doctor had anticipated, causing a small commotion in the delivery room. Screwing up his tiny red face in the glare of the bright lights, he screamed loudly at the unfriendly reception. Continuing to complain long and heartily, he finally fell into an exhausted sleep while Elsa held him in the crook of her arm. Gazing at his tiny face she felt her heart expand, filling her chest with a love such as she had never before felt.

Tired herself, Elsa smiled at her young son, unable to take her eyes from his small face with the plumply rounded cheeks, the tiny rosebud mouth and the light brown fuzz on the top of his perfectly shaped head. His tiny hand curled around her finger and she felt as if her heart was going to explode with the love she felt for this child.

Peter arrived at eleven a.m. the following morning full of his accomplishments of the night before. His son was hardly mentioned after a cursory glance into the nursery. "Without me, they wouldn't have been able to do it. We'll have the union in the plant now. All because of me," he said beaming. "Of course the bosses aren't too happy but the union will look after the workers now. We're going to demand better wages, better working conditions and shorter working hours."

"Do you think you'll get your demands?" Elsa asked wearily.

"We will. Everyone is solidly behind the union one hundred percent and we're all ready to fight and the bosses know it."

"Is it possible that you could lose your jobs?"

"Haven't you been listening to me? There's not a chance of that. The union wouldn't allow it. That's the point of having a union; to protect the workers against unscrupulous and unfair bosses."

"What do you think of your son, Peter?"

"Husky looking fellow. We'll breed our own little communists." He laughed heartily.

Elsa lay back against her pillow feeling suddenly very tired. *'I will never, never let you brainwash my child,'* she silently promised as she closed her eyes so he wouldn't see her anger.

During the ten days that Elsa remained in the hospital, she tried not to feel pangs of jealousy at the happiness other couples seemed to share over the births of their babies. Peter came to the hospital only four times during that period claiming heavy demands on his time with union duties and he brought neither flowers, smiles or reassurances of love. She tried not to care, choking back the tears when she saw the loving husbands around her, walking happily arm-in-arm with their wives, smiling proudly through the nursery window at their new offspring.

When Elsa returned home, nothing had changed between her and Peter. However, it no longer mattered as she kept herself busy happily caring for wee Willie. He was a contented and healthy baby, smiling readily at those around him and he had a devoted and loving audience in his mother and Auntie Katrin.

"He is beautiful, Elsa. Now that Michael and I are married, we plan to have several children. But we don't want to bring children into such an unsettled world right now – but soon, I hope."

"I know that times aren't good and everything is so unsettled but I'm so happy that I have Willie. Now I know that my life has a purpose," Elsa smiled at Katrin.

The union activities seemed to be a springboard for Peter and he next organized a political group that began meeting weekly in their small apartment. They drank heavily and the apartment was soon filled with a pall of hazy blue cigarette smoke while they discussed the various philosophies of Lenin, Marx and Trotsky.

Often arguments would erupt and voices would be raised angrily as each person argued their own particular ideology. Elsa often thought that each person's theory seemed to be as unique as their own personal fingerprints, each agreeing on nothing.

That seemed to be the glue that stuck these people together. During those days there seemed little glue sticking Elsa and Peter together, not even wee Willie.

Elsa hated the meetings; and the noise and the ashes scattered on her polished floor. She seethed at the overturned ashtrays and the butts pressed onto saucers, into plant pots or floating in half-drunk cups of coffee and beer.

The group that Peter was involved with were loud and obnoxious but Peter was the loudest of them all. He was the centre of attention and he revelled in it; again he was the flashy teenager with no respect for the police or right-wing government officials. "We'll infiltrate the government at the lower levels," Peter suggested at one of the meetings.

"They act like nothing more than small bickering children," Elsa confided one day to Katrin, "but I'm frightened of them and their ideas and I suspect that many of them have twisted and dangerous minds. They're the misfits of society and they're in our apartment with wee Willie.

"Have you heard about the speeches Peter gives wherever he can about the injustices of the blacks in the United States, about the disgrace of poverty around the world, about the oppression of the poor by the rich ruling class? He has left-wing propaganda printed and his group distribute it on street corners calling for the overthrow of all bureaucrats, landlords and capitalists. 'Workers unite', and 'Fight the bourgois bosses,' is their rallying call.

"He's trying to get me to follow his left-wing propaganda and he's told me stories of children of left-wing parents being put into hospitals with relatively non life-threatening illnesses and never coming out alive because extreme right-wing doctors work together with the police and government in an effort to get rid of all the communists. He told me that he and his group are under surveillance and they may have to go underground with their activities to save the workers of the world."

Elsa began having nightmares and dreamed of being chased and running and hiding while trying to keep young Willie from crying out and giving their hiding place away. She never saw the faces of her pursuers, only heard their running feet behind her, pounding the pavement or crashing through brush in a dark forest. Every night the dream returned and each night she would waken in a cold sweat. Her daytimes also became living hells and she suspected all strangers of watching and waiting for her and Willie in an effort to get to Peter and his group.

"Katrin, I keep thinking that we're going to be kidnapped and held hostage so they can get at Peter. The awful thing is, Peter wouldn't care. While he spends every spare moment of his time trying to better the world for these unknown workers, the proletariat, who are one day supposed to rise up and overthrow the right-wing ruling class, we are suffering the abuses of his temper and neglect. I constantly look over my shoulder; I don't know what I'm going to do and he's becoming more involved with his political group."

Katrin shook her head sadly, "Oh Elsa. I don't blame you for being frightened. I would be terrified. Do you think that they're trying to start a revolution like they had in Russia?"

"I don't know," Elsa shrugged. "He's become so secretive lately that I just don't know. They don't even meet here anymore. Don't you think if they were trying to do that, they'd have had a better chance before the war when no one had jobs and everyone was frustrated and unhappy. They can't have a revolution without people to follow them, can they? And anyway, his group is not very large unless a lot more people have joined since they've been meeting here. I'm afraid because I think some of the people in his group are evil and dangerous and they scare me. I think some of them would be capable of doing just about anything. But at least they don't meet here any more so for that I am glad."

"Are you afraid of Peter?"

"Sometimes but I'm more afraid of what all of this might be doing to Willie. And Katrin, I think I'm going to have another baby. If things were different, I would be so happy to have another child."

Katrin laid her hand on her friend's arm. "Perhaps he's just telling you all of these stories to keep you frightened so that he can dominate you and keep control over you.

"He wants you under his thumb and afraid so you won't ever complain about what he's doing. I don't know how you tolerate it, Elsa." Katrin smiled sadly at her friend.

"But I have some news for you also. I just came from seeing the doctor and Michael and I are going to have a baby too. I know we hadn't planned to now because of the way the world is but we both agreed that we're very happy about it. So Elsa, our babies will be very nearly the same age. Won't that be nice? And they'll be as good friends as we are, I'm sure of it."

Elsa smiled for the first time since her friend had stopped in to visit and felt a little of the gloom lift from her trampled spirits. Katrin always had a warming affect on her.

"I hope they will be." She glanced at the kitchen clock and jumped up, fear stark on her face. "Oh Katrin, I have to get dinner started. Peter will be home soon and he'll start yelling if it's not ready when he gets here."

"Why do you let him treat you like that? You're his wife, not his slave. Has he ever hit you, Elsa?"

"No." She lowered her head. "But I'm never sure that he won't," she whispered. "He yells a lot and he's very critical and I never seem to be able to do anything that pleases him. But sometimes words can cut just as deeply." Elsa's eyes filled with tears.

"Oh Elsa, poor Elsa," Katrin hugged her friend.

"It's not really so bad. I've got Willie and I have you Katrin, and Michael."

"You'll always have us, dear." Katrin smiled affectionately at her friend. "Now I must go but I'll talk to you in a few days." and she was out of the door in a swirl of happiness to hurry home to tell Michael the good news that they had both already suspected.

Chapter III

Sarah Ann was born on a cold wind-whipped day in March of 1942. She came into the world spirited. She had spunk; she was indomitable; full of energy and determination. People in her life learned quite quickly to see things her way or she screamed gustily in frustration. No one minded because there was a sweet side to Sarah as well and as she grew older, her fairness became well known and was nicely tempered with her perseverence.

Elsa adored her daughter from the minute she saw the dark wise eyes peering so intently into her own. As her heart expanded within her chest, she traced the tiny heart-shaped face, with the turned-up button nose, gently with her finger. Touching the small hands with the curled-up fingers lovingly, she smiled at her beautiful daughter wondering as she did so, how she of the plain face and mousey contenance could have given birth to this perfection.

Katrin's baby, born a month earlier, had been a daughter also. Elsa had prayed fervently for a daughter so the two children could become fast friends, as she and Katrin were, growing and playing together.

Elsa was anxious to leave the hospital as quickly as possible, worrying constantly about the stories Peter had told her. She watched diligently over the safety of her brand-new infant, her face pressed constantly against the nursery window, fearful of reactionaries in the hospital system that might be waiting for the opportunity to snatch her infant from her. At each feeding when the baby was brought to her, she completely unwrapped her, checking to make sure that she was still as perfect as she had been when last she'd seen her.

Peter had told her that people were paid large sums of money to get rid of people they didn't want and that they were everywhere and so she trusted no one. She was afraid to fall asleep at night in case little Sarah

Ann disappeared during the long hours that she was forced to be apart from her child. She feared that she would be kidnapped, or tortured or taken to be raised by someone else; a stranger who didn't love her like she did. Her fears were endless and by the time Elsa left the hospital, she was a nervous wreck.

Shortly after Sarah Ann's birth, Janet visited Elsa at home. "Are you alright Mam, you look very tired. Have you not been well?"

Janet stared wordlessly at her daughter, her eyes seemingly bright wth unshed tears. *'But perhaps it was just the way the light shone on her face,'* Elsa decided.

"Would you like to see your newest grandchild? She's beautiful." Elsa picked Sarah Ann out of the nearby cot.

"May I hold her?" Janet asked.

With surprise Elsa placed the sleeping baby into her mother's arms. "Sarah Ann is a lovely name. It suits her." Looking at her daughter with sadness, she finally asked, "How are things between you and Peter?"

Unsure of where this conversation was leading, Elsa merely shrugged.

"I've heard things," her mother continued. "I've heard about the speeches Peter gives. They say he's a troublemaker." Searching her daughter's face, she finally asked, "Does he mistreat you and the children?"

Elsa felt laughter bubble inside her and thought of the irony of the question. *'Different than my own parents did?'* she thought angrily. Instead she said, "Peter isn't here much. He goes to meetings most evenings, he gives speeches and he tries to get converts for his small group of followers. He's worked long hours agitating to get unions into other plants. I think he's had some successes with this but I'm not sure. I don't ask because every question becomes a long lecture. And I'm not interested in his political beliefs."

"Well, I should certainly hope not. That is not a woman's role. Are there women in this....this movement?"

"I have no idea and I don't care what a woman's role is supposed to be. I just know that my life is with my children and I do not want to be lectured about an ideology I care nothing about. I have no interest in unions or Marxism. How is Papa?"

With her eyes downcast Janet muttered, "Your father is fine."

"Elizabeth said he's working now."

"Yes, with all the young men at war, he's been able to get some work. He'll never be a happy man though." Standing up quickly, "Is wee Willie sleeping? Oh well, perhaps I'll see him another time."

The war in Europe was still being fought and more men were going across the waters to fight every day. Even women were becoming involved and losses in terms of human life were high. Rationing of petro and food was everywhere. The stories Elsa heard were frightening about the atrocities of the German Nazis; about the plundering, the looting, the concentration camps, the killing of Jews in gas chambers and the experiments that were being done on prisoners. Every story told of cruelty, killing, maiming and abuses.

When Elsa heard that Alexander William had been sent home, she decided to visit him, choosing a time she knew her father would be at work.

"Hello Mam. Elizabeth told me about Alexander William. May I come in?"

Elsa was shocked by her mother's appearance. Janet had aged considerably since she had been to visit her a few weeks previously. Nodding, Janet stepped aside while tears streamed down her face. "He's asleep now but we'll sit in here so we don't disturb him."

"What happened, Mam?"

Janet put her face in her hands. "It's so terrible. He's lost his left leg below the knee. It happened when a grenade landed in his foxhole. He was the only one that escaped; nine of his comrades died in the blast. He's returned, and I thank God that he's alive, but besides the loss of most of his leg, his spirit was destroyed with the explosion of that grenade.

"He has aged twenty years and he's bitter and resentful of those who have not joined in the war effort. He says that it's a man's duty to protect our country against men like Adolf Hitler. He said that if it could happen there, it could happen here too."

"When did it happen?"

"A couple of months ago but I didn't hear until shortly before he arrived home. Thank God he was able to come home."

Elsa looked at her mother's shrunken, pathetic figure and wasn't sure what she felt for her. "William Alexander is strong. I think once he gets over the worst of the shock and his health recovers, he'll be fine."

"I didn't see him," Elsa told Katrin when she picked up the children. "Mam said he was sleeping and she doesn't disturb him when he is because he has problems getting to sleep because of the pain. She looked so old, I almost didn't recognize her when she answered the door. She said he just sits and reads and listens to his favorite shows on the radio. She said he never misses the Green Hornet and will turn his back on whoever is there when it comes on."

"I'm sure he'll be fine. I remember William Alexander as being very vibrant. I'm sure the shock will take him awhile to overcome but he'll be fine, Elsa."

"Mam said that he's very angry about those men who don't go to war and those who do nothing for the war effort. Most are doing something for the war effort. There are fewer men in the stores and on the streetcars and women are now doing jobs previously done by men."

"I've certainly noticed. And you and I are knitting socks for the soldiers overseas as our contribution to the war effort. Everyone is becoming involved. I've heard of grandmothers who send care packages and even young children collect foil from cigarette packages for its lead content. I believe most are helping one way or another."

"And women are becoming more vocal now that they are the ones who have to make the decisions that men used to make—I know I'm not one of those women," Elsa smiled. "My life hasn't changed because of the war."

"No," Katrin agreed. "Not with Peter around. I know you won't mind me saying this but your husband possesses a great number of traits and characteristics that are neither pleasant nor desirable."

Elsa laughed. "Katrin, I can always trust you for your honesty." Elsa was unsure whether these characteristics had always been there or not but he seemed to have become a stranger even while they shared the same home.

"I'll admit that he does tend to have an arrogant and aggressive personality with tendencies towards being self-centered and egotistical. But Katrin, he is the father of my children and I can't change that. I love my children dearly and will do nothing that would alter their lives or bring disgrace upon our family."

"Elsa, my dear, I was merely making an observation."

*   *   *   *   *

William and Sarah were as different as night was from day. Willie's placid nature always gave way to Sarah's more head-strong personality but it always appeared to be a mutual agreement with no friction evident. Both children were as devoted to each other as their mother was to them.

"Elizabeth," Elsa confided in her sister when she discovered that she was again pregnant, "I don't know how my heart will be able to expand to love another child as much as I love these two."

"You will be able to. I envy you, Elsa. I would love to have children but I haven't found the father I want for them yet."

*   *   *   *   *

When in June of 1944 twin sons were born to Elsa and Peter, she discovered that her heart easily expanded to love not one, but two extra little people. The twins, named Elliott and Martin, although carbon copies of each other, looked like neither their older brother or their sister. Elsa was quite besotted with them as well.

"Elsa, with all of these children, you should have some conveniences. You have nothing that would make it easier for you." Katrin was incensed.

"Peter insists that only the necessities are required. He feels that anything that makes life more comfortable or easier for me is bourgeois. He said I can't be one of the proletariat if I'm not prepared for a life of struggle."

"But it's not you who wants to be one of the proletariat."

"I don't quite understand his logic either because he gets to sit down to a meal immediately upon his return home from work every day and I keep the children quiet so he can read the evening newspaper in a relaxed and quiet atmosphere. And I always make sure that the children are fed ahead of time so as not to ruin his digestion which would cause him to be in a foul mood. So you're right, who is bourgeouis?"

"I can't believe you do all of that for that man. They're his children too."

"Actually it works quite well because as he's eating, I read to them until after he's left the house for one of his important assignations. Then I get them ready for bed."

"The man doesn't know how lucky he is. And then, knowing you, you probably kiss them once for yourself and once for their father when you tuck them into bed for the night. And I know that Peter never comes home to a messy, toy-strewn house because it would put him out-of-sorts."

Elsa laughed. "Well it makes my life much easier when Peter is pleasant than when he's 'out-of-sorts'."

"You're going to wear yourself out catering to that man, Elsa. Are you still having those nightmares?"

"I shouldn't tell you because you'll lecture me. It's easier to do what Peter wants than to argue with him."

"I only lecture you because I love you. Peter is a bully. Bullies always back down when someone stands up to them, Elsa. You always look so tired."

"I have been having the nightmares and now they're all the more frightening because I have more children to protect against the unseen pursuers. They visit all my night dreams. And during the day I'm so afraid of letting the children out of my sight for fear someone will take them."

"Your daytime fears are probably a lingering residue from your night dreams. We have to think of something because this can't go on, Elsa."

Chapter IV

In 1945, the war ended and the soldiers returned home jubilant that the war was finally over. Many were broken in body and spirits, refusing to talk about the horrors they had witnessed. Most were changed in ways they would never be able to explain, not to wives, not to lovers and not to mothers. They wanted to forget; get on with their lives, take up where they had left off. They returned home to wives who would be like strangers and many returned to children they had never seen.

It was an adjustment for the returning soldiers as well as for the wives who had been left in charge and were now expected to take a back-seat again. Some women relinquished their new roles with gladness in their hearts while others chafed at the change in their status. Some of the returning soldiers had received 'Dear John' letters while they had been overseas and were coming home to loneliness and despair. A few found jobs waiting for them but many others found work difficult to find.

Elsa knew little of this except what she heard from Katrin who was more involved in life outside of her home than what Elsa was permitted. "Why don't you tell him that you want more freedom? Why can't you even go to a movie with me once in awhile?

"You're a prisoner, Elsa. Why do you put up with it?" Katrin was often exasperated with her friend's passiveness.

"I... I can't," Elsa's voice trembled. "I've tried Katrin, really I have but my knees buckle beneath me everytime I think of the words I would need to say," Elsa's eyes glistened brightly with unshed tears.

Katrin put her arm around her friend. "I just don't understand. I know you've got the children but you need more out of life than what you've got and you'll never get it unless you fight for it. You seem to be more nervous lately when Peter's name is mentioned, is there a reason?"

The tears rolled slowly down Elsa's thin cheeks. "Never mind," Katrin threw up her arms in frustration and the matter was dropped, yet once again.

*   *   *   *   *

Two years after the twins were born, Kathleen made her appearance, followed eighteen months later by Melissa.

And then Alexander, Elsa's father, died of a massive heart attack shortly after Melissa was born. Those who saw it happen, said there had been no warning. In the middle of a verbal altercation with his supervisor, he had fallen, clutching his chest. Some said that if he hadn't died, he'd have been fired.

"Papa died, Elsa." She had remained dry-eyed while her sister had cried softly when she'd told her the news. After Elizabeth had left, she thought about her father and could only feel pity for him. She was by far the luckier one. She could love and be loved by her children and her friend, Katrin whereas her father had the love of no one, with the possible exception of Elizabeth.

"I know you weren't close to your father, Elsa but I was sorry to hear about his death," Katrin said.

"I don't feel anything. I know I should but I don't. I don't ever remember him being a happy man. He came to Canada looking for riches but his dream of wealth died an early death. There were many reasons; the Depression, a sour personality, a bad temper, impatience and his frustration with life. Admittedly bad luck did play a small part but my father placed the entire responsibility for the death of his dreams on bad luck.

"My father had nothing that he thought was of any worth. William Alexander was only there until he got stronger, Elizabeth had moved out on her own and you know how often I've seen my parents even though they only live a dozen blocks away.

"My father wanted so much but had nothing of substance in his personality that warranted what he craved. He gave nothing so he received little, only what pity now demands."

"How is your mother taking it," Katrina asked.

"I don't know but I'm sure living with my father has not been easy for her either. It's made her into what she has now become. I feel pity for her as well but the wall is too thick where my parents are concerned and I don't feel that I owe them anything. At this point I don't even care to know why they became the way they are."

"Are you going to attend your father's funeral?"

"I will because of Elizabeth. Are you and Michael planning to go?"

"I will go with you and we'll leave all the children with Michael." Katrin gave her friend a hug.

Elsa had not seen her mother for two years and was shocked to see that at fifty-three years old, Janet could easily have passed for a woman of at least ten years older. It was easy to see that life had not been kind to her and Elsa was forced to feel a slight softening towards her. When she looked into the open coffin at the face of the father she hadn't seen for five years, she realized he was no more than a stranger. The lines of anger, frustration and discontentment had been erased from his face and Elsa wondered what he'd have been like if things had been different for him. Raising her head, Elsa looked into the eyes of her mother and was puzzled by what she saw there. If she didn't believe otherwise, she would have thought tenderness filled her age-worn eyes as she looked at her husband.

"How do you feel Elsa?" Katrin took her friend by the arm. "You have a strange expression on your face."

"I was just wondering what my father would have been like if he had found what he was looking for. Then I remembered that life has gone wrong for many of us in different ways so I won't waste my tears on him. Each person has to learn to make the best out of what they have and deal with what life gives them."

*   *   *   *   *

Three years after the sudden death of Alexander, Rebecca made a late appearance in the Hall family.

Sarah Ann, at nine years old, was growing into a lovely young girl, mature and dependable beyond her years, a result of the responsibility she had shouldered at such a young age. Her hair was a mass of honey brown curls, her brown eyes were large and twinkling and her smile mischievous. There was none of her mother's timidity in her nature and she stood up defiantly to injustices, speaking her mind with confidence. Sarah Ann quickly took on the role of 'mother's helper' for her new baby sister.

Chapter V

Shortly after Rebecca's birth in 1951, Elsa realized that Peter's interest in the political movement was waning as he began spending more time at home.

"Peter doesn't seem to be as involved with politics, I've noticed," Katrin commented one afternoon when they had taken the children to a nearby park.

"No. It was easier though when he was in his political groups," Elsa confided, "because he was rarely home so at least he wasn't there to criticize the children and me all the time. Now there are strangers coming every evening and there's always the smell of cigarette smoke and stale beer. The children and I lie in bed and have to listen to the drunks and the all-night poker games. Their language is obscene and they tell dirty jokes. I don't feel as if it's my home anymore; it has been taken over by virtual strangers. They walk through the house, ignoring me and the children as if we don't exist. It gives me more work than I ever had before cleaning up the mess these men, and a few women leave before they stagger home near morning.

"Peter doesn't want the children being noisy when his friends are there. Sarah Ann helps me to try and keep them quiet. It's hard on them to be yelled at all the time."

"Elsa, things just go from bad to worse as far as Peter is concerned. It's not fair that the children have to be quiet for drunks. And it's not fair that Sarah Ann has to try and keep them quiet. She's only a child herself."

"I know Katrin; the responsibility lies with me. It isn't fair and like my wise little daughter said, 'they haven't done anything wrong.' They are just being children.

"But when I think about confronting Peter about anything, I break out in a cold sweat. The problem of co-existing with Peter without confrontation and yet making life bearable for the children is becoming an ever increasingly difficult situation."

There were other things that made life more difficult for Elsa as well; things that she couldn't even discuss with Katrin. Often after a night of heavy drinking, Peter would climb into bed, roughly shaking Elsa awake and demand 'his rights as her husband'.

"Wha' else would I keep you 'round for?" he would mumble drunkenly. "you're not attractive and you can't carry on an intelligent conversation with any of my friends." Then pulling her toward him, he'd force her legs apart. And then when he couldn't perform, as often happened when he was drunk, he took his anger and embarrassment out on her.

When he took her like that she was reminded of Frank Wilson and the tears would slide from beneath her closed eyelids. Trying to push the memory from her thoughts, she forced her mind to go blank so she didn't have to think about either Peter or Frank Wilson. *'If Peter loved me, if he was affectionate, if we could talk, I know the memories could be laid to rest once and for all. They never will be though as long as I'm with Peter,'* she thought.

Elsa continued to guard her secret closely, telling no one, not even Katrin. She still felt the shame and guilt of that day as if it had been only yesterday.

After a time Peter's habits altered again and Elsa gradually realized that he was spending less time at home but since both she and the children were relieved at this change, no one queried it. The tension lifted, the children laughed again and the house became a home once more, alive with the sounds of happy, squabbling children. While they played, Elsa did her household tasks listening to the tales of Ozzie and Harriet and wished their family could be as happy as the Nelsons were.

"Peter seems to have changed," Katrin remarked to Elsa one day.

"Not just Peter, everything has. We don't have all the drunks here any more. He's starting to spend a lot of money on clothes for himself now and he's more like the Peter I first met – glib, confident, brash and commanding. He hums while he shaves and smirks when he walks out the door with his hair all plastered down with Brylcreem and smelling of cheap cologne. I think he's trying to do a Dick Tracey imitation. You saw his bright shiny blue Studebaker, didn't you? And I always know when he leaves that he'll be home very late, if at all. But the funny thing Katrin, is that no one minds his absences. And because it is such a relief when he drives away, I never care where he goes. It's good enough that he's gone. He's away now almost as much as he had been when he was involved in politics, if not more."

"It's nice that you've finally got a telephone installed. It will be much easier for you and I to stay in touch now. I've often worried that you wouldn't be able to get hold of me quickly if you ever really needed us."

"Peter would have thought before that having a telephone was bourgeouis; now we were almost the first on the street to have one. When Peter talks on the telephone, he doesn't talk in his usual booming voice but in his new softer voice." Elsa shrugged unconcernedly. "A quieter Peter means a more peaceful house so I don't mind what secrets he's hiding.

"I feel uncomfortable and silly speaking into a telephone without being able to see the person I'm talking to so I rarely answer it. It doesn't matter anyway because Peter is usually the first one to it when it rings. When he's home, he's constantly talking on it."

*　　　*　　　*　　　*　　　*

One hot summer evening after Peter had climbed jauntily into his Studebaker and driven off down the drive, the telephone had rung insistently. Elsa reluctantly answered. A female voice on the other end demanded, "Let me speak to Peter."

"He's... .he's... .just left," Elsa stammered nervously.

"Just left? Are you sure?""

"Y... yes. Who's... .calling please?"

"Never mind. I"ll see him later." Trembling, Elsa replaced the receiver. She disliked the faceless voices especially when they were rude as so many of Peter's friends were.

As time passed, there were other incidents. Often late at night, before Peter had returned home from his evening out, a caller would remain on the line without speaking and Elsa, already nervous, could hear the other person breathing loudly into her ear.

Once in the middle of the night, after the telephone had rung on three separate occasions, Elsa had buried the offensive instrument beneath a pile of pillows.

Elsa's suspicions were finally confirmed when she saw traces of bright red lipstick smeared on Peter's shirt collar and white handkerchief. However, it wasn't until she found his soiled underwear in the laundry hamper with the incriminating tell-tale stains of semen that she knew what she could no longer deny to herself was really happening.

She thought briefly of confronting him with her suspicions but would it make a difference? Would he care that she felt betrayed, used and unloved? Even knowing deep within herself that he hadn't loved her in the beginning of their marriage, hurt her deeply enough. Each night, long after the children were in bed and long before Peter would arrive home, she would sit in the darkened room and ponder the question.

"Elsa, you've been very quiet lately. Is there something wrong?"

"You have probably suspected the same as I have about Peter's behaviour, Katrin. My dilemma is how to handle it. I feel ill when I think about approaching him with my suspicions and I know that with his verbal skills and knack of taking the offensive, I would immediately be put on the defensive and before long, he'd have me apologizing to him for all the wrongs I've committed in our marriage. He does it – you've seen him do it with everyone. Then he'll be on his way again feeling that the problem has been solved and no blame need be attached to him."

"Yes, I've seen how he can manipulate people. It takes someone who can think on their feet to best him but you can't just keep taking it, Elsa. He keeps using you as a doormat."

"You know that saying, 'what goes around, comes around'? I believe that. Look at my father – he died quite young. He could've had a good life. Peter counts on my cowardice and timidity for not bringing him to account for his behaviour and he congratulates himself on his superior intelligence while he figuratively thumbs his nose at me. I think things will eventually change for him. I don't know if it'll be because I'll finally decide to do something or whether he'll get too cocky one day, but they'll change."

"But doesn't it make you angry that he thinks he's getting away with it," Katrin's face was red with self-righteous anger.

"Yes, I'm angry and I resent his smug attitude, overbearing confidence, his deceit and that secret smirk of his at my assumed ignorance. And I won't tell you that there aren't times that I don't feel depressed. I also have to admit that when I sometimes feel depressed, I give poor Sarah Ann more responsibility than she should have to deal with.

"There are times when I will cry at the slightest provocation and when I'm in that type of mood, I think back to my childhood. I have tried to put all that behind me but sometimes, when I'm down, it all comes back."

During her low periods when the face of Frank Wilson intruded upon her thoughts, she felt unworthy, unclean and unloved. But she couldn't tell Katrin. *'Why?'* she asked herself a hundred times. *'Why did that horrid, dirty man touch me, hurt me? Why does Peter treat me this way?' During those times her hurts were inconsolable and the questions endless. There are no answers. Others find answers. Why not I?'*

"Elsa, Peter is not worth getting upset about," Katrin told her friend.

"I think the best thing to do is to go about as if you're the happiest person in the world. Then he has no control over you. That's what he wants. He likes to control and dominate you; act like he doesn't even exist."

"I know what you're saying, Katrin but what he is doing hurts a lot. You've got Michael; someone that loves you. I don't have anyone that loves me."

Katrin snorted loudly. "What are you talking about? You've got your children, Elsa. They love you and they need you. Who loves Peter, Elsa? I don't think you do anymore and the children don't. Think about it – you've got a lot more than he has. Don't get depressed because of him – he's certainly not worth it."

"Sometimes I just feel overwhelmed."

"You're going to have to give your head a good shake because you can't let the burden of the care of the children fall to Sarah Ann, Elsa. She's too young to carry that much responsibility.

"Elsa, you don't have to confront Peter. Just take a good look at him and say over and over to yourself until you know that it's true, 'I'm better than you are and I'm not going to let you ruin my life or the lives of my children.' Let him do what he wants and it will only hurt you if you let it."

Katrin squeezed her friends cold fingers. "I know dear that I can't really feel what you're feeling but you've got to face the fact that you won't be able to change Peter so you will have to decide to either live with it, confront him or leave. Michael says that you've had the rough end of the stick and it isn't fair but you and I learned a long time ago that nothing is fair in life, didn't we?"

Elsa nodded her head as a tear dropped onto her clasped hands. "Most of the time I'm fine but once I begin to feel depressed, it takes hold of me and I can't seem to stop crying."

"I know I can say these things because we're friends. Try to force yourself to do things that will keep your mind active so you won't think about what Peter is doing. And smile, even when you don't feel like smiling and the next time it'll come easier. Unhappiness is like a merry-go-round—you can't just step away from it. You have to work at jumping as far from it as you can so you aren't caught up in it again. Michael and I will help you all we can."

Elsa smiled through her tears; her first smile in months.

"See that's a start. Listen, I have an idea. Let's have a party next week for Sarah's tenth birthday. We'll have it at our place and Michael will come 'round to pick you all up. Helen will be so excited; she's been wanting to see Sarah for several weeks now but Sarah has been telling her that she's too busy."

The tears began to form in Elsa's eyes again. "Now, now," Katrin playfully wagged a finger at her friend. "No more of that now. Remember, we're going to do something about it. You're going to be so busy doing things that Peter will think he's missing out on something."

"I was thinking about Sarah Ann. She works so hard."

"She's a spunky one, alright. You can be very proud of that child Elsa and I'll make a bet that no grass will ever grow beneath her feet. She'll put the world in its place, that one. There, you're smiling again. It'll get easier and I'll bet you're feeling better already."

Elsa shrugged. "The party sounds like a good idea."

"The girls will love it. Sarah Ann told Helen that she loves hot dogs. And we'll have jello and kool-aid and of course, a nice big birthday cake which Helen and I will bake and some ice cream. What do you think about making it a surprise for all of the children?"

"I don't know if Peter will give me any money. He'll think that it's a waste of money to have a party."

"Don't you worry about that. This is our treat. Now what I want you to do between now and then is some sewing. I bought some material to make Helen a dress and I don't know what I was thinking about but I bought far too much. They wouldn't let me return it and Helen doesn't need two dresses of the same material so why don't you make Sarah Ann a dress to wear to her birthday party?"

Elsa threw her arms around her friend. "Oh Katrin, you're such a good friend. I don't know what I would ever do without you."

"And so are you, my dear. I'll get Michael to drop the material off to you tomorrow so that you can get started on it right away. Now no more tears. Promise?"

"I'll try." Elsa's voice trembled. "I really will."

"You can do it. Now let's go and see what the children are doing so that Sarah Ann can go back to being a child again."

"I don't think she will ever be able to do that. I think she was born an adult."

*　　　*　　　*　　　*　　　*

Shortly after Sarah's tenth birthday party, Elsa answered the door to two police officers. "Mrs. Hall?" one of the uniformed officers showed her his police badge. "Is your husband home?"

"No, he isn't. Has something happened?"

"It's a matter of great urgency that we speak with your husband. We have some questions to ask him. Do you know where we can reach him?"

"He… .he didn't… .come home last night," she whispered in embarrassment. "I don't know… .where he is."

"We have had a serious report involving your husband. When did you last see him?"

"He left … about eight o'clock… .I think it was, last evening."

"Does he drive a bright blue Studebaker, license number FVR 723?"

"Yes he does. Can you tell me what has happened?"

"We have to speak with your husband, Ma'am." He nodded his head slightly. "We'll be in touch with you again. However, if he returns home, please let us know." The younger officer handed her a card with the precinct's telephone number.

While Elsa watched the car pull away from the curb in front of the house, the telephone jangled abruptly causing her to jump nervously. "Has anyone been there?" Peter demanded.

"The.... Police were. What has happened, Peter?"

"What did you tell them?"

"Nothing....except.... .."

"Except? What do you mean, except? I don't want you to tell anyone anything."

"Except that you weren't here last night."

"Okay, now shut up and listen to me. If they come back again, tell them nothing. Have you got that? Absolutely nothing. You don't tell them where I work; you don't tell them anything about me. I won't be home for a few days. I'll stay someplace until this whole thing blows over."

"But ... .what happened? Why do they want to talk to you?"

"Never mind. The less you know, the better it will be so you can't open your big mouth and screw everything up."

"Where will you be staying? In case I have to be in touch with you."

Peter gave a loud snort of laughter. "Like I said, the less you know, the better. I'll call again in a few days. Now remember what I said." Elsa slowly replaced the receiver.

The following day in the newspaper Elsa read the headlines and realized what the story was that Peter hadn't told her. '*Hit-and-Run*', the headline blazed. '*A blue Studebaker, License No. FVR 723, struck Harold Gowan, 78, of Burnaby late yesterday as he crossed the street at Broadway and Main. The impact of the vehicle threw Mr. Gowan twenty feet into the intersection. The driver of the vehicle did not stop but witnesses were able to give the license number and description of the hit-and-run vehicle to police when they arrived at the scene of the crime.*' Elsa put the newspaper down and felt nausea well up within her. *'How could he?'* she cried to herself. *'And to just leave the poor man lying there. What kind of a person is Peter?'*

She had no doubt that the driver was Peter and that he would be capable of doing just that. Peter always thought first about himself.

Later in the day, the same two officers came again to question her on Peter's whereabouts. "Have you spoken with your husband yet, Mrs. Hall?"

"Yesterday… .he called but he didn't say where he was and… .I haven't talked to him since then."

"Mrs. Hall, this is an extremely serious matter that we are investigating and your husband is only making matters worse for himself. An elderly man is in hospital in critical condition because of your husband's suspected negligence. We need to know where we can reach him."

"I… .don't know. He wouldn't tell me."

The officers stared at her in disbelief and finally, shaking their heads, left. "Good day, Mrs. Hall. We had hoped that you would be able to assist us."

When on the third day the newspaper headline read, *'Hit-and-Run Victim Dies',* Elsa sat down and cried. "The poor man," she moaned. "And his family, how they must be suffering."

When finally Peter telephoned again late one evening, Elsa could tell from the slow way he spoke that he had been drinking. "Have they been there lately?"

"Who Peter?"

"The police, you dummy!"

"No… .not for almost a week."

"Good. Did you tell them anything? Did they ask where I worked? I haven't been back to work this week just in case they showed up there. I've probably lost my job by now because the old bastard is mean enough to let me go."

"No, I didn't tell them anything." Elsa heard a woman's laughter in the background. "Where are you?"

"At a friend's place. I'll be staying here a while longer."

"We have practically no groceries left, Peter. I will have to get some things."

"What do you expect me to do about it? I've got enough problems of my own without worrying about whether you've got groceries. Think of something for yourself for once in your life. The whole lot of you have kept me poor. I'm telling you, I'm sick to death of it. Everytime I turn around, it's money for this or money for that. Do you know how many hours of my paycheque it takes just to put food on the table for all of you?"

Elsa felt tears spring to her eyes. "Maybe I'll be able to get some money to you and maybe I won't," he continued. "I'll just see how I feel and I don't know when I'll be back. I'll talk to you again sometime later," and with that he was gone.

Elsa's first thought was Katrin. "We can help a little to tide you over but if it's for a longer period of time, you'll have to speak to someone about getting some financial assistance, Elsa. I'm sorry."

The next bit of news Elsa heard was when she read in the newspaper that *'A blue Studebaker has been found in what police had first believed was a vacant garage and investigators now feel they are closer to finding the driver of the vehicle connected with the hit-and-run death of Mr. Gowan. A few leads have come to light that investigators hadn't been aware of previously and now they feel that it is just a matter of time before the callous hit-and-run driver will be called to account for his criminal act.'*

Elsa had not heard from Peter again, nor had she received any money from him. She had finally been forced to speak with a government agency about receiving some assistance for her and the children. Although Katrin had gone with her, it hadn't lessened her feelings of embarrassment.

"I have never felt so degraded and humiliated – just to get some assistance so I can feed my children. I'll have to look for a job because I don't want to take hand-outs. Thank you for coming with me, Katrin."

"You know I'm here for you always, Elsa. When I was coming over to pick you up, I heard on the news that Peter has been apprehended and is in jail pending a court date. No bail has been set."

"I feel only relief. And it must be a relief for Mr. Gowan's family too."

Elsa and Katrin had gone to the trial but it was only on the final day at the end of the proceedings that Peter had noticed them sitting near the back of the courtroom. Until then, he had looked at no one other than the Judge, the prosecutor, his own defence lawyer and a well-dressed, slim, slightly flamboyant bleached blonde woman who had sat near the prisoners dock for the entire proceedings. He had occasionally smiled a slight, tired smile in her direction and she had returned his smiles. Elsa had felt dowdy and poorly-dressed in comparison and wondered sadly how she could possibly compete with someone like her.

'But do I even want to?' she wondered.

"I can see the lines of strain on Peter's face but I know they are more for himself than for the poor man he killed," Elsa whispered to Katrin. "I've been watching him these last few days and he could be someone else – not the man I've been married to. I have no idea what I feel for him any longer."

"You will be sentenced to one year for vehicular manslaughter while driving with undue care and attention while in an intoxicated state. Your inebriation resulted in the death of Harold Gowan," the judge pronounced. Peter had shown no obvious emotion when the verdict was delivered.

It was while the sentence was being pronounced that Peter had looked around and seeing Elsa at the back of the room had frowned slightly, his face flushing before quickly turning away. Keeping his eyes fixed on his lawyer he had refused to look in Elsa's direction again.

Chapter VI

Elsa made no attempt to visit Peter while he was in jail.

"I'm not sure how things stand regarding Peter and I," Elsa confided to Katrin. "Are we separated or what? With all the things that Peter has done, this is the most embarrassing and humiliating. I almost feel that I have been partly responsible for his actions and I know that's silly. The children have heard at school that their father is a 'killer' and that's been very difficult for them. The one good thing is that there's less tension in the house than there was when their father was home."

"You'll do fine, Elsa. Money will probably be the most difficult problem and although I know you're thrifty, it will be hard to stretch what you have to the end of each month. We'll help as much as we can."

"I feel bad taking from you and Michael. You've both been so good to us. I've been going to a few places looking for work so I hope something will turn up. But right now I am resenting Peter and am more angry with him than I have ever been before. It's disgraceful that he has left his children like this with no thought to how we were going to live. But that's Peter, he always only thinks of himself.

"When the court case was going on, I remember telling you that I had no idea what I felt for him. Now I know. It's almost... .almost like I hate him. I hate to say that but sometimes I get these feelings where I could actually do him... .harm. Where I want something... .terrible to happen to him."

"I can understand how you feel Elsa, but those feelings will hurt you more than they will him. Don't let them eat you up. We'll have to get you out doing things – things that are fun."

"But there's no extra money for anything. We can barely make it as it is. I hate being so poor. I hate always scrimping and never having enough. And yet," she watched the children playing, a small smile on her pale lips, "my children are healthy and right now they're happy so I really am fortunate."

"Why don't you try to think of something you can do involving children, where you can earn some extra money? You enjoy children."

"But what?"

"I know! How about starting an afternoon story-telling session and charge a small fee for each child who attends. That would give you a little extra money and give you an interest outside of your problems."

"I couldn't do that, Katrin. Who would come to it?"

"You can do anything. If you want to, that is. I'm sure there's a lot of people who probably want a little break and they can send their children to you for awhile and the children get a chance to learn at the same time.

"Michael could do up some notices and they could be delivered in both our neighborhoods and at the schools. They could be posted at the churches and food markets too. It would work, Elsa. I know it would."

"It sounds scary. All those people. What would I say to them?"

"They'd be dropping off their children and picking them up. You would hardly have to say anything. Let's try it. I'll help you for the first few times."

"Do you really think it would work?"

"Yes. Now end of discussion. I'll get Michael to do up the notices right away and all of us will deliver them and then we'll wait until the business starts to pour in."

*   *   *   *   *

One day, looking at her friend, Katrin said, "Elsa, I am so happy that you are enjoying life now and you almost always have a smile on your face."

"I never thought it would work but now I have almost more children than I can handle. What a great idea you had, Katrin. Do you know that some of the mothers are putting their children's names on a waiting list? I feel more fulfilled and useful than I've ever felt before. And I enjoy it immensely. Children are wonderful. They sit and listen to the stories, they're non-judgmental and they don't expect me to be anything other than who I am; too bad adults aren't more like that."

"It's a win-win situation, isn't it? Your finances have improved, you're happy and you love what you're doing."

"The only thing I'm dreading is the day that Peter will be released from prison. Life is good now and I hate for it to end. But maybe he won't come back here. Maybe he'll go to that blonde woman again."

*　　　*　　　*　　　*　　　*

When Peter was released in the summer of 1953, he returned home; a sudden presence out of the wall of silence and virtually a stranger. In a very short time the children's reading sessions were disbanded, as Elsa knew they would be. The noise bothered Peter; he didn't like the new confidence he saw in Elsa; and he didn't like her to be independent.

Elsa missed them as much as she missed her recently-acquired feelings of self-worth. She never asked about the blonde woman or about anything that had happened before that fateful day. Nor did Peter offer any explanations because it had never been necessary for him to do so in the past.

Her life returned to what it had been before Peter had gone to jail and those who knew her saw the transition in her at his return. Peter looked for a job but without any immediacy and Elsa began to despair that he would ever find one. She felt that his prison record was probably a hindrance in his ability to find work even assuming that he had been prepared to look with any greater effort.

Hanging around the house, he complained incessantly and his voice became a thorne in Elsa's side. But finally the hoped for happened; Peter found work at a factory on Water Street. He spent his days making bags for holding grain for the country feed stores.

"I hate the evenings," Elsa confided to Katrin. "Peter paces continuously; he's so restless and discontented. He telephoned his father to see if he could borrow some money to buy another car. He told him that we needed a station wagon for all the children.

"His father was so pleased to hear from Peter. He hadn't been in contact with them for years. They wired him some money after Peter promised that he would write soon sending pictures of all the children.

They had no idea that Peter had so many children. And he's their only child; how sad for them."

"And you've never met them. Do you even know where they live?"

"No, Peter is pretty secretive about a lot of things. And, of course, you've seen the car Peter bought—a two year old Chevrolet with shining paint and polished chrome; it's not exactly a station wagon."

"I'll bet with a new car it won't be long and he'll be going out evenings to visit old friends," Katrin laughed. "With him at work during the day and out in the evenings maybe you'll be able to start having your reading groups again. That would be nice for you and a little extra money that hopefully he won't find out about."

*   *   *   *   *

Christmas was a quiet affair with a goose dinner at Katrin's and Michael's home. In the background Bing Crosby softly crooned, 'I'm Dreaming of a White Christmas.' In spite of the calm and friendly atmosphere, Elsa could feel Peter becoming more restless and edgey as the day progressed. Elsa glanced nervously at Katrin and knew that she also realized that Peter was working himself up to something.

"Come on," he finally growled irritably. "We're going home now."

"But it's still early and the children are enjoying themselves. Can't you stay a little longer, Peter?" Katrin implored.

"I said it's time that we left. I've got things that I've got to do."

"But it's Christmas Day. What is so important to do on Christmas Day that can't wait? Can't you convince Peter to stay longer, Michael?"

"Looks like he's made up his mind already, Katrin."

Katrin looked at her friend but Elsa avoided her eyes, not wishing to say anything to further irritate Peter. She recognized the signs and knew if pushed, he would become embarrassingly unreasonable.

Peter turned to Elsa, "Get the children and I'll meet you outside in the car."

Elsa waited until Peter had closed the door before she spoke. "I'm sorry Michael and Katrin. You are my two dearest friends and we've ruined your Christmas."

"You haven't ruined anything, Elsa. Now don't you take responsibility for that man's actions," Michael told her firmly. "We hold Peter responsible for what he does."

Elsa smiled sadly. "Thank you, Michael. You're both so good to the children and I. And it was a lovely dinner. Sarah Ann, would you please tell the children that your father said it's time to leave."

"Already?" Then becoming aware of the look on her mother's face, "Alright, I'll tell them," she answered unhappily.

On the way home, the children were subdued, sensing their father's restive mood. No one wanted to be on the receiving end of an angry outburst from him.

"Out," he bellowed when they arrived home. "I've got an appointment," he told Elsa, "and I don't know how long I'll be."

"Mommy, where's Daddy going?" Melissa asked as she watched her father drive away. "Why did we have to leave? I was having fun at Auntie Katrin's."

"Come on Melissa," Sarah Ann took her younger sister's hand, "We'll have fun here too."

"But it doesn't seem like Christmas here," Melissa pouted, "not like at Auntie Katrin's."

"I'll read you all some Christmas stories and then we'll play a game. Can we make some hot chocolate?" she asked her mother.

*   *   *   *   *

Elsa was not surprised, nor overly upset, when Peter didn't come home that night. But as one day went into another she became progressively more angry. When he finally showed up late on New Years Day, he was hungover and miserable. Staring belligerently at Elsa, he challenged her to make an issue of his absence.

"Well," he finally approached her when she remained silent, "don't you have anything to say, my dear little wife?"

"No."

"No, she says. The little woman says she has nothing to say," he taunted her. "You're not going to ask me where I've been all week?"

"I would've thought you'd have telephoned me while you were away if you had wanted me to know where you were."

"You're crazy. You're nothing but a crazy stupid bitch."

Elsa shrugged, well aware that he wanted to fight, trying to bait her, so he'd feel justified in leaving again. She wasn't going to make it that easy for him.

"I'll bet you've been crying to that friend of yours all week too."

Elsa forced herself to think of other things so as not to hear what he was saying to her. She concentrated on the directions for the cake she was baking.

"Are you listening to me?" He grabbed her shoulders and spun her around to face him.

Staring at him, she watched his mouth move in his face and examined the large pores on his nose, the deep crease between his eyebrows, and the lines that ran from his nose to the corners of his mouth. She noticed that his ears protruded slightly from the sides of his head and that they were now red. His cheeks were flushed and for the first time she was aware of the network of tiny red veins beside his nose which extended onto his cheeks.

"I said, do you hear what I'm saying?" His fingers dug into her shoulders cruelly.

She nodded. "Yes, I did Peter," she said, looking directly into his face.

He pushed her roughly away, muttering something unintelligible before stomping into the living room where she heard the newspaper rustling moments later.

"Two teaspoons of baking powder," she whispered to herself while the words *'stupid bitch, stupid bitch'* swam around in her head. She forced herself to remember what Katrin had told her to keep reminding herself of, *'I am better than you and I'm not going to let you ruin my life and the lives of my children. Stupid bitch! I am better than you.'* "Two cups of flour."

"I'm going to get a beer. I can't stand this Gawd forsaken place any longer," he broke into her mind wanderings as she tried to concentrate, keeping her anger at bay.

Opening her mouth to say, *'but they'll be closed'*, she shut it before the words could be uttered.

He stared at her waiting. "You were going to say something?"

"No, nothing." "One and a half cups of sugar." *I'm better than you. Stupid bitch.'* 'Three eggs."

She heard the front door close behind him and breathed a sigh of relief. "One half cup of milk and one teaspoon of vanilla. Now we're done."

As the months passed, Peter continued to taunt her, seemingly trying to provoke her for some unknown reason, into fighting. She was unsure of his motive but refused to get drawn into whatever game he was playing. Instead, to keep her sanity, she closed her ears when he railed at her and dissected his face, feature by feature, analyzing each absurd little detail; his thinning hair, the wort on the side of his nose, the beginnings of his double chin and the gray in his whiskers.

It was her defence against his offensive attacks and only she was aware of her strategy. He thought he had her cowed and speechless. He thought he was breaking her down but she never heard a word he said. She was becoming quite adept at making her mind a blank page when he was around.

Although he was rarely there, he did continue to pay the rent and the basic living expenses. Being out almost every evening, he often didn't return until the early hours of the morning and sometimes not at all. Elsa never worried or complained because the relief at his absences was too great.

She knew there must be other women or at least one, because he hadn't touched her as a husband since well before Christmas. She also sensed that he was working up to something and felt that whatever it was, she wouldn't have long to wait before she found out what it was. As each day passed he became angrier and more verbally abusive. She was sure that there would soon be a final blow-up.

Living on tenderhooks in anticipation of what was going to happen, Elsa surprisingly felt emotionally stronger as each day passed. "I have a feeling Peter is up to something," she told Katrin. "Either he's going to really blow up or do something major. I'm hoping he'll finally decide to leave and then I can climb down off this roller coaster that I've been on for all these years."

*　　　*　　　*　　　*　　　*

One day in June of 1955, Peter announced that he was going fishing to an Interior lake for the weekend. "I'll be renting a small motor boat at that place out on the highway. I'll leave Friday night and be back late Sunday evening. I'm going alone because I have to do some thinking about my life and what I want out of it."

Elsa nodded her head. There was nothing for her to say. Since he was rarely home at any time on the weekend, she wondered vaguely why he was telling her now why he wouldn't be and especially why he was going into so much detail about his whereabouts.

"Can't you ever say anything?" he yelled. "All you ever do is nod or shake your head. Are you so stupid that you can't even answer me?"

But Elsa's ears had already closed and she was busily dissecting the features on his face.

"Oh, you make me so sick," he finally said and slamming the door, he left.

Elsa spent the next day washing and ironing his clothes.

"Where's my new shirt?" he growled at her as he was packing.

"To go fishing?" Elsa asked with surprise. "I thought you only took your old clothes with you when you go fishing."

"Are you trying to tell me what I can and what I can't take with me?"

Elsa shook her head nervously.

"There you go shaking your head again. If I want to take all of my clothes, I'll take them. No stupid woman is going to tell me what to do. Now get that shirt."

On the Saturday that Peter was gone, Elsa and Katrin had lunch together at Woolworth's lunch counter while Michael took the children to the park. "How are things going between you and Peter now, Elsa?"

"I keep remembering what you told me; to keep thinking that I'm better than he is when he puts me down. It's so hard sometimes to keep telling myself that but I am trying. Something is going to happen soon though, I can feel it."

"Why do you think that?"

"I don't know. I just know he's building up to something. He's always trying to pick a fight and when I won't fight, he gets even angrier. He's away almost every week-end and most evenings now."

"Does he give you any excuses for where he's been?"

"No, and to be absolutely truthful, I don't really care. Peter being out of the house makes life more pleasant for everyone."

"It probably helps that you don't care. When is he getting back from this fishing trip?"

"Late Sunday night, he said."

"Then why don't you and the children come over for roast beef dinner tomorrow?"

"Michael will be tired of seeing the children after having them at the park all afternoon."

"Don't be silly, Elsa. Michael loves spending time with them. He always wished we were able to have more children. He wanted six but since that didn't happen, he can enjoy yours. Now, since we've got the whole afternoon to ourselves, why don't we see a movie? Abbott and Costello is playing." Elsa wrinkled up her nose.

"I know. I think they're silly too but Michael likes them. There's one that Rita Hayworth is playing in at the Orpheum. I forget the name of it but... what do you think?"

"The Rita Hayworth one would probably be good. Should we walk or take the street car?"

*   *   *   *   *

Elsa lay awake in bed that night after the children were tucked in and thought about the movie, one of the very few she had seen in her life, and about her lunch with Katrin. It had been an enjoyable day and especially so knowing that Peter wouldn't be popping home demanding to know where she was and what she had been doing and where his dinner was. He'd have been wanting her to do this and that for him; things that he could easily do for himself. He always chose a time when it was obvious that she was already busy. To save herself an argument she didn't want and didn't have the energy to handle, she always did as he demanded.

'What is he up to?' she wondered again as she had so many times over the last few months.

The following day, Elsa and the children spent the afternoon and early evening with Michael and Katrin. Michael had played horseshoes in the backyard with the older children and later they had played Dominoes and Pick-Up-Sticks while Katrin and Elsa had gossiped and kept an eye on Rebecca who was too young yet for most of the other childrens' activities. *'Another enjoyable day,'* Elsa thought to herself as she watched her children enjoying themselves and, appreciating as she always did, how good Michael was with them.

"I guess we should get you all home," Michael said to Elsa, "so Peter doesn't become anxious about where you are if he gets there before you do."

Elsa's eyes flew to the clock. She had totally forgotten the time in the relaxed atmosphere. "Oh yes, Michael. Thank you for reminding me." Jumping to her feet, she called, "Children, gather your things up quickly. It's time to leave."

"Aw, do we have to go now?" several small voices wailed.

"Yes, now hurry."

At home Elsa got the children into bed anxious about what Peter's mood would be like when he returned. 'Would he be in a temper? Would he tell her he was leaving her for someone else?' She listened to The Great Gildersleeves and George Burns and Gracie Allan on the radio but found it difficult to concentrate on what they were saying. Feeling slightly nauseous, as she always did before Peter was expected to return from wherever he had been, she wandered aimlessly through the house.

When, at eleven o'clock he still wasn't home, she went to bed and said a little prayer that he wouldn't come home drunk and in a mood to fight. Exhausted and not wishing to fight after such a nice weekend, she sensed she may say things she would later regret. And tired as she was, it would be difficult tuning his harassment out and closing her ears to his taunts. Finally exhausted, she fell into a troubled sleep.

In the morning she realized that Peter's side of the bed hadn't been slept in. *'He's probably gone to wherever he usually goes on weekends,'* she thought as she prepared the childrens' lunches, *'but he's always home on Sunday evenings. Strange!'* she mused.

Later in the morning Mr. Hanson, Peter's boss called, "Mrs. Hall, is Peter sick today? He hasn't come in to work yet."

"He hasn't come in today? I really don't know, Mr. Hanson. He went fishing this weekend. I haven't seen him since he left here Friday evening."

"When did you expect him back?"

"Well... .last night but... .then I thought maybe he... had made arrangements to stay... ..an extra night."

"Is there somewhere else he might have gone? Never mind. When he returns, Mrs. Hall, have him call me before he comes in to work. This isn't the first time he's done this and I don't believe we will be needing him any longer. Have a good day."

Elsa wasn't worried that Peter hadn't returned since he had never been known for his dependability. The job, however, was a different matter. *'I'll give the Police a call and have them check out the area of the lake, if he isn't back by tonight,'* she thought finally becoming concerned. *'But if he's someplace else, he'll be angry that I've dragged the Police into something that he'll think is his business.'*

It was always difficult to make a decision where Peter was involved because regardless of whatever decision she made, it was always a decision he disapproved of, berating her for it until long after she had stopped listening to him.

Suddenly she was snapped out of her dilemma by a firm knock at the door. A tall, serious looking man stood on her front step, with Peter's jacket slung over his arm; the one he had been wearing when he'd left on Friday. "Mrs. Hall? I'm Detective Cooper of Special Divisions. We don't want to alarm you but I have some questions that I would like to ask you." He raised his eyebrows questioningly and Elsa nodded fearfully.

"May I come in, Mrs. Hall? Have you seen your husband in the last few days?"

"He... went fishing... .on Friday. I expected him back... .last night."

"We're not sure what this means but a hiker in the area of Green Lake spotted an abandoned car in the parking lot and also reported that there was a boat drifting with no one in it. They had seen the car there all weekend but surmised that someone was doing an overnight hike.

They finally decided to call us. When we investigated, we discovered that the car was registered in your husband's name. We also found a receipt for the boat rental on the front seat of the car." Holding up Peter's jacket, he asked, "Does this belong to your husband, Mrs. Hall?"

"Yes," she whispered. "Do you think he drowned?"

"We don't know yet. We've searched the surrounding woods and discovered his tent with some of his belongings. There was no wallet in the tent, but this jacket was there so we're quite sure that it was his tent. We will be doing a thorough investigation of the surrounding area but I'm afraid Mrs. Hall, that it does not look good. We will be sending divers into the lake to look as well. I know this must be difficult for you but I'm afraid there is no easy way of telling bad news. Can I get anything for you or is there someone that I can call to come and stay with you?"

Shaking her head, she muttered, "I'm fine, thank you."

Shrugging, he said, "Well, if you think you'll be alright. I'll be keeping in touch with you to let you know how our investigation is progressing. I hope we'll be able to bring you some good news."

"Thank you." Elsa closed the door behind him and sat with her arms wrapped tightly around her body. She thought about the way Peter had been acting since he'd gotten out of prison; how frustrated and angry he'd been. *'Has he drowned? Has he gotten lost in the woods? Maybe some animal had attacked him? Or,'* and she shuddered at the thought, *'has he committed suicide? Would he or could he do such a thing? No,'* she decided, *'he liked himself too well. He wouldn't just throw his life away like that. If something happened to him, it would have had to be an accident.'*

'But he was always so careful,' the other side of her argued. *'Except when he'd been drinking. And he'd have been drinking while he was fishing,'* she reminded herself.

She reached for the telephone. "Katrin? The Police think something has happened to Peter. They found his boat... on the lake... .but they... don't know where... Peter is." Elsa felt breathless and her teeth chattered as she spoke.

"Elsa, I'll be right there."

"You poor dear," Katrin put her arms around her friend. "You need a nice strong cup of coffee and then you can tell me what happened."

"I don't know. The only thing... .I know is... they can't... .can't find Peter."

"Alright now, try to relax. We'll find out what's going on. Michael will be able to get some information. Men always listen to another man before they'll listen to a woman. Everything will work out."

"I... .don't know... . He's... .he's been acting... .so strangely lately."

Katrin tried not to smile. In her opinion, Peter had always been a little strange but it wasn't for her to say. "Here's some coffee. Drink it up and you'll feel much better."

Elsa clasped the warm mug and stared in front of her. "It's strange, isn't it?" she whispered. "All of it. I could almost believe that he's planned the whole thing." She took a sip of the hot coffee. "I just don't understand."

"Planned it? Listen Elsa, we don't know anything yet so there's absolutely no sense in getting upset or trying to second guess what has happened until we've heard what the Police have to say. I'll telephone Michael and let him know what has been going on and then we're going to do all the regular things you would be doing. We'll make the beds and do the laundry. Do you have any ironing that has to be done?"

"Ironing?" Elsa repeated the word as if she'd never heard it before.

"Yes, the ironing. We'll get it all done. Where's Rebecca, Elsa?"

"Uh, she's playing next door."

Later in the day Michael called. "Hi Honey," he said when Katrin picked up the telephone. "I've got some information but not a lot. They've got people out searching the woods surrounding the lake and there are divers in the lake. Apparently, it's very difficult for the divers because there are a lot of submerged stumps and logs and the centre apparently is very deep. So far they haven't come up with anything. They have no evidence that he was attacked by an animal or anything else either. He seems to have disappeared into thin air or the lake has swallowed him up. But don't mention that to Elsa."

"No, no, I won't. If they find out anything, will they be getting in touch with you or Elsa?"

"I've asked them to keep me apprised of everything that happens. It'll be much easier on Elsa that way. We can give her any bad news much gentler than the authorities would. Also, I really don't think that Elsa can handle much more. She's been through so much lately so we'll have to help her as much as possible."

"I think you're right and thanks, Michael. You are a darling and I love you."

*   *   *   *   *

When the children came home from school, they were surprised to see their Aunt Katrin folding the laundry. "Is anything wrong, Aunt Katrin?" Sarah Ann asked, her large eyes serious and too knowing for a child her age.

"You're mother isn't feeling well so I'm giving her a hand. Helen is on her way over too. How would you and Helen like to make us all dinner? It can be a surprise for everyone."

"We can? That would be so much fun." Sarah Ann's face brightened. "Can we make anything we want; something special?"

"Within reason dear. We want to eat before we all starve so just don't get too elaborate. Something nice and simple will do."

"What's wrong with Mother?"

"Don't look so worried darling. I'll talk to you later about it but your mother is going to be fine. Where's Willie?"

"Oh, you know Willie. He always has a crush on some girl or other. This time it's Mary Beth Williams so he and his friend James followed her home. Willie said he was going to carry her books but more likely, he's got her convinced to carry his books."

"Sounds like Willie alright," Katrin agreed. She looked out the window and saw Elliott and Martin, the energetic eleven year old twins racing up and down the driveway on their battered old bicycles. After eleven years, Katrin still found it difficult to tell them apart from appearances only but after watching them for a few minutes she was able to discern the subtle differences between them by their actions.

Glancing into the girl's bedroom, she saw Kathleen and Melissa playing quietly together with their dolls.

"Sh-h, don't wake her up," Kathleen cautioned her younger sister as she gently placed her baby doll in a box she had made into a doll bed.

"I won't wake her. See, my baby's going to sleep too."

Katrin tiptoed away from the open doorway and glanced into the backyard where Rebecca was busily building roads and tunnels in the sandbox with the little boy next door. Her face was dirty and her blonde hair, coming loose from their pigtails hung down her back.

In the livingroom, Elsa was sitting quietly in a chair by the window watching the antics of the twins. Turning when she heard Katrin enter the room, a small smile appeared on her thin lips. "I was just watching Elliott and Martin; so alike and yet like day and night. They're like a long-married couple whose personalities complement each other. What one lacks, the other has; in every aspect."

"You're very fortunate with your children, Elsa."

"I know Katrin. I'm so glad I have them. And to think I worried so much about whether my heart would expand to love them all. What a silly thought that was. Has Michael heard any more news yet?"

"No, but you know what they say, 'No news is good news.'"

"That's not necessarily true. You know Katrin, I've been sitting here thinking and I don't believe they're going to find Peter."

"Why do you think that?"

Elsa shrugged. "I don't know. Just a feeling, I guess. I have been feeling lately that he's been working up to something. I think he's decided to disappear."

"Elsa, that's a silly notion. Why would he go to all this trouble to disappear? He could've just not come back one of the times he's been away. If he was going to do something like that, why wouldn't he have taken all of his things. If he's disappeared like you're saying, he'll have to start all over again from scratch. I don't for a minute believe that he would do that, Elsa. He always makes sure he gets everything he thinks he deserves."

"You're wrong, Katrin. It's something he would do. For the attention. He's probably laughing at all the people who are looking for him right now. He'd think it was one big joke."

"That's crazy. He can't hide from tracking dogs. They'd get his scent. The investigators will come up with something. He won't want to start from scratch again."

"Material things aren't important to Peter. Remember Katrin? And look around, what have we really got? We don't own our house. There were still payments to be made on the car. And look at our furniture. We don't have much and he could save a lot, as he has so often told me, if his paycheques didn't have to go to feed and clothe all of us. He's always telling me how many hours each day he has to work to do that."

Katrin had forgotten about Peter's previous communistic tendencies. "Does he still believe in all that stuff? He doesn't seem to with the new car, the new clothes and his fast-paced social life. Well, I guess we'll find out soon enough."

Elsa turned to look out the window again and Katrin left her, wondering as she did, about the questions Elsa had raised. *'No, it's too farfetched. Even for someone like Peter,'* she thought.

The search continued the following day and Katrin remained with Elsa, helping her with the children and trying to keep her spirits up. She had managed to avoid any further questions from Sarah Ann, hoping she wouldn't have to tell her anything until they knew exactly what had happened.

Michael called in the afternoon to say that there had been a new development. "Peter's shirt has been found snagged on one of the submerged stumps and his shoe was on the lake bottom not far from the shirt. The divers say that there are a lot of undercurrents in that section of the lake and that his body could have drifted quite a distance away. Or they said he could be caught under one of the submerged stumps. Apparently the whole bottom of the lake is a jumbled mass of logs and stumps and they may never find him. They're quite sure that's what has happened to him. Even the dogs have found no scent of him in the woods except around his tent and car and near the lake where he would've gone in with his boat. There's also no evidence of him walking back down the road and getting picked up by another car. The dogs would have picked up his scent if that had been the case. Elsa's theory is really quite unrealistic. My guess is that he had been drinking and fell into the lake while he was drunk and drowned. He was probably pulled down by the undercurrents. That kind of thing happens in the river too. I don't think he swam that well either if I remember right."

"No, he didn't. I recall Elsa saying once that he didn't like swimming after his father threw him into the middle of a pool trying to teach him to swim when he was quite young. Are they going to keep looking for him?"

"The divers will continue searching the lake tomorrow and if they haven't found anything by then, I think they're assuming that he's snagged under one of the logs and likely will never be found. They've almost completed their search of the area surrounding the lake so by tomorrow we should have some definite conclusions. How is Elsa holding up?"

"About the same as yesterday; not badly. I've been keeping her busy. She's holding up better than I expected she would."

"I wouldn't think she'd be taking it too hard considering how badly he's treated her all these years. He was unbelievable."

"I know but Elsa is a very loyal person and I think she's always hoped that things would get better between them for the sake of the children. I never thought there was any hope for their relationship and personally think she's better off without him. I know you and I both agree on that, Michael."

"Yes, but it won't be easy with all those children. Financially, it will be a terrible struggle. I'm sure Peter hasn't put anything away for a rainy day."

"He handled everything. So if he did put anything away, Elsa won't ever know about it and she's always been too frightened of him to ask. She did manage not too badly while he was in prison so maybe she'll continue with that. If she does, she'll be alright."

"She knew that was only for a short time. If he's dead, emotionally I'm not sure that she'll hold up for the long term. That's a lot of children to be solely responsible for and Rebecca is still so young."

"I think she'll do fine once she adjusts. She really is a strong person. I'll stay with her again tonight but come by on your way home from work, darling. We'll all have dinner together. I miss you."

By Wednesday even little Rebecca knew that there was something more wrong than what their Aunt Katrin had told them. "I know something is wrong, Aunt Katrin. Are you going to tell us?" Sarah Ann approached her aunt, in her typically no-nonsense way as she was making their lunches for school.

"This evening after dinner we'll all sit down and have a talk. We'll wait until Willie is home."

"The younger ones too?"

"We'll see about that," Katrin gave Sarah Ann a hug. "Off you go girls. Willie, hurry up or you're going to be late. And Willie, no hanging out with the girls today after school. Come straight home, please."

Before the children returned from school, Michael showed up with Detective Cooper from Special Divisions. "Elsa, sit down on the sofa beside me. This gentleman would like to talk to you." Michael took her cold hand in his.

"Mrs. Hall, I'm afraid the news is not good. There seems to be no doubt that your husband has drowned. Divers have found his shirt snagged on a stump and his shoe in the lake as you have already been told, and today they found his wallet not far from where the shoe was found. There was some money in it although there wasn't anything else. It was partially hidden beneath a log. No doubt that's why it was overlooked yesterday when they searched. All of these items were near the mouth of the creek. The creek is the reason the currents are so strong in that area. The divers say that because of the number of submerged stumps and logs, and because of the size of the lake, your husband's body may never be discovered. I want to emphasize this very strongly so you won't hold out any false hopes. There is no doubt in any of the investigator's minds that your husband drowned in that lake. I am very sorry."

Michael squeezed Elsa's limp hand. "Are you alright?"

She nodded. "So they are absolutely sure?"

"Mrs. Hall, the dogs didn't pick up anything to indicate otherwise and nor did the searchers. If he left the lake area, he would have had to fly out. I know this has all been very difficult for you."

"Are the divers going to continue searching?"

"No, Mrs. Hall. The search will be called off. The evidence seems to be conclusive and there seems little to be gained for the expense involved in continuing with the search. The divers hold very little hope of the possibility of ever finding his body. If you wished a search to continue, the expense would have to be bourne by yourself."

Elsa shook her head. "If there's nothing to be gained, and you're absolutely sure, there doesn't seem to be any point and—I couldn't afford the cost anyway, I'm afraid."

"I'm very sorry Ma'am to be the bearer of such bad news."

Elsa inclined her head but remained dry-eyed.

Mr. Cooper got up to leave and Michael saw him to the door. "Elsa, do you want me to get you anything?" Katrin sat down beside her friend.

"I really... .I thought he had just decided to leave. These last few days I didn't really think anything had happened to him." Her voice sounded faraway. "But maybe .... when I wished... ."

"Don't hold out any hopes, Elsa. He's gone; he won't be coming back this time.

Come and lie down, dear. Michael and I will look after telling the children when they're all together."

"Are they sure he's never coming back?" Elsa searched her friend's face.

"Yes, very sure." Katrin didn't understand the look in Elsa's eyes and reminded herself to mention the strangeness of it to Michael when they were alone together.

Elsa lay in her darkened room after she had been told the conclusion of the investigation. She felt guilty for the harm she had often wished on him when she had been angry. Remembering these thoughts she knew even Katrin must not know of her ill will towards him. *'IF he is really dead,'* she sighed. *'But if this is just another game to him and he's decided to disappear for awhile until he gets tired of playing the game then I will really wish him harm. I know Peter, he could turn up at anytime and make life miserable for me again. I'll never really know. The question will always be there so I'll never really be free of him. He'll always be with us, haunting us, neither dead nor alive.'*

Chapter VII

Resuming her children's reading group, Elsa gradually lost her fear that Peter would return to control her life. "Mom," Sarah Ann said after watching her mother with the young children, "you're very good at keeping the children's interest and getting them to behave for you. Have you thought about branching out?"

Looking at her eldest daughter, Elsa realized with a shock that Sarah Ann was growing up. She noticed, as if for the first time, the way her daughter's dark auburn hair fell in natural waves over her shoulders but it was her eyes that held the attention of all who saw her. At fifteen years old, Sarah Ann was becoming quite a beautiful young lady. A slight frown formed between Elsa's eyebrows. "I haven't Sarah Ann. Did you have something particular in mind?"

"I was thinking that perhaps you could approach some of the community organizations to see if your reading groups could become part of their curriculum. That way you would be able to have more children each time and have, maybe one hour sessions. If you had several sessions in a day, you'd be able to make far more money than you do now. Maybe you could even hire other readers to read to the children and you could supervise the sessions. You've got the confidence now so I know you could do it. I've seen the change in you lately. Even Aunt Katrin said what a big change there has been in you. She said you look happier now than you have ever looked in all the years she has known you." Sarah Ann smiled fondly at her mother.

"I've been so busy that I hadn't thought about it but yes, I am much happier. I certainly am more relaxed and not so nervous. And I'm beginning to feel that I'm capable of doing something on my own and succeeding at it. I've never felt that way before. And I finally believe that your father really did drown and is not coming back. The not knowing was driving me crazy. I kept looking over my shoulder, expecting him back at any time."

"I never believed he was coming back. You always were capable, Mom, at least when Father wasn't around. I saw what he did to you. What he did to all of us, in fact. Even the children are happier now. They no longer cringe whenever they hear the front door open."

Sarah Ann saw the look that passed quickly over her mother's face. "I'm glad you've got that silly notion out of your head, Mom. He died in that lake. He'll never be coming back." Sarah Ann herself would not have been happy either had her father returned from the dead.

Smiling, she hugged her mother. "I saw how Father treated you and how you didn't fight him on anything. You took whatever he dished out. I can remember when I was as young as five, I had already made up my mind that no one would ever do that to me. And I tried to make it so he didn't do the same thing to us children. I tried to keep them out of his way so we wouldn't be in the line of fire when he was at his worst. As long as we were out of the way, he didn't really care if we were here or not. In a way, I hope it made it a little bit easier for you too. If he couldn't say to you that what we were doing was annoying him, it gave him less to complain about. But Mom, I wish you had stood up to him."

Elsa nodded her head. "I should have but he terrified me when he was in a rant, especially if he had been drinking. It was the same with my father and when I think about it, they were the same type of men. The same but for very different reasons. Both of them liked to control those around them.

"It's been almost two years now. I think we can breath a sigh of relief. If he was alive, I'm sure we would have heard something by now." Elsa put her arm around her daughter and held her close. Sarah Ann had been her strength often during the difficult road they had traveled but Elsa knew that her own strength had grown since Peter had been gone. And now for the first time in her life, she didn't have to live with belittlement or fear.

"How is it Sarah Ann that you have been so strong? You've often acted as a surrogate mother for the younger children when I was upset or was having trouble managing things?"

"Remember I was born spunky. You've often told me that. I've learned a lot of things by being my father's daughter. I'm not sure that I will ever want to marry but if I did, I would be very, very careful of the type of man I choose. And if somebody didn't treat me well, I'd be gone before he could blink; or he would be."

Elsa started to speak and then quickly closed her mouth.

"What were you going to say, Mom?"

"I was going to say something about loyalty and for better or worse but there has to be loyalty on both sides and if there's more worse than better then you're right, it's better to be gone from the situation. I can see that now. I hope all of my children choose better than I did and marry for the right reasons. And I can see now that if a person keeps accepting bad treatment, the other person will expect you to keep taking it once a precedence has been set."

PART III SARAH ANN

Chapter I

Having had responsibility for her siblings at a very young age Sarah Ann instinctively felt that it was her job to protect them against their father. She had often compared her father with her friends' fathers and realized, even as a young child, that he was different from most of them. Wondering somewhat guiltily why her mother had married him, Sarah Ann found no redeeming features that would make him attractive to her mother.

Sometimes, in a childish game with friends, they would list the qualities they wanted in their husbands when they got married. Every time Sarah Ann looked at her father, she knew the qualities she didn't want her husband to have. Of those she was very sure. In fact, she wasn't even sure if marriage would ever be in her future. She saw how her father became another person when he was with others. She knew he portrayed himself quite differently when it suited him and she knew she wouldn't want to take a chance on marrying someone who felt he should treat strangers better than he treated his wife, his children and those closest to him. And although she loved her siblings, she wasn't sure either if children were what she wanted. Her friends were determined that marriage and children were the most important things in life and were planning their futures accordingly and most were choosing not to further their education. Sarah Ann had definite plans of attending University and she was quite sure that she would have an important career someday. Her friends felt that she would eventually change her mind because what woman wouldn't want to be married and have children. She was far less convinced than they were.

*   *   *   *   *

Sarah Ann studied hard and graduated in 1960 as the valedictorian of her class with the class comment of being 'the girl most likely to succeed in the business world'. She had smiled to herself when she had first heard the comments and was determined to make their assessment of her come true.

Enrolling in college, Sarah Ann had taken business management courses while continuing to work at the local greenhouses to help subsidize her education. Living at home, she helped her mother with household chores and assisted in keeping the younger children in line and on track.

Sarah Ann was happy that her mother was enjoying the reading groups she supervised through the community services and had eventually joined a couple of women's groups. She realized that her mother was probably busier now than when all the children were small. Even Aunt Katrin complained that she rarely got to see her friend.

"Sarah Ann," Elsa's face wore a happy smile. "Two of the ladies from my book club are planning to take a cruise in the Fall. They have invited me to join them.

You are already so busy that I hate to ask you but....would you be able to keep an eye on the three girls while I'm gone? It's a ten day cruise."

Sarah Ann threw her arms around her mother's neck. "Of course I will. You really deserve to take a trip. I'll be here to watch the children. I'm so excited for you; what a wonderful opportunity."

A tear trickled down Elsa's cheek as she smiled at her daughter. "I am very proud of you, Sarah Ann and I appreciate everything you do to help me. You won't have to worry about the twins. They're pretty good; they won't give you any trouble."

"Mom, you will go on your trip and you are not to worry about a thing. None of them will be any trouble, believe me. Come on, let's have a glass of wine to celebrate your independence and your new life as a world traveler."

Elsa laughed nervously. "I'm so excited that they asked me and that I will be able to go. They go almost every year, well at least somewhere, not always on a cruise, and they said they have great times. With the money that I'm making with the reading groups and now that even the twins are helping towards buying their own clothes and helping to pay for extra things, it is much easier for me financially. In fact," she smiled happily at her daughter, "this last year has probably been the easiest year financially that I can remember. I have you to thank for it. If you hadn't come up with that idea of the reading groups in the community centres, things wouldn't be so easy for me now."

"You can probably thank the fact that I'm taking business management courses. They have given me a new way of looking at things. I've got a lot of plans for the future myself which I can hardly wait to put into action." Sarah Ann toasted her mother. "Come on, let's sit down. We haven't had a chance for a nice long chat, just the two of us, for quite awhile. We've both been so busy."

*　　　*　　　*　　　*　　　*

Sarah Ann now thought about her mother as she worked at her desk sorting through her case files and putting them into priority order.

Elsa had done well over the last few years. Sarah Ann often saw her laughing with friends as they planned their many excursions together. She had taken several cruises, gone on walking trips and had even recently taken up cross country skiing. On one of her cross country skiing trips she had met a well-mannered, quiet spoken gentleman who she now went to the occasional movie and dinner with. She insisted, when Sarah Ann had asked, that he was only a friend for the occasional social activity, and nothing more. Sarah Ann didn't question her mother further and was happy for her obvious enjoyment of life; more than she had ever had, she suspected.

Sarah Ann knew very well what it was like to have a male friend for the occasional movie and dinner. She'd had several male friends over the years herself. But none became serious relationships. Whenever a male friend became more serious than she wished, he would very quickly become, as her family came to call them, 'things of the past'. That is until she'd met Adam. From the first time she'd seen him across the room at the Conference Centre, she knew she wanted to meet him. She also knew from that first meeting that it would be difficult to continue to follow her self-imposed rule to have her friendship with Adam remain a friends only relationship. Shuffling her files, she thought back to their first meeting.

*   *   *   *   *

Feeling a tap on her shoulder, she had turned around, "Excuse me, I was wondering if I could get you a cup of coffee?"

"No thank you. I'm afraid I only have one cup of coffee a day but thank you for asking. By the way, my name is Sarah Ann Hall," she smiled, holding out her hand.

Laughing, he said, "Hello Sarah Ann, I'm very happy to meet you. I have to confess though that I already asked someone what your name was. My name is Adam Bennett. I'm the school counselor at St. George High, over on Broadway."

"Really? So you are the counselor from there! I've heard so many good things about the progress you have made with the children in that school. From everything I've been told, it's a pretty tough school. Is that right?"

"A lot of the inner-city schools are tough. Most of the children are on their fifth or sixth dad with many of them not knowing who their original dad ever was, so it's no wonder really that they have a tough time. In fact I wonder sometimes if the mothers even know, remember or care. Alcohol and drug addictions are rampant in the area. How can any child grow up unscathed under those conditions? Many also have lived on welfare most of their lives and move as often as they change their socks; keeping just ahead of the rent collector. A lot of the children don't have a thing that they can call their own so stealing at a young age is not considered by them to be a crime, it's purely a matter of survival. They don't have the books or the clothes that they need for school but they know where they can get them, real quick. It's just a quick stop at the local store, a quick look around, a grab and they're gone. Most are quite proud of their ability not to get caught. It's enough to make a person cry when you see how so many of them live. I should say how they exist because that's all they're really doing. But on a happier note, it's surprising how many of them actually do make it in spite of their difficult backgrounds. Enough about what I do. I was told that you have your own counseling practice."

"You have been doing your homework. Yes, I do. It took me a while to get there though. I initially took business management courses before I realized that what I really wanted to do was to become a counselor. I know what you mean about the poor homes and the difficulties they experience. I go into a lot of those homes and try to turn families around but for most the extreme poverty has beaten their spirits into the ground. However, over the years there are a few that I have had some luck with, especially if we have been able to build up their self-esteem and self-confidence."

"I agree that self-esteem and confidence are the key issues involved with these children. Not just the children but with their parents as well, especially some of the single mothers. If the parents can feel confident about their abilities, they will be able to pass that on to their children. But if they don't, their negative attitudes will be passed on to their children instead. I try to drum into their heads that negative attitudes will get them nowhere; only more negativity. How are you enjoying the Seminar so far?"

Sarah Ann shrugged her shoulders. "I'm enjoying it but I was hoping it offered a little more information than what there seems to be here today. A lot of the classes are quite similar to others I have taken in the past."

"I know what you mean. There is one class at three o'clock that I'm looking forward to but other than that, there hasn't been anything really new for me either. But you never know when you sign up for them." Adam smiled, his blue eyes crinkling at the corners. "Um, are you free for dinner this evening? I don't want to put you on the spot but I'd really like it if you would join me."

Sarah Ann hesitated momentarily. "As a matter of fact, I am available. I would love to, Adam."

They had gone to a Greek Taverna where a belly dancer had entertained them, swishing her colourful scarves in their direction as she danced past. "How long have you had your practice?" Adam asked as he picked at his calamarie appetizer. Offering some to Sarah Ann, she had wrinkled her nose before turning it down.

"I've had my own office for three years now and practiced for two years before that. What made you decide that you wanted to become a school counselor?"

Adam looked uncomfortable before he finally looked her in the eye. "I have an older brother that…shall we say….. he got off on the wrong foot and got himself into some very serious trouble. He's in jail now, unfortunately. Neither my mother or my father knew how to handle him so they finally threw up their hands and did nothing at all. As I grew older I realized that something probably could have been done to prevent it had he been given a strong steer in the right direction at an early age. If he'd had some strong guidance, he no doubt wouldn't be where he is now. I think you have to work with the young, before they get into trouble. I believe it's much more difficult to change someone after their life has already been established and they're headed down the wrong path. What about you?"

"It's somewhat similar. My father treated my mother and us children very badly. We were all afraid of him and it affected all of us in various ways. My oldest brother is very easy going and he lets everything slide off him. He chose to be away from home whenever my father was there. My twin brothers, who are two years younger than me, handled the situation in much the same way as my brother Willie did, as they got older. They were able to because boys are allowed a little more freedom than girls are, I think. My three younger sisters were as intimidated as my mother was and for that reason tended to be treated as badly as my mother. My mother was afraid to stand up to my father in any way so even as a young child, I felt that since she wasn't going to, I would have to. I'm afraid, looking back on it now, that I was the toughest of all of us. I decided then and there that I would never let anyone treat me the way he had treated my mother."

"So Sarah Ann was the fighter for the group, heh?" Adam smiled.

"I was because even when I was very young, I decided that no one should treat others like my father treated his family. Then when I was deciding what I was going to do, I suddenly realized that by being a counselor I could possibly help other families that were in similar situations where there is abuse happening within the family. When I was young I thought it was just our family. Now that I'm a counselor I've discovered how rampant the problem really is."

Adam nodded his head in understanding. "It's a serious problem alright. If we could only get to the root of problems within families, we'd have emotionally healthier children. But it'll be a long time in coming, I think. What we're doing now is like trying to plug the holes in a dyke or fix an amputation with a bandage. But to get onto a more pleasant subject, why don't you tell me more about Sarah Ann."

Taking a sip of her wine she smiled, "There's not an awful lot to tell. I've already mentioned that I'm second oldest in a large family; the eldest girl."

Adam smiled, "That tells a story in itself. Besides being a fighter, were you the bossy older sister?"

"I was never bossy." In an attempt to look stern, a frown creased Sarah's forehead. "I led and encouraged but I was never bossy. How about you?"

"There was just my older brother and myself. He's eight years older than I am. And believe me, after seeing where he went, I was not likely to follow in his footsteps. He was an excellent teacher in helping me to learn what not to do. My parents both died a few years ago, at fairly young ages. I've always suspected it was because of the worry and stress he put them through. Outside of that, I grew up much the same as any other boy. I played soccer. I still do, in fact and I ski, when we have enough snow and golf when I have enough time. What are your interests?"

"Well I don't play soccer but I do ski. Whether or not I golf is debatable, depending on who you are talking to. It seems like it should be so easy to hit a tiny, little ball along on grass but I seem to be having some difficulty grasping the ability to do so. I like to hike and I enjoy entertaining. I also spend quite a bit of time with my family. After my father died, we all became very close."

"I would be happy to give you a few golf lessons. But don't worry about your ability because no one has ever said that golfing is easy. It may only be little but there's no doubt that those little balls definitely have minds of their own."

Sarah Ann smiled at Adam thinking that any man who offered to take her golfing after she had disclosed how badly she played the game must be a gem. Looking at him, she admired the way his dark brown hair fell into natural waves across his forehead. She also liked the way his eyes twinkled when he talked well before the smile had reached his lips. And when he smiled, she felt as if he was sharing a huge secret with her.

"If you did that, I'm not sure that the word happy is the one you would use but if the invitation is still open, I would like to take you up on your offer." Sarah Ann took a bite of her Moussaka while she watched Adam beckon the waiter over.

"Could you bring us each another glass of wine, please. Actually, on second thought bring us half a litre of the same wine. Thank you."

Laughing, Adam said, "We'll see. Tell me more about your family. I'm always interested in what the effects are on people after they become adults when they have had difficult childhoods. Even your mother's situation is interesting having been intimidated by first her father and then by her husband. How is she doing now? And your sisters, how are they doing now that they've grown up?"

"My mother is doing wonderfully well, happier than she's ever been. She's a very strong woman. My sisters, well, they are three very different personalities. The youngest, Rebecca is doing fine. She was quite young when my father died so her memories aren't as vivid and there seem to be no effects at all. I think what she remembers, if anything, has been effectively swept under the proverbial carpet. Kathleen, the one that is four years younger than me has a bit of a chip on her shoulder so she tends to be argumentative and a little difficult to get along with at times. With everyone, not just family. Any man that could get along with her will be a Saint. She does have a heart of gold though where family is concerned, under the hard crust. Melissa appears to be relatively unscathed as far as any major hang-ups are concerned. Although she said she'll probably never marry; she thinks she'll be quite happy remaining single. She does date occasionally but they're only friends, she says. She's twenty-three years old and she's planning to be a lawyer so most of her time is spent studying."

"And what about you, Sarah Ann?" Adam smiled gently at her. "I suspect you have some rather definite opinions and a lifestyle that relates directly back to your childhood. I'm sorry, I shouldn't have asked you that. I don't want to see you get up and walk out of here. I have some tickets for a concert on the weekend. Would you like to go with me?"

"What time is the concert? I'm taking a group of some of the children I work with on an outing for the day. I do it on my own time with the help of two of my sisters and my mother. Most of these children wouldn't get a chance to go anywhere if we didn't take them once in a while. We've been doing this for about a year now."

"I'm very impressed. I can give you a hand if you need extra help."

"Thanks Adam but most of these children's problems have been related to the men in their lives, mostly step-fathers so they have difficulty trusting men that they don't know. Perhaps another time." Sarah Ann smiled at Adam, wondering if there would be other times that they would get together.

"Anytime I can help, I would like to. The concert doors open at seven. There are a couple of warm-up bands so the main group doesn't come on until about eight thirty. They're a new group from England. I hadn't heard of them before but apparently they're supposed to be very good. Even if we miss the warm-up bands, it doesn't matter. How does that work for you?"

Leaving the restaurant, they made arrangements about where they would meet for the Concert. Sarah Ann had always made it a practice when first dating someone new to meet at an appointed place because then she was in control of when she could leave. Adam had smiled when she had made the suggestion but had not insisted otherwise. She made a note of that in the pro side of her mind. It might be nice, she decided, to date someone who understands a little bit about why people do the things they do.

*   *   *   *   *

At the Concert they had seen the Beatles, a group of young men with interesting hairstyles and wonderful accents. The crowd had gone wild and the excitement in the building had flowed over, around and through Sarah Ann until she was almost as excited as the other concert goers.

They had also gone golfing and Adam, being true to his word, had been patient while trying to teach her the basics of the game. Although it may be difficult he had told her, he was convinced that she would eventually become a good golfer. In the meantime, they played 'best ball' on his ball and she enjoyed herself more than she had ever enjoyed a game of golf before.

As Sarah Ann looked back over the four months since she had first met Adam, she couldn't recall a more exciting time in her life. She was aware that as they did more things together, and as they became closer, they would become more intimate and before long the relationship would change. In other relationships this had not been a problem because she had felt no strong emotional attachment. The relationship with Adam was different and she wasn't sure how she was going to handle it or even if she wanted to have a relationship where she felt so emotionally involved.

'Am I ready for a serious relationship?' she often thought. *'Do I want to be this involved? Life was much easier before I met Adam, but not nearly as much fun,'* she had to admit.

What would Adam's expectations be as the relationship became more serious? She had always been adamantly adverse to marriage; never wanting to be in a position of vulnerability. If she allowed herself to become emotionally involved, as she knew she was becoming with Adam, she knew she would be opening the door to the possibility of being hurt, as her mother had been. Did she want to take the risk? She knew her feelings for him were very different than she had ever experienced before. In the past, she had always been able to walk away without ever once looking back. She wasn't sure that she would be able to do that with Adam. She wondered if she should dissolve their relationship while she still could. But could she do it?

"Sarah Ann," Adam sounded excited when he called her, "I've volunteered to transport a boy to Prince George, to his father's home. He's been living here with his mother but it hasn't been working out. The mother has had a few scrapes with the law and the father has stepped in and wants to have the boy live with him.

"Fortunately, the boy is agreeable to the arrangement. I'm hoping that you would like to join me on the trip." Adam hesitated, waiting for her reply.

Sarah Ann had been afraid that something similar to this would happen and then she would be forced to make a decision. Until now she had been able to keep the relationship on a casual level. Remembering her worries over becoming too involved with Adam, she knew if she spent the entire weekend with him, their relationship would be different. Over the last few weeks she was beginning to get that feeling she sometimes got when a relationship felt like it was closing in on her.

"Is something wrong, Sarah Ann?"

"Uh, I'm sorry Adam but I won't be able to go along with you."

"Oh! I was hoping that you could." Sarah Ann could hear the disappointment in his voice. "I thought it would be a good chance to have a nice long weekend together. I thought we could drop the boy off at his father's place and do some exploring on our way back." Adam hesitated before adding, "Well, maybe another time. There will be other times, I hope Sarah Ann?"

"Yes, another time. When will you be leaving?"

"I was planning to leave Friday evening but if you're unable to come, maybe I'll leave on Saturday morning Are you free for dinner on Friday evening?" Adam's voice sounded slightly deflated.

"I'd like that. I really am sorry about the weekend, Adam."

"Are you sure everything is alright, Sarah Ann? You sound a little different. Nothing is bothering you, is there?"

"Honestly, Adam, I'm just fine. I'll see you on Friday for dinner."

*   *   *   *   *

Sarah Ann sipped her wine as she watched Adam over the rim of her glass. Knowing that he sensed there was something wrong, she was apprehensive about what he might say to her and how she would answer. She didn't enjoy serious conversations where she was put in the position of having to explain her actions. And she especially didn't want to have to explain why she was backing away from their relationship.

Laying down his knife and fork, Adam picked up his glass of wine and looked across the table at Sarah Ann. The smile had disappeared from his face. "Do you want to tell me what's bothering you? I know you well enough to know there's something going on in that pretty head of yours. How will we be able to have a relationship if we're not going to be able to talk about things that bother us? Have I said or done something to offend you?"

Sarah Ann could feel her cheeks flush, the heat spreading to her neck. "It's nothing you've done or said Adam. You're a great person."

"If I'm great, why do I get the feeling that you're pulling away from me? I felt it as soon as I asked if you wanted to join me when I go to Prince George. I thought we had something special going but now I'm confused."

Sarah Ann looked unhappily at her plate. The seafood, which she normally loved, looked unappetizing and she felt nauseous as she considered how she was going to answer him. In her confusion, her stomach churned. She didn't want to lose what they had but she was also afraid of where the relationship might take her.

She was very attracted to Adam but her feelings for him were much stronger than what she was comfortable with. She was beginning to get that closed in feeling that she had experienced in the past when she was in a relationship that was getting too serious. Normally when the closed in feeling hit her, she was off and running. But she didn't really want to do a disappearing act this time. Although she didn't like the feeling of not being in control of her emotions, she also didn't want to lose what they had either. She had to admit to herself that she enjoyed how he treated her, how he made her feel special, the fun they had when they were together, the things they had in common and how they could talk for hours.

Sarah Ann slowly raised her eyes to meet Adam's across the table. "I hope you will understand what I'm going to say, Adam." She fidgeted restlessly before continuing, "Because of the way my father treated my mother, I swore that I would never allow myself to be treated in the same way. I know what you're going to say, 'that you never would treat me like that' and I know you wouldn't, but because of that I've avoided all serious relationships where I haven't felt that I could just walk away with no explanations. The problem is that now I don't want to just walk away because I do care about what we have." Sarah Ann felt the tears as they stung behind her eyelids.

"Is that what this is all about? I suspected that you were very cautious about relationships and I also suspected what the reason for it was. Sarah Ann, that's why I have tried not to rush you about anything. I'm sorry if I made you feel as if I was closing in on you. I was trying to be very careful. I thought a nice casual weekend drive to Prince George would be a good way to get out of the city and enjoy ourselves. I wasn't trying to put any pressure on you. If it makes you feel any better, I'll emphasize 'casual' weekend. Eventually you will trust me though, you know." He smiled, squeezing her hand across the table..

Sarah Ann smiled slightly. "I'm sorry Adam, I've overreacted rather badly, haven't I? I do know that you have been making an effort not to put any pressure on me. But as soon as you mentioned weekend away, I got that edgey feeling." Smiling more broadly, she asked hesitantly, "But I'd like to go if the invitation is still open for a 'casual' weekend?"

"Of course it is. But are you sure? I don't want you to do anything that you don't feel comfortable with."

"I really would like to come along. I guess it's been all the years of practice I've had at avoiding serious relationships. If you could be a little patient with me, I might be able to overcome the feelings of panic I get when I think I'm getting myself in too deep."

"We'll work at this together, Sarah Ann. And Sarah, I'm very happy you're coming along with us. And," Adam hesitated, "I'm glad you told me and didn't just run."

*   *   *   *   *

The weekend had been a wonderful getaway. Driving the freeway route, they had arrived in Prince George late in the evening on Saturday. Sarah Ann had been pleased that the boy had been genuinely happy to see his father. It was not always the case in these situations but Adam had mentioned that the father had been keeping in close contact with the boy and had seen him regularly over the past several years.

After they had dropped the boy off, Adam said, "I've made reservations at a hotel here in town. I thought it would be better to stay here and then head out early in the morning. I don't think I could look at another stretch of highway right now. We've got two days to get back so we'll have time to explore a little on our way. I thought we could go back through the canyon route which is much more scenic than the Freeway."

The following morning Adam had knocked on their connecting door at what Sarah Ann considered the crack of dawn. "Get up lazy bones, we're getting a late start."

Taking the highway through Quesnel, Williams Lake and 100 Mile House, Adam had turned to Sarah Ann and smiling said, "Another time maybe we could stop and visit Barkerville if we're up here again. Have you ever been there? It's an interesting place. There's a saloon and in the summer they have spectacular entertainment. They also have horse and carriages that visitors can take rides on. Also there's an old cemetery that I was particularly interested in when I visited. It was surprising to find that there were so many young people buried in it. They had difficult lives in those days. And throughout the whole town, there is a lot of the history about the entire area."

"That would be wonderful. Exploring ghost towns has always interested me. I've got some books on ghost towns."

"Barkerville isn't really a ghost town. It never has been although for many years there were only a few residents before the government decided to commercialize it. But I agree with you, I'm interested in exploring ghost towns as well. There are a couple around the Princeton area. From what I've heard in one of them there is practically nothing left and the other one is starting to be commercialized as well."

They had driven in silence for a while. "The landscape is so different up here compared to the Vancouver area," Sarah Ann commented as she watched the terrain change over the miles while they drove. "Where will we be staying this evening?" she said, turning to Adam.

Laughing he said, "You took the words right out of my mouth. I was just going to suggest that we can stay in either 100 Mile House, which we'll be coming up to shortly, or drive a little further and stay at Cache Creek. Do you want to call it a day or are you up for driving a little further?"

"Since you're doing the driving, you should make the decision. I'm just sitting here enjoying the scenery and," Sarah Ann turned to Adam with a smile, "the company. But you must be awfully tired since you had such a long day of driving yesterday and now again today."

"I'm fine. I enjoy driving, especially when I have such charming company beside me. I am so happy you decided to come along with me. " Adam smiled and Sarah Ann noticed the sparkle in his eyes. "Let's drive to Cache Creek and then we'll have more time for exploring tomorrow. Hopefully we'll find a place that has a hot tub. Doesn't that sound like a bit of heaven?"

$$* \qquad * \qquad * \qquad * \qquad *$$

During the week since they had returned Sarah Ann thought often about the weekend they had spent together. By the second night when they had finally found a place to stay, Sarah Ann knew without a doubt how she felt about Adam and she was terrified. Commitment to any man was a scary thought. Talking to herself, she knew deep down within her that Adam was different than her father had been and he was different than anyone else she had ever known. She had seen nothing yet that would indicate that he was anything different than the person he appeared to be. She had seen nothing either to make her believe that she couldn't trust him. But trust was almost as scary a word as commitment was. But at least she wasn't running. That was progress.

Adam had been loving, gentle and thoughtful and when he had looked into her eyes, she saw the words he had not as yet spoken. She knew that he hadn't wanted her to feel pressured by their weekend together so he showed her in every other way possible that he loved her. She knew the words would be difficult for her to speak as well because once spoken she would be fearful that her feeling of independence would be gone and she would begin to feel suffocated.

Sarah Ann's thoughts were broken by the ringing of the telephone, "Hello there! How are you doing today, Princess?"

"Hi Adam, I'm fine. I was just thinking about you." She gulped when she realized that by telling him he had been in her thoughts, she had allowed a little vulnerability into her life. Her aloof shell had slipped slightly.

"I'm glad to hear that Sarah Ann and I'm glad that I'm not the only one with thoughts." Adam laughed good naturedly. "Since you're in such good spirits, I'd like to run something by you. I have a student who is in grade eight; a very nice girl but she has some very serious problems with her home life. I wonder if, between us, we'd be able to help her so that she doesn't enter her adult life with a lot of severe baggage. The big problem is that her family are not in a financial position to pay for counseling nor are they interested in doing so because they think that their lifestyle isn't a problem and in fact, have become quite angry when anyone tries to talk to them. Other counselors have apparently tried over the years. So unfortunately, it would have to be on a volunteer basis." Hesitating Adam continued, "But this girl has such great potential that I feel it would be a shame not to help her because I don't think she has the fortitude to overcome her problems on her own, at least not at this time." Adam paused again, "Would you be interested in helping me with this project, Sarah Ann?"

"I will help but I don't usually make a habit of doing volunteer counseling because if I was to let my heart rule me, my whole practice could become a volunteer one. Do you think she would be agreeable to having me counsel her?"

"I think so. I will talk to her and let you know if she agrees. I'm still trying to get through her extreme reserve but Heather is finally beginning to, albeit rarely, open up with me."

"What are her specific problems? She's about thirteen, I assume?"

"Yes. I have a file on her so it's probably best for you to see what I've got in the way of information on her and what I've been able to accomplish so far, if she agrees. It hasn't been a lot unfortunately because, as I said, she's extremely reserved."

"Thirteen is such a difficult age anyway. They've already got the hormones going full-tilt without having additional problems as well. I'd like to take a look at the file before I meet with her, if I could."

"Thanks, Sarah Ann. I'll confirm with Heather and if she is still agreeable, I'll bring it with me when we go for dinner tonight. Would you like to try Japanese this time?"

"I would love that. In fact, it's one of my favourite types of foods; teriyaki chicken and sushi, now what could be better than that? But I'll pass on the saki."

"Not my favourite beverage either. I won't be able to get to your place until about seven p.m. There's a staff meeting after school and some of the teachers whose students come to see me on a regular basis usually have questions over and above the reports that I give them routinely. Heather especially is of concern to several of them. She's very well liked by the staff because she's not a behavioral problem."

*　　*　　*　　*　　*

Later that evening, Sarah Ann opened the file intending to take a cursory look at the contents but was drawn in from the minute she saw the picture of the lonely looking girl. The picture showed an extremely shy girl with her eyes cast downward rather than looking directly at the camera as most girls her age would do. Appearing very small for her age, she was small-boned and delicate and extremely thin. Her bony arms stuck out of a shirt that was too big for her and her worn jeans looked as if they stayed up by a wish as there were no hips to hold them in place. Her heart went out to this waif of a girl.

Heather, the third child of five daughters and a son, were all born in a nine year period. The mother was overworked and overwhelmed with the responsibility of six children in a short period of time. Her first child had been born when she was seventeen years old; not much more than a child herself. Her common law husband, father of the last three children, was a laborer. Not working regularly, money was a constant problem causing many bitter fights. Most of the father's anger was directed at the three older children and his wife. But because of Heather's timidity, she appeared to bear the brunt of his anger.

Arriving at school with welts and bruises was a common occurrence for the child but the reason was always adamantly denied by Heather when she was asked. At one time, while in grade six, she had come to school with a broken arm. Adam had made a notation that Heather rarely lifted her head when spoken to, mumbled replies only to questions and never initiated any conversation on her own. It had only been in the last few weeks that Heather had offered slightly more information than was usual.

She had recently mentioned that her mother was in the hospital but she appeared to be unaware of the reason for it.

Sarah Ann thought about the similarities within her own family and felt a strong kinship with Heather. The girl, from what she had read, appeared to be in the same situation as her own mother, Elsa had been with the same resultant problems. Thinking about how happy her mother was now, she found herself anxious to help Heather with her problems. She was tempted to call Adam but looking at her watch, she realized that she had been so engrossed in the file that it was now two-thirty a.m. She hadn't been aware of the passing of the time and realized that she'd be tired tomorrow if she didn't get some sleep.

*   *   *   *   *

Phoning the following day Adam said, "Did you get a chance to review that file yet, Sarah Ann? I met with Heather this morning and it appears as if it wasn't a very good weekend for her. She is refusing to talk. In fact, she refused to look at me the entire time she was in my office. She also seemed to be shivering but she shook her head when I asked if she was cold. I was hoping that we could get together with her soon. I think that she might be more comfortable with a woman than she is with a man."

"I was up until late last night reading through the file. I really want to help her because I can see resemblances to my own family. My heart went out to her."

"From what you've told me about your family, I thought the same thing. For that reason, I think that if you talk to her, it might do her a world of good. Right now she probably thinks that she's the only one who has ever been in a position like this. But if she realizes that it happens to others as well and that there is a way to live better than how she is living now, I'm sure she will open up more. How is your time for later today?"

Checking her schedule, Sarah Ann replied, "I could be available around four or four-thirty. Why don't you check with her to see if she is agreeable to meeting with me then and let me know."

Chapter II

When Sarah Ann walked into Adam's office and saw the thin child sitting hunched into a chair, staring at the floor, she felt tears gathering and with difficulty held them back. Glancing in the direction of Adam, she smiled slightly in greeting.

"Hello Heather, my name is Ms. Hall." The child instinctively looked in the direction of Sarah Ann before timidly lowering her eyes to the floor.

"Heather, Mr. Bennett has asked me to speak with you. He said you have agreed to meet with me. Do you still feel that you want to?"

The child's eyes quickly searched Sarah Ann's face before she slowly nodded her head.

"Today we'll get to know each other, Heather. I have a private practice but occasionally I work with counselors in the various schools. If you have any problems that you want to talk to us about, we can help you once we know what they are. Do you have any questions you would like to ask me?"

The child looked fully at Sarah Ann for the first time since she had entered the room. "Would you like us to help you?"

With a hesitant nod of her head, Heather quietly mumbled "I think so. But what ....will happen .....to me if I..... tell you....things?" She seemed to fade further into the chair.

"Nothing, Heather. We will only do what will help you. We will never do anything that could place you in more harm. We promise you that."

Sarah Ann could see out of the corner of her eye that Adam was smiling and realized that she had probably made more headway with the child than he had been able to do thus far.

"Is there anything you would like to talk to us about now, Heather?"

The child appeared undecided before she slowly shook her head.

"We'll set up another appointment but if you wish to talk to us before then, all you have to do is call either one of us. Okay Heather?"

* * * * *

"Things seem to be going quite well with you and Heather in your last few meetings. She's opening up a little bit more each time, I've noticed," Adam said one evening over dinner. "Would you be able to meet with her sometime tomorrow? She came to school today with some nasty bruises on her face and arms. I think she feels much more comfortable with you than she does with me."

"Yes. I could see her sometime tomorrow afternoon. Do you think she's ready to tell me what happened?"

Adam picked up his glass of wine and slowly swirled the amber liquid. "If she's going to talk to anyone, it will be you. She has developed a bit of a bond with you and she does seem to trust you."

* * * * *

"You have a lot of bruises and scrapes on your face, Heather." Sarah Ann said.

Shrugging her shoulders, Heather kept her eyes fastened to the floor. "If my father…finds out that…I've told you…I'll be in more…trouble." Her eyes shone brightly with unshed tears.

"He won't find out, Heather. Can you tell us what happened?"

Heather nodded her head but refused to look up. "I asked why… my…mother was in the…..hospital. He hit me…I fell down. He…said it was…none of my…b..b..business."

The tears spilled down her face and Sarah Ann ached to take her into her arms but knew she couldn't. "I'm so sorry, Heather. Would you like us to see how your mother is doing? We could find out for you; would you like us to do that?"

Heather nodded her head, the hint of a smile on her unhappy face. "Would you see if she's okay?"

"How will things be for you at home tonight, Heather?"

"My father is... working an afternoon shift today... so he won't be home."

"Ms. Hall will drive you home and I'll check with the hospital to see how your mother is doing," Adam told the child. "I'll talk to you tomorrow morning or would you rather wait until Ms. Hall is here also?"

Heather looked a little fearful. "I'd like...Ms Hall to be here too."

"Ms. Hall will have to check her schedule to see when she will be available so I'll let you know tomorrow morning what time we'll meet."

*   *   *   *   *

Adam, as he told Sarah Ann later, was not surprised with what he saw when he met Barbara Carter, Heather's mother, at the hospital. "She's small, like her daughter, and has obviously been badly beaten, however she insisted she had fallen down the stairs in her home when she had gotten up in the middle of the night. She had to whisper through swollen lips when she told me it was her fault. She said she didn't turn on the light when she got up.

"She said, 'Has Heather been telling you stories? That one has always been trouble. She has caused more problems than the rest of them put together.' Disgust was clearly etched on her swollen face when she talked about her daughter. She said that Heather has always been a very clumsy child. She asked if I was accusing her husband of beating her? 'Is that what she told you,' she asked me?

"I told her that Heather has not told us anything and in fact, Heather hardly says anything at all. I said that as counselors, the fact that she rarely speaks has us concerned and that's why we're looking into the situation.

"Well, there's nothing to look into," she told me. She tried to convince me that they get along just fine as a family. 'My husband is a good man,' she said. 'We always have enough to eat and we have a house to live in. When he gets after the kids, it's because they deserve it. If anyone says differently, they're lying.

"And if it's those neighbors," she continued, "they have been nothing but troublemakers since we moved there.

"I told her that we were not accusing her husband of anything; we were only talking to her because it was difficult not to wonder when a child turns up at school, as often as Heather does, with bruises, welts and broken bones.

"She turned her face to the wall and refused to participate in any further conversation. When I left the hospital, I thought the visit was a complete waste of time. It always amazes me how these women will protect abusive husbands and fathers. There is more than the father's abuse that is a problem in that family.

"Anyway, we can't do anything more tonight. Shall we go for dinner?"

"Dinner sounds great but I don't think talking to her was entirely a waste of time. We do know now how badly she was beaten so we know what the man is capable of doing. It's interesting that she was willing to blame Heather rather than her husband. She could have covered for her husband without blaming her daughter. The poor child! We have our work cut out for us in trying to help her."

"You're getting more than you bargained for, I think Princess." Adam leaned over and kissed her. "I love you."

Staring at Adam, she felt as if the air had been knocked out of her, "You've never said that before, Adam." She could feel the little fingers of vulnerability starting to creep in the direction of her heart.

"You know it's been there almost from the start, don't you, Sarah Ann? I was trying to wait until I thought you were ready to hear it but I'm afraid the words tumbled off the tip of my tongue before I could stop them." Smiling, he took her face in his hands and kissed her before pulling her tightly into his arms. "You're not going to run off, are you? I would have trouble handling that. My ego, you know," he laughed in an attempt to lighten the suddenly tense situation.

"No," hesitating she added, "I won't. At least I don't think so. It's strange that I can counsel others on all of their problems but I've been realizing since I've met you that I have my own set of baggage. I guess I've been carrying it around for a long time. I'm working on it, Adam.

Really I am. But I have to admit that I felt a moment of panic when you said it, and still do," she smiled nervously.

"The 'it' you are referring to is called love. And, even though I realize you can't speak those words yet, I know they are there. I can tell even though you don't want to admit it, even to yourself. I can be patient. The words will come." Smiling at her, he put her arm through his. "Don't worry, I'm not going to smother you, I'm just going to love you. Are you hungry?"

"A little. What are we going to tell Heather?" Sarah Ann was happy to turn the conversation back to Heather.

"I can't believe that she didn't know why her mother was in the hospital. My gut feeling is just to say she'll be out shortly and try to get her to open up as much as possible. It's more to change her perception of why she's being treated that way and help her to realize that it's not because of who she is but because of who her parents are. Maybe she'll be able to understand that circumstances mould people into becoming who they are, as they have done with both you and I. If she could realize that it's because of the problems they've got and that they more than likely don't even know how to act any differently than they do. I would love to see her removed from that environment but if we can't prove what's happening, we can't remove her. And it seems that no one is willing to talk, including Heather."

"Most counselors would say after seeing her that it would be an almost impossible job to help her with self-esteem and confidence but I saw how much my mother changed after she began to feel better about herself. But Heather has to have things in her life that will make her feel happy. Does she have any friends?"

"No, she seems to stay pretty much to herself. I wouldn't be surprised if she is depressed as well. Perhaps she should be taken to a medical doctor for his opinion on that. Also I think we should try to discover if she has any particular interests or talents and give her an opportunity to be involved with them." Adam shook his head sadly as he thought about the lonely young girl.

"A nice haircut and some special clothes would probably help her too." Sarah Ann laughed. "She may become our full-time project if we're not careful. Before we know it we'll be taking her to dinner with us. Actually that may not be a bad idea to do occasionally. I'll bet she's never been to a real restaurant before."

"You're getting quite involved in this, aren't you?" Adam smiled lovingly at her.

"Often all a child needs to succeed in the world, no matter what their background has been, is to have one person who truly believes in them and who cares about them. We can be that one person." Sarah Ann laughed. "My mother didn't have anyone who ever truly loved her or believed in her as a child, except for such short periods of time that it didn't accomplish what it should've done. But her friend, my Aunt Katrin, did a lot for her by gradually helping her to build her self-esteem. I would like Heather to have the opportunity to develop some confidence before she becomes an adult. If she does, she won't likely fall into the same situation as her mother, or my mother for that matter. I call it the 'sins of the fathers' but I guess it could be called the 'sins of the mothers' as well, in many cases."

"Yes, we could be that one person but I won't say anything more along those lines in case you find your running legs." Adam smiled as he took her hand.

Sniffing at the delicious aromas, Sarah Ann realized how hungry she really was. After deciding on grilled salmon, she took a sip of wine. "I was talking to my mother earlier today and she's going on another cruise. I'm so happy that her life has finally come together and that she's enjoying the years she's got left."

"I would like to meet your mother one day. She sounds like a great person. In fact, I would like to meet your whole family someday. They all sound like such wonderful and interesting people. Would that feel like too much of a commitment for me to meet them?" Adam smiled innocently at her.

"They've all been asking when they're going to meet you too. I told them that if they got to meet you, they weren't to make anything out of it. They said that I had some crazy ideas and probably shouldn't be a counselor. It's a family joke – theirs, not mine."

"I promise that I won't make anything out of it either if it makes you feel better. So when will I meet them? This weekend?"

"Are you pressuring me, Adam?"

"No, I'm not. I was trying to be funny but obviously I'm not."

"Obviously," Sarah Ann answered dryly.

*   *   *   *   *

"You're bringing Adam for dinner on Sunday? That's wonderful, Sarah Ann. You've never invited a man for a family dinner before. You must be serious about him," her mother was ecstatic.

"Don't jump to conclusions, Mom," Sarah Ann snapped. But seeing the hurt expression on her mother's face said, "I'm sorry, Mom but the word serious is a pretty scary word. It's almost as bad as the word commitment. We are not serious. We are friends. I know," she smiled at her mother, "I've been carrying those pieces of baggage with me my whole adult life. Maybe someday I'll be able to say that I'm serious because I'm ready for a committed relationship. And when I can do that, I'm hoping it will be with Adam; if he's patient while I work through my hang-ups. Right now he's coming as a very dear friend, nothing more."

"He can come as Donald Duck if he wants to, I'm just looking forward to meeting him. I hope you are able to work through your issues too, Sarah Ann." Holding up her hands, Elsa smiled, "And those words are not criticism, my dear, they are a hope. From what you've said about Adam, he sounds like a very nice man. Since Willie and the twins have found such nice girls, I've been hoping the same for my daughters too."

"It's easy to tell that you spend the day reading children's stories but Donald Duck, he won't be. Unfortunately we have all been tarnished with the brush of Father but I think we will all eventually work through it one way or another. I've been trying to work on how I feel about relationships ever since I've met Adam and I do think that those little tentacles of fear don't threaten to strangle me quite as often as they once did."

"It would be a shame to let a good one go because of fear if your gut feeling tells you that he's the right man. How do his colleagues treat him? His friends? With respect? Do they obviously like him? It's usually a good indication of who he is if he's well liked and respected by the people he works with."

"He is. That was the first thing that struck me. The students he works with all seem to adore him too. Even this little girl we're both counseling but she's another story. She comes from a background similar to yours and she's rather fearful of men, like many of the young girls I work with who are experiencing such traumatic happenings in their lives."

Elsa shook her head. "What we do to our children. When all of you were born, I loved you so much and tried to make up to you what your father didn't give in the way of love. I'm afraid there was no love in him to give anyone. But I wasn't able to stop the harm he did. If I had been a stronger person, the harm he did might not have caused the problems they have. I wanted so much for all of you to be happy. I wanted everything for you that I didn't have. Unfortunately, that didn't happen."

"Don't feel badly; you did the best you could under the circumstances. We were far luckier than you were Mom because we all knew we had your absolute love and for that reason, you have nothing to feel badly about. You, and only you, made us the people we are. So if we have a few problems, they're not your responsibility and you have to admit that we are all quite successful. That's something! We all should get down on our knees and thank you for what you were able to do against so much adversity."

Elsa smiled at her eldest daughter. "My wonderful daughter; how proud of you I am." Giving Sarah Ann a hug, she continued, "Well, I can hardly wait to meet Adam. I think everyone will be here for dinner so we'll have quite a houseful."

*   *   *   *   *

"Hello, Mrs. Stewart," Adam extended his hand. "I've been looking forward to meeting you and the rest of the family." Sarah Ann noticed how Adam looked around the room, including all of her large family with his smile.

During the visit, Kathleen pulled Sarah Ann aside and in typically Kathleen-style said, "Umph, he's pretty good looking but is he as nice as he appears? Most aren't, you know."

"Oh Sarah Ann, if there was another man around like Adam, I think I'd have trouble doing my studying so it's probably a good thing that I haven't found one like him yet," Melissa whispered.

Rebecca threw her arms around Sarah Ann's neck and whispering in her ear said, "Good catch. If you find another one like him, let me know and I'll be there quick as a wink."

While Adam was chatting with Willie and the twins, Elsa put her arm around her daughter's shoulders. "He seems like a lovely man, Sarah Ann and he seems to be genuinely fond of you. I've been noticing how thoughtful he is with you and how his eyes light up when he looks at you. The eyes can speak more loudly than any simple words could ever do. I feel very happy just seeing the expression on his face when he looks at you, Sarah Ann."

Sarah Ann smiled warmly at her mother. "I know he's a wonderful man, Mom. He and Willie and the twins seem to be getting along very nicely."

"I would think Adam could get along with everyone. I don't think you have to worry about him in that respect, Sarah Ann."

*   *   *   *   *

As they left her mother's place later that evening, Adam reached across to take her hand. "I had a wonderful time, Sarah Ann. Your family is great. Your brothers and I are planning to go golfing together. You didn't tell me that they were all such avid golfers."

"It seemed a moot point. I didn't really think that you would be meeting them quite this quickly, Adam." Sarah Ann smiled, squeezing his hand as she spoke.

"Was it so scary allowing me a little further into your life?" Adam looked sideways at her, a quizzical expression on his face.

"I have to admit that it felt more comfortable than I thought it would. You fit in with my family very well, Adam. Everyone seemed to enjoy your company."

"I'm glad to hear that because I very much want to be part of your life. Part of your whole life, Sarah Ann."

"When are we meeting again with Heather?"

"You have a habit Sarah Ann of changing the subject when you don't like the conversation. What would a psychiatrist have to say about that, I wonder?"

"You're not answering my question, so who is changing the subject?"

"You know what I mean but that's alright. One of these days I'll break through your reserve and your reluctance to become seriously involved. I'm convinced that it will happen, Sarah Ann. As for Heather, I have another meeting with her on Monday. I hope it hasn't been another bad weekend for her. I would think her mother is out of the hospital by now. Are you available to meet with her too?"

"I have Monday morning free of appointments if that was when you were meeting with her."

*   *   *   *   *

"Hello Heather, it's nice to see you again. How was your weekend?" Sarah Ann smiled at the young girl huddled in the corner chair.

Shrugging, she said, "Okay." Looking up briefly she added, "My mom's home. She looks different."

"I'm glad to hear that she's home, Heather. Perhaps she lost weight while she was in the hospital; that would make her look different. Were there any problems over the weekend?"

Heather shrugged her thin shoulders. "It was okay."

"I'm glad. I have been thinking about you the last few days and wondered if there is anything that you are interested in and would like to do but haven't had a chance to do. Perhaps you would like to do some painting? The art teacher said that you have quite a lot of talent in that area. We could get you some of the materials you would require."

Shrugging again, in a low voice she said, "I couldn't do it at home, my father would throw everything away if I took it there."

"Why is that, Heather?" Sarah Ann put her hand on the young girl's arm.

"He'd say it was a waste of time and I should be helping my mom with the chores."

"Well I'm sure we could arrange for you to have a place to paint here, if that's what you would really like to do, Heather," Adam interjected. "Would you?"

"You'd do that? I could really paint?" Heather sat up straighter in the chair, a look of excitement transformed her face.

"Yes, we'll get some supplies for you. In fact Heather, you and I could go one day after school to get your painting supplies. Also, I was thinking that we could get our hair cut too. I need a haircut and I think you'd really like my hairdresser. Would you like to do that?"

Heather shifted slightly, interest evident in the shy look she turned on Sarah Ann. Whispering, she said, "A haircut? A real haircut? And paint supplies?" With a look of disbelief, she quietly asked, "When can we do that?"

"I'm free Thursday afternoon, how about then?"

*　　　*　　　*　　　*　　　*

After Heather had left the office, Sarah Ann and Adam smiled conspiratorily. "I think you're making some headway," Adam said as he hugged Sarah Ann. "I've never got more than a few words out of her at any one time before. I'll bet from now on we'll start to see a huge change in her although I hope her parents don't negate everything we're trying to do. From what I hear the girl has a lot of potential with her artistic talent."

"Hopefully our influence, and what we're doing for her, will help give her enough self-esteem and confidence so she will be able to see her parents more objectively than how she sees them now. If she doesn't take everything personally, she will become stronger and will be able to avoid a lot of what is now happening to her."

"You're right but now she's intimidated and frightened. When she feels that she looks better and realizes that she's very talented, she will look at herself differently.

Hopefully we can get her to where she will look at herself in the mirror and say, 'I don't deserve to be treated like this and I'm not going to take it any longer'."

"It'll happen." Sarah Ann glanced at her watch. "Oh dear, I didn't realize it was so late. I'd better get back so I can get ready for my afternoon appointments."

"I appreciate what you're doing for Heather, Sarah Ann. I was also thinking last night that we had such a nice weekend when we drove back from Prince George, why don't we go away again. Perhaps this weekend; what do you think?"

Sarah Ann felt the familiar gripping of nerves in the pit of her stomach but she had to admit that it was much less than she would have expected. Smiling at Adam, she said, "Uh....it would be nice but....."

Adam pulled Sarah Ann into his arms. "No 'buts' Sarah Ann and no pressure. At least you didn't say a definite no. Are we starting to make headway with you as well, Princess?"

"Maybe just a little bit, but we'll see. Where were you thinking we could go?"

"I know a great little island; it's one of the gulf islands. But if we go there we should leave on the Friday evening so we have more time to enjoy ourselves because travel takes so long with the ferries. Do you think you would like to do that?"

*   *   *   *   *

Holding hands while they walked along the shalestone beach, Sarah Ann smiled at Adam, "This was a wonderful idea. It's such a romantic place to be. Look at how the sun sparkles on the water. I almost feel hypnotized when I watch the waves roll onto shore."

Laughing, Adam said, "I'm glad to hear you say that. Especially since you have avoided romance as strongly as you have. Maybe we really are making some progress with our Sarah Ann. Hypnotized you say? That opens up a whole other field."

"A figure of speech only Adam. Although I admit you do seem to weave a bit of a magic spell in the air around you, the word commitment is still a scary sounding word."

"I'll have to work on it then, won't I? How are you feeling about the word trust?"

Sarah Ann laughed. "I'm doing a little better with that than I am with commitment."

"I'm glad to hear that too. How would you like to test trust a little?"

Sarah Ann hesitated. "Uhm. I'm not sure, Adam. What do you have in mind?"

"Well I know you're a little uncomfortable around the water but I was going to suggest that we go kayaking, maybe just in a bay until you get comfortable with it. You'd be wearing a life jacket and I'm an excellent swimmer. I wouldn't let anything happen to you, Sarah Ann. Are you willing to give it a try? It's not the same kind of trust that you're afraid of but it would be a beginning."

Sarah Ann froze at the idea of being in a kayak remembering that her father had died at the bottom of a lake. "I don't know, Adam. I can't swim very well. I don't think I can do it. It isn't about trust. It's about fear."

"It is about trust, and facing your fears, Sarah Ann. It's a different kind of fear but fears are fears. First of all it is almost impossible to tip a double kayak, secondly I wouldn't go where there were waves, we'd be in a sheltered cove and thirdly, you would be wearing a life jacket. But even assuming the unlikely event happened and you fell out, I used to be a lifeguard so you would be completely safe with me. I hope that you would trust me enough not to let any harm come to you. So you see, it is very much about trust. I also think it's a good idea to get over your fear of the water. You did say, didn't you that there was some speculation that your father didn't drown; that he may have disappeared instead. So maybe your fear of the water, at least based on your father drowning, can be dispensed with."

"I know there were some that thought he may have planned his disappearance but what if he did really drown? I'll think about it, Adam and if we do practice the trust thing, maybe we could do it tomorrow – not today."

Adam nodded his head and they walked along the beach in silence for a short time. As they walked, Sarah Ann saw several things she would've commented on to Adam, but feeling he was disappointed with her, she made none. Giving herself a mental kick, she was determined to trust Adam the following day.

Adam was the first to break the silence. "There are some hiking trails just up from the point here. Do you want to explore them? It's a beautiful view so you'll be able to get some really great pictures," he said looking at her camera. "I'm afraid I forgot to bring mine along."

"I'd love to. I'm glad you brought me here; it's so beautiful. Oh look Adam, you can see some of the other islands from up here."

"That's the mainland over there. And those are some of the other gulf islands, smaller ones than this one though. Listen Sarah Ann, I'm sorry. I wasn't angry with you; only disappointed." Putting his arms around her, he pulled her to him.

"And I'm sorry too. I really will try tomorrow, I promise."

"Don't worry about it if you're not ready. It's just that you probably miss out on a lot of wonderful opportunities in life because of your hang-ups and fears." Adam kissed her on the forehead, her nose and finally a lingering kiss on her lips.

Later as they watched the sun sink lower in the sky, Adam smiled down at Sarah Ann, kissing her briefly. "I didn't know it could be this wonderful," he told her. "I think we are good together, Sarah Ann."

Sarah Ann hesitated momentarily before gently letting her fingertips trace the outline of Adam's cheek. Gently she kissed the corner of his mouth, "Yes, I think we are good together but don't read more into that comment than I'm prepared for right now."

"I love you, Sarah Ann. I can't imagine my life without you. And I hope that one day soon you will be able to say those words too." Not waiting for an answer, because he knew there would be none, he took her in his arms and kissed her more fiercely than he had previously.

Later she had lain awake, tormented with her thoughts. She had wanted to say the words she knew he wanted to hear. The words and the feelings were there; but to say them would have made her feel as if she had given something of herself away and she didn't think she was ready for that yet. Even if it was to Adam.

*   *   *   *   *

The following morning Adam had been up early. After his shower, he lay quietly on the bed beside her. "Wake up Princess, I have a surprise for you."

Sarah Ann's eyes fluttered open. "What is it?"

"Ha, I knew that would wake you up. We're having champagne and orange juice. We're celebrating."

Sarah Ann sat up quickly, panic beginning to take hold of her. "What...," she looked nervously around, "are we celebrating?"

Handing her a tall, bubbling glass, he said, "We're celebrating 'Us'."

The panic was beginning to take a stronger grip of her. "What do you mean we're celebrating 'Us'?

"We're celebrating 'Us', as a couple who have fun together, who enjoy being together, who can converse and who have the same interests. I for one like being part of the 'Us' team. I can only assume that you do too or you wouldn't be here. Am I right, Princess?"

Sarah Ann wasn't sure where Adam was going with all of this and her feeling of panic was threatening to consume her. "Uh, we do have fun together and we do have the same interests." Hesitating, not sure if she wanted to hear the answer, she asked, "Is that the only reason for the champagne and the celebration?"

"Yes. There will be other reasons sometime but for today, that's the main reason. Don't look so worried, we're just celebrating being 'Us'. Have you thought anymore about going kayaking today, Sarah Ann?"

"I did. After you fell asleep last night, I did quite a bit of thinking about being out on the water and I would like to go. And you're right, it's about time that I gave trust at least a little bit of a test." Sarah Ann felt a nervous shiver go through her as she said the words.

Adam smiled, his eyes lighting up his face. "Are you sure, Sarah Ann because I'm not going to force you if you're not sure?"

"We'll do it Adam, before I change my mind." Laughing she grabbed his hand.

*   *   *   *   *

"Heather, I've seen some of your paintings. You do beautiful work. Have you taken any of them home to show your parents," Sarah Ann smiled at the young girl.

"Thanks," she answered shyly. "I'm not going to take any of them home. My father would burn them or tear them up."

"Would you mind if I took a couple of them and hung them in my office? Also Mr. Bennett said he was hoping that you would agree to have some of them framed and hung in the hallway near the school office."

Heather's face was wreathed in the first real smile that Sarah Ann had seen on the child. "You will? No one has ever said my paintings were that good before."

"They are excellent. I like your new hairstyle too, Heather. It's very becoming and I've heard you've received a lot of compliments about it."

Nodding, Heather said, "A couple of girls told me they really liked my hair. They even asked if I wanted to have lunch with them."

"So things are going better at school, are they?"

"School is better. It's pretty much the same at home though, at least when my father is there. He works away more though and we all like that. I think even my mother likes it better since she's been in the hospital."

"I'm glad things are improving," Sarah Ann commented quietly. Sarah Ann glanced quickly towards Adam hoping that her words wouldn't cause Heather to clam up.

"He seems to yell more than he hits now. I think it has something to do with my mother having been in the hospital. A lady came and talked to both of them."

"I have a story I'd like to tell you about a family and how things turned out for them. There is quite often a happy ending to a sometimes sad story."

Glancing briefly at Sarah Ann, Heather smiled hesitantly.

"The story begins when a young child was born into a family where she didn't feel she was loved by either her mother or her father. They were extremely poor and her mother was tired and overwhelmed and mistreated by her husband. Her father treated his family poorly because of the many disappointments and frustrations and the way he felt life had treated him. As her father began to realize that life was not going to be the way he thought it would be, he took his anger out on his wife and his children. He was a blamer; he blamed everyone but himself for all of his misfortunes. He later thought drinking would make his world better. In time he was not able to go through a day when he didn't drink in an effort to drown his frustrations. Of course that didn't solve his problems and, in fact it only increased them twofold. As his behaviour worsened, her mother became even more unhappy. Raising her children became an even more difficult task and eventually she fell into the bitterness and frustration trap that her husband was enmeshed in. This child grew up with no confidence or self-esteem and as a result, she married a man who was much like her father. This often happens. Her husband also was not happy with his life and took his anger and bitterness out on his wife and later his children in the same way that her father had. It became a vicious circle. As a result her children all suffered in much the same way she had suffered at the hands of her father. Fortunately for them, their mother had a lot of love to give – love she never received as a child – and she had a determination to do better than her own mother had done. Later her husband disappeared and she discovered she was stronger than she thought she had been. She established a business for herself and raised all of her children by herself. Her confidence and self-esteem grew each day. She is now happy with her life, as are the children and as a result, they have become a very close-knit family. I like stories with happy endings and this is one that I like to tell.

"Also, I've told you about my mother; she reads stories to children. She has been looking for someone who might be interested in helping her occasionally in the afternoons. If you are interested in meeting her and working with children reading stories, it would mean earning some spending money. How do you feel about that? Mr. Bennett and I would be with you if you wanted to meet her. Would you like that?"

Looking down at the floor, Heather shrugged. "I don't know. I would like to but I don't know. Maybe she won't like me."

"If that's all you're worried about Heather, I can assure you that my mother, Mrs. Hall, will like you very much. Also, I was wondering if you would like to come shopping with me? I need to buy some things and I saw an outfit that I thought would look spectacular on you. Would you like to come along on a girl's shopping trip?"

$*$ $*$ $*$ $*$ $*$

Elsa pulled her daughter aside. "I can hardly believe this is the quiet, shy girl you told me she was. She's been quite talkative with the children since she got here and she seems to have a way with the little ones."

"I was hoping that the two of you would get along together but I have to admit I'm a little surprised myself that she is this talkative. She seems to have completely opened up to you and the children. Watching her with them, I think she'll do very well with the reading groups. What do you think?. And if she earned a little money for helping, she'd be able to buy a few clothes and other things that girls her age would like to buy. I bought her a few clothes and got her a hair cut but I think it would be much better for her self-esteem if she felt she was earning the money herself."

"I agree. I could start her off immediately with one or two afternoons a week. And if she works out well, I could give her more hours as long as it doesn't interfere with her school work." Elsa smiled at her daughter.

"Also Sarah Ann, I've been spending more time with your grandmother. William Alexander doesn't get around that well with his leg so he doesn't see her very often and with Elizabeth away, I try to do what I can for her. She hasn't been doing very well lately. If you have time, I'm sure she would enjoy seeing you."

"Mom, you are wonderful. Letting Heather help you will mean so much to her. As for Gram, I feel guilty that I haven't been over to see her for a while. I'll try to do that this weekend."

"You should take that wonderful man of yours along with you." Elsa laughed when she saw the expression on her daughter's face. "As I said before, you could do a lot worse than being serious about Adam."

"When we were away last weekend, I think I mastered my trust issue. Adam convinced me to go kayaking with him. I went, even though you know how I am about deep water. That was a big step for me but I finally made a decision to put my trust in him. I think I may even be mastering serious – just a little."

"So that leaves commitment. It looks like you're doing almost as well as some of the young people you work with at overcoming your problems." Elsa drew her daughter close to her, a tear slowly trickling down her cheek. "I feel so much guilt about what was done to all of you children! A crime was committed," she whispered.

"Mom, you committed no crime. The sins were father's and you were the victim as much as we were."

*   *   *   *   *

"Hello Gram, I'd like you to meet Adam Bennett. He's a very good friend of mine." Sarah Ann was surprised when she saw how frail her grandmother had become since she'd seen her last.

Janet's small, veined hand lay on the coverlet of her bed, her gnarled fingers playing with the folds of the material. The faded blue eyes carefully searched Sarah Ann's face trying to remember which of her many grandchildren this one was. "Ah, Sarah Ann. You haven't changed, dear. You never change. You are as beautiful as when you were a child. And as I've told you before, you are the most faithful of all of my grandchildren. I'm not complaining, dear, I know how busy all you young people are. It is always a treat to see you."

Sarah Ann smiled, "You remember that Aunt Elizabeth and her family live in Alberta now, don't you, Gram? And Alexander William only has his one son, Douglas and he's away in England now. So that just leaves us. And I'm sure the others will come to see you as soon as they are able."

"Yes, yes dear, I remember all that. I'm not senile, you know." Her watery eyes drifted in the direction of Adam. "And who did you say this young man was again?"

"Adam. He's a school counselor. The work that we do is very similar."

"I understand you're from Scotland, Mrs. Stewart? I was there some years ago on a teacher exchange program. It's a lovely place."

Her eyes shone brightly with unshed tears as Adam spoke about her homeland. "'Tis sad—never to have gone back to my home. Mam Stewart was like a mother to me. I missed her when we left. I didn't want to leave Scotland but my husband insisted. He said that the streets would be paved with gold when we got here." She shook her head sadly. "Things weren't good back there but they weren't good here either; at least not most of the time. Your mother can tell you that, dear." She looked off in the distance before turning again to look at Sarah Ann and Adam.

"Life plays strange tricks while it leads us along different paths, Sarah Ann. Elsa, your mother, now she didn't have it good but she's done more for me than could have been expected of her, and more than the rest all put together. People have different stuff in them and you never know and appreciate it until sometimes it's almos' too late. Your mother has good stuff in her, Sarah Ann and I feel a huge guilt that I didn't appreciate it before now." A tear trickled slowly down her wrinkled cheek. "Your mother," she looked away momentarily, "now she deserved much better than she got."

"I'm sure you deserved better than you got also, Gram." Sarah squeezed the frail, old hand. "Mom has told me stories about Grandpa. I guess he didn't die very happily either. It's a shame though that he took his unhappiness out on so many people. I think we could all be happier if we looked at the positive things we have in our lives rather than concentrate on the negative things. From what I've heard about Grandpa, his eyes and heart only saw problems, he never appreciated what was good." She felt Adam squeeze her hand.

"We won't talk 'bout him, Sarah Ann. He's been gone a long time and there's no point in dredging up a lot of painful things that nothing can be done about." Smiling at Sarah Ann and Adam, she said, "It was very nice of you two young people to come and visit an old lady. I think I'm just about worn out for today. I hope young man that you will come back another time." Looking at Sarah Ann, she whispered, "What was his name again, dear?"

Chapter III

"All of Heather's teachers are amazed at the change in her. She's made several friends, she walks with confidence, she smiles, she can answer questions when asked but the biggest change is in her appearance. Since she's been working with your mother, and has money to be able to buy new clothes, she has taken so much pride in her appearance. I kind of suspect though, that she keeps her new clothes in her locker and changes when she gets to school. She'd probably have to share them with her sisters if she took them home."

"I'm so glad to hear things are going well for her. Even if she has to keep her new clothes in her locker, she has learned to adapt to her situation and learned how to make things easier for herself. I wish that all of our clients had that ability. My mother has become quite fond of her and thinks she's quite an amazing girl. Heather gave Mom one of her paintings. She has it hanging in her bedroom on the wall above her bed."

"So we've got Heather on the right track towards becoming an emotionally healthy young lady. How is Sarah Ann doing with her hang-ups?"

"My hang-ups? Haven't you noticed a huge difference? I think trust has been pretty much taken care of, wouldn't you say?" Smiling she added, "Is there any other young person you're dealing with that requires my help?"

"Not at the moment, Princess. You haven't finished answering my question. What about serious?"

"I think I'm doing pretty well with serious too." Leaning forward she kissed Adam gently on the lips. "Elliott and Charlotte have invited us over for dinner this weekend. Would you like to go?"

"You're doing it again. You change the subject every time you don't want to answer a question. Okay, you're doing not too badly with serious too since I assume that taking me to Elliott's and Charlotte's for dinner is a first for you. Now what about the big one, commitment?"

"Adam, you know how I feel about you. Do you want to go to Elliott's place?"

"I'm fairly sure that I know how you feel about me but I would like to hear you say it, Sarah Ann. Why is that so difficult, Princess?"

Sarah Ann could feel the tears stinging behind her eyelids. Why couldn't she? She knew that Adam deserved an answer. "I guess because I feel that I would be owned; that I would lose part of me; part of my independence and if things didn't work out between us, that I would be stuck; like my mother was." The tears spilled from the pools of her eyes and streamed down her face. Wiping them away, she looked away from Adam.

Nodding slowly, he lifted her chin so that she was forced to look into his eyes. "I'll wait, but not forever. I want marriage to be in my future. And children. I want a family, Sarah Ann."

*   *   *   *   *

Sarah Ann had lain in bed that night, sleep alluding her. She had felt the cold sliver of fear as it had sliced through her body at his words. In previous relationships, with those words she'd have been gone with a flip of her hair and not a backward glance but with Adam, everything was different. She loved him but she wasn't sure if she'd ever be able to tell him how she felt. Even to her, 'I love you but I don't want to be married to you', didn't sound much like love. At least it didn't sound like any story book tales of love she had ever read about. *'But,'* she shrugged defensively, *'real life isn't like story book tales.'*

The phrase 'commitment phobia' came back to her; she remembered it from her training but at that time there had been no need to apply it to herself. There had always been sane and reasonable explanations why she had left previous relationships. Sometimes they were too possessive and if there was anything she disliked, it was someone who wanted to possess and control her. She had been accused in the past also of being too picky but she really didn't believe that had ever been the case. She just couldn't imagine spending her life with someone who she didn't feel comfortable with or that she felt wasn't the right person for her. Thinking about it, she definitely didn't feel that 'phobia' was the right word to use in her case either. However, she had to admit that she did have a small commitment issue. Glancing at the clock, she realized that it was three-thirty a.m. and sleep was still a long way off.

With her training she was forced to realize that her commitment problem went back to the days of how her father had behaved and particularly with how he had treated her mother. She knew she had a fear of giving up her freedom; the ability to control all aspects of her own life and the fear of feeling trapped in something she couldn't easily get out of if she wished. For this reason, she realized as she lay there that she had kept a distance between herself and Adam in order to avoid having to make any strong commitment that would lead to marriage.

'But I do love Adam!' The thought startled her into a new awareness. Thinking of the look in Adam's eyes when he had said he 'would not wait forever', she knew she loved him and didn't want to lose him. *'Do the good things in the relationship outweigh the bad things? Silly question,'* she smiled to herself. Offhand she couldn't think of anything negative with respect to Adam. *'Is our relationship worth fighting for?'* She knew it was. *'If only I can get over my fear of commitment. Do I want to be with Adam more than I fear what commitment will mean to me?'* In the early morning light Sarah Ann decided she would have to think about what she really wanted in life.

*   *   *   *   *

During the following weeks Sarah Ann and Adam had gone to her brother Elliott's home for dinner where they had both enjoyed the children; gone for a hike around Bunzen Lake and had taken in a movie one evening. And everytime they were together Sarah Ann could feel Adam watching her and waiting to hear the words she hadn't yet been able to say.

"Have you thought at all about the conversation we had about your commitment problem, Sarah Ann?" Adam had finally asked one evening when they had gone to a quiet restaurant for dinner.

Looking around the restaurant, her eyes rested on a young couple at a nearby table. Reaching across the table the man had gently stroked the lady's cheek. Taking his hand, she had smiled into his eyes and Sarah Ann saw the whispered words of endearment and the look of love softening the young woman's features. She felt a wrench in her heart. She knew she felt the same kind of love. It was alive but hidden deeply within her like a caged animal fighting to escape and not knowing how. Tears stung her eyes, she kept her face turned from Adam for fear that he would see them.

Reluctantly she finally turned to face him, managing a small smile. "I have," she whispered. But seeing the look of unhappiness on his face, she turned quickly away. Her eyes again rested on the young couple chatting animatedly together. They appeared to be so happy and in love. Still not prepared to face Adam, she continued to watch them.

"Do you want to tell me what you have been thinking, Sarah Ann?" Adam gently intruded upon her thoughts.

Sighing she turned to face the man she loved. "I realize I have a problem with commitment, Adam but I think it will just take more time." She searched his face but wasn't sure what she saw there.

Adam sighed deeply. "Sarah Ann, you're a counselor and you admit you have a problem. Have you ever considered getting help with your problem?"

Sarah Ann shook her head. "It has never been a problem until now but I think I can work it out on my own without having to go to a counselor." She looked around as if searching for an answer. "I really do think I can, Adam."

Adam refused to let up on her. "What will you do, Sarah Ann? Do you think the problem will just disappear on its own? It's such a deep-rooted problem that I don't think it will. I told you before that I would like to marry you. I would like to have children with you. I would like us to be a family. I know we could be happy together. Will you get help, Sarah Ann?"

She had given him no answer. She had felt that saying she was going to get help with her commitment problem was almost the same as telling him she loved him. She would be losing her independence and she would not be in control of her own life.

*   *   *   *   *

The following week she heard nothing from Adam and another type of fear began to grip her with a force that took her by surprise. A part of her wanted to call and tell him she loved him. But she couldn't. As time went on, she knew she didn't want to live her life without him but still she hesitated to set up an appointment with a counselor.

"Sarah Ann, we haven't seen you for a couple of weeks. Can you and Adam come for dinner on the weekend?"

"I've been busy lately Mom and, uh, Adam and I haven't seen each other for awhile."

"Sarah Ann, I'm sorry. I thought you two were getting along so well. He seems to care so much for you."

"Maybe that's the problem. You know how I feel about commitment. I've been burying myself in my work and…well, I haven't heard from him for over two weeks."

"Have you thought about seeing a counselor, Sarah Ann. Even doctors see other doctors, you know. I think if you could get over this problem, you and Adam would be happy together."

"Adam suggested the same thing as well. I thought I'd be able to work it out for myself."

"You haven't been able to so far, my dear."

"Adam said he wanted to get married and have children. We had a discussion and then he just walked away and he's left me with the responsibility of contacting him. I can't believe he's gone this long without calling me."

"I don't blame him, Sarah Ann. He's told you exactly how he feels and I can't see that you've made an effort. From my point of view, I can see you have three options. Either you decide that you can make a commitment to Adam, or if you are unable to on your own and still want to have a relationship with him then you will have to see a counselor or you just walk away and never see him again."

The thought of never seeing Adam again caused a sharp pain to knife through her heart. "You're right, Mom. I have never felt like this before and I do miss him desperately. You know that old adage, 'if you love something, set it free…'. That's what Adam did. I think I will go and see a counselor."

However, after a third week had rolled around, Sarah Ann still hadn't gotten around to making an appointment with a counselor.

"If you haven't seen a counselor, have you at least spoken with Adam, Sarah Ann?"

"No Mom, but I'm going to call him. I think we have to at least talk although maybe he's given up on me by now. Because this is such a difficult issue for me, I'd almost forgotten the importance of communication. As counselor's we're always telling our clients that there has to be communication and I haven't followed my own advice."

Her hand reached for the telephone and then drew back. *'What is wrong with me?'* she asked herself. *'Do I really need to talk to a counselor? No,'* she decided with determination.

Finally with her heart pounding and her fingers trembling, she dialed the phone. "Adam, I've been doing a lot of thinking. Can we get together and talk?" She could hear the tremor in her voice.

"Of course, Sarah Ann. I was hoping you would call but I was going to leave it up to you. When do you want to get together?"

*   *   *   *   *

"We've got a lot of things to discuss, Adam. At least I have a lot of things that I would like to discuss with you; things that I have been thinking about since I saw you last. It's been very difficult. I've had to do a lot of soul-searching; a lot of dredging up of my past and I realize now that there are a few things about myself that I am not happy about or proud of. For a counselor, I have to admit that I have some very major hang-ups. I've discovered that it's a whole lot easier to be objective about other people's problems and lives than about my own. I hope you will be patient and will try to understand how I have been feeling."

"You've made a start by thinking about the problem and by deciding to discuss it with me. That's a huge start, Sarah Ann and I'm very glad that you've made it."

"I've thought about the relationships that I've had in the past and realize that as soon as anyone got too close to me or I started to feel engulfed, I backed off and left the relationship. I always had very good excuses for why I had left. But when I look back at those relationships now, I realize my excuses were exactly that – excuses to get out of them.

188

I feel badly now because I know I've hurt some who loved me very much. With many, I left with some very flimsy excuses; I realize that now. I didn't do that with you because I knew that what we had was very, very special. So I allowed it to go beyond where I have allowed other relationships to go. But then I became frightened when I felt I was being pressured to commit further to our relationship. You were right and I was wrong. It wasn't an unreasonable expectation on your part. I knew you sensed that I had distanced myself, especially as I began to feel more closed in. I think it was then that you became more serious about getting to the root of my hang-ups. It is probably a good thing that you forced me to really look within myself to see how I truly felt and to decide what I really wanted. When you left and didn't call me, I was shocked. That has never happened to me before. I was always the one who did the leaving. Besides forcing me to think about how I felt about you, it also forced me to look at my own role in my relationships."

Adam looked apprehensive, nodding occasionally while Sarah Ann spoke. "And have you decided now what you want?"

Sarah Ann nodded her head without taking her eyes from Adam. "Yes, I have. I've decided that I'm going to face the challenge of overcoming my commitment issue because I do love you, Adam. There, now I've said it, and I mean it; with all of my heart, Adam." She squeezed his hand and smiling nervously she whispered, "I really do."

Adam pulled her into his arms. Kissing her, he softly replied, "You have no idea how much that means to me, Princess. While I was letting you think through your commitment issue, I wondered if I had done the right thing. You have no idea how happy I am that you got the courage to utter those three little words. Was it really so difficult?"

Laughing, she said, "No surprisingly. I guess because the words came from my heart and were just waiting to be spoken. I finally decided that now was the time."

"What other challenge has to be addressed now, do you think?" Adam asked her, a questioning look on his face.

"I think we should discuss that soon but not right now. I feel like such a weight has been lifted off me now."

"This isn't more about changing the subject is it, Sarah Ann?"

"No it isn't, Adam. With everything I've been thinking and worrying about for the last few weeks, I feel as if I've been on a treadmill for a month. Could we jump one hurdle at a time, Adam?"

"I understand that," Adam smiled hopefully at her, "but admitting that you love me is just the beginning. You know that I want to get married and have a family. Loving each other is where that will take us. Are you ready for that?"

Sarah Ann put her arms around his neck and drawing him down to her, she kissed him gently. "I really do want 'Us' to work, Adam. Just be patient with me for a little while longer and help me if I happen to go off track a bit."

Chapter IV

"I was talking to Heather today. You wouldn't recognize her from that skinny, frightened little girl you met, Sarah Ann. She's so busy lately between her painting, working with your mother and her school work that you'll have to make an appointment to see her. Her grades are very good too; unbelievable in fact. I wouldn't have thought there could ever have been such a turnaround in such a relatively short time in anyone before."

"I'm glad. I would like to see her, it's been quite a while. I became quite fond of her." Sarah Ann took Adam's hand as she climbed over a log. "I love it down here. The sunsets are always so beautiful. Maybe we should bring her down for fish 'n' chips sometime soon."

"We could do that one day. Would you like to go for dinner on Friday at The Horizon, Sarah Ann? We can see great sunsets from up there too."

"I'd like that, Adam. I love all the wonderful seafood they have and like you say, the sunsets are fantastic."

"We haven't been since shortly after we met and on Friday, it will be one year. Did you remember that?"

Sarah Ann squeezed Adam's hand and smiling said, "I did remember. Where did the year go? It's hard to believe."

Adam pulled her into the circle of his arm. "It's been a pretty good year all in all, hasn't it, Princess?"

Looking into his eyes, Sarah Ann knew that he was thinking about the three weeks when their relationship had not been going very well. Smiling, she kissed him quickly before they headed back to the car.

*   *   *   *   *

Sarah Ann smiled as she looked around the restaurant. Plants hung from the ceiling and small white lights shone subtly through the small shrubs in the oversized pots on the deck. Miniature evergreen trees in large tubs were placed strategically beside each table, allowing privacy for each diner. They had been placed at a window seat in a cozy corner of the restaurant where they had an unbelievable view of the city below them. As the sky darkened, the sunset would be breathtaking and the lights of the city would be like jewels strewn at their feet. It would be a scene fit for royalty.

"This is even better than the last time we were here. We didn't have a window seat then." Sarah Ann had noticed that Adam had worn a tie which he usually wore only in dire circumstances or special occasions. Smiling, she pointed to his tie, "In honour of our special occasion, I see. I can't think of a nicer way to celebrate our one year anniversary of meeting each other than by coming here. What a perfect idea, Adam." Breathing deeply she thought, as she so often did, about how thoughtful Adam always was and, how lucky she was to have met him.

"I asked specifically for a window seat when I made the reservations. I thought you might like to enjoy the view of the city while we eat." Adam reached across the table to take her hand, squeezing it as he did so. "As for the tie," he smiled boyishly, "a special occasion warrants a tie, don't you think?"

Nodding she smiled before popping a sizzling shrimp into her mouth. Her eyes opened widely, "Wow, that's spicy! But delicious. I've never had the sizzling shrimp appetizer before. I'll need more wine, I think." Laughing she held out her glass so Adam could refill it.

The sun was starting to set on the horizon when Adam said, "Come on, bring your wine glass. Let's go out on the deck and watch the sun go down before our dinner arrives."

Sarah Ann looked around before whispering, "Can we do that?"

"Certainly we can." Putting his arm around her shoulder, he led her out into the cool evening. The air was heavy with the scent of flowers hanging in baskets above their heads and in the planters on the deck at their feet.

"Isn't this lovely? It surpasses even what we can see from our table." Putting his glass on top of the railing, he took her glass and placed it beside his. "This is the first anniversary of our meeting Sarah Ann and I wanted it to be special because for me, it was a very important day of my life. I hope it means as much to you as it does to me."

"I know I've had a few issues to deal with, Adam but I am so very happy that we met. I had thought my life was good before. I was happy and contented, but I didn't realize what was missing in my life until I met you."

"I would like to be able to spend the rest of my life with you and I hope you feel the same way." He hesitated before asking, "Do you, Sarah Ann?"

Sarah Ann's mind raced. Sensing that this was going to be a serious conversation she quickly reasoned that she was okay with serious now. She was even quite sure, after that bad three week period, that she was fine with commitment as well. Looking into his face, she saw his love for her deep in his eyes.

"I know how awful those three weeks were when I didn't see you and wondering if I ever would see you again. I can't imagine not having you in my life forever. I also know without a doubt that I love you too, Adam."

"I'm very happy that you feel that way and I'm happy that you've been able to tell me. I wanted this dinner to be very special, not only because it is the first anniversary of our meeting, but..." Adam hesitated, searching her face.

Sarah Ann suddenly realized what Adam was going to say next and felt a momentary flash of panic that left her feeling breathless. She knew that she loved Adam but marriage? Marriage was so final; it was the ultimate commitment. Was she ready yet for that?

"What I'm trying to say, Sarah Ann, is that I'd like you to be my wife for the rest of my life. I'm not saying that we have to get married right away but I would like us to be engaged. We can wait as long as you want, until you feel comfortable about getting married. Will you say that you will marry me when you're ready to get married?" He drew a jeweller's box from the inside pocket of his jacket and opening the lid, took a sparkling diamond and emerald ring out of the satin interior.

Hesitating, Sarah Ann looked at the ring, a design of diamonds set within a horseshoe shape of tiny emeralds. She searched Adam's face, then whispered softly, "I do love you Adam. And I would like us to be engaged, but not right now." Putting her arms around his neck, she kissed him, whispering, "And I do want to get married – eventually – but not yet. Do you understand, Adam?" She saw the disappointment reflected on his face as he replaced the ring inside the velvety box.

"I won't rush you, Sarah. But," he reminded her, "I won't wait forever. Let's get our dinner now."

Dinner was a quiet affair and Sarah Ann despaired when she looked into Adam's eyes. She realized that she had hurt him and she wasn't being fair to him. *'Perhaps,'* she thought as the silence lengthened, *'I should tell him not to wait for me. If I can't commit now, maybe I will never be able to.'* But the thought of living life without Adam created another train of thought. *'What am I afraid of? I love him. I want to be with him. I know he would never try to control me. I would have his love and...'* her heart lurched, *'his children. We would be a family.'*

"Adam, could we go out on the deck and talk again – where it's quieter and more private." Putting down his fork, he followed her outside.

Standing on her toes, she pulled him down so she could kiss him gently on the lips. "I did some thinking while we were eating, Adam. You surprised me; caught me off guard. I would like to be engaged now – that is, if your offer is still open. But I would like a long engagement." She smiled, tears forming in the corners of her eyes.

"Princess, are you sure?"

Sarah Ann nodded her head, "I'm sure Adam."

Taking her hand, he unsteadily placed the ring on her finger. "I'm not used to doing this," he smiled, his eyes bright. "You have no idea how happy you have made me."

Adam smiled down at her before taking her in his arms and kissing her tenderly on the lips.

"I had ordered champagne earlier hoping that this was the occasion we would be celebrating. Shall we go inside now? You look as if you're getting a little cold out here. Or is it nerves?"

"Probably a little bit of both," she laughed.

Inside, at a nod from Adam, the waiter brought the champagne to their table in a silver ice bucket. With the bubbles tickling her nose, Sarah Ann smiled at Adam.

"You had this very well planned, didn't you, Adam? I guess I very nearly ruined all your plans."

"That thought occurred to me when I made the reservations but I was hoping with all the thinking you've been doing lately that it would work out as well as it has. And I was hoping that you would come to the realization that marriage isn't an end but a new and wonderful beginning. And it will be for us, Sarah Ann. We have so much to look forward to together. I believe that if ever there were two people suited for each other, it's you and I." Smiling, he picked up her hand and looking at the ring said, "It suits your hand. I had it custom-made for you."

"It is beautiful, Adam. I can see the significance to 'Us' in your design of the ring. That makes it even more special to me." Sarah Ann looked at the 'S' design of the diamonds with the raised portion of emeralds in the shape of a horseshoe surrounding them. Her eyes filled with tears when she thought of Adam designing it to signify their own unique relationship.

*   *   *   *   *

"You did it. I'm happy for you, Sarah Ann. I feel very strongly that Adam will be a good husband to you. I have seen nothing that would make me think otherwise. At least one of my daughters is going to get married!"

Sarah Ann laughed. "We haven't talked about a wedding date yet Mom. We're in no rush. I would like to have a long engagement period – it will make the lead-up to the wedding more exciting, don't you think?." Elsa eyed her daughter suspiciously.

"I thought I would invite everyone to come for dinner this Sunday as a celebration of your engagement. Do you mind if I invite Heather as well?"

"It's been quite some time since I've seen her. How is she doing?"

"She does so well with the children that I'm encouraging her to become a teacher. She said she thinks that's what she would like to be;

she would like to help children who come from homes like hers. She wants to be like you and Adam. I knew from the first time I met her that she had a lot of potential. You both gave her the tools to work with. Her painting abilities have improved vastly too."

"I hope she can make it; I would love to see her again. Don't go to any trouble Mom; just a nice simple meal with the family would be great."

*   *   *   *   *

The weather was warm and sunny when they arrived at Elsa's and the family rushed to them with congratulations. Sarah Ann noticed that Heather held back shyly but there was a bright smile on her face when she saw them.

"Congratulations, old man," Willie shook Adam's hand. "I didn't think anyone would ever manage to capture our elusive butterfly here."

"I don't believe anyone captures your sister, Willie. I believe it's a mutual decision but thank you for your good wishes," Adam laughed.

"Sarah Ann," Melissa danced happily around her. "I'm so happy for you." Smiling at Adam, she asked, "Do you have a brother, Adam?"

"Not one that is available, Melissa but if you're looking, I'll keep my eyes open for you."

"I didn't think you'd ever do it, Sarah Ann." Kathleen looked as out of sorts as she always did. "I thought you and I would be the last ones to succumb, if ever we did. I'm still not convinced that marriage is what it's cracked up to be, as nice as Adam seems to be." Sarah Ann ignored Kathleen's typically 'Kathleen' comment.

"I'm going to be writing my end of the term exams in six months so you can keep your eyes open for me too, Adam," Melissa smiled.

"So when is the wedding going to take place, you two?" Elliott was pleased with the engagement announcement. "Now I won't have to take Sarah Ann golfing with me." He winked at Adam. "Looks like you get the honors."

"We haven't set a date yet, Elliott. We're not in any rush at all," Sarah Ann quickly answered her brother. "We plan on having a long engagement."

"Considering what Sarah Ann's attitude has always been about marriage, I'm surprised you got her as far as an engagement." Martin spoke quietly, laying his hand on Adam's shoulder. "I think she's left a trail of broken hearts behind her."

"Your family seem to be convinced that I'll never get you to the altar. Shall we set a date now to prove to them that we really do plan to get married?" Adam smiled at Sarah Ann and taking her hand, he gently pulled her over to stand beside him. Holding up his hand, he said, "I'm not saying that it has to be soon," he added, whispering in her ear. "We could make it a year from now if it would make you feel more comfortable."

"Can we all make some suggestions?" Rebecca excitedly took Sarah Ann's other hand. "Are you going to have a big wedding or a small one?"

"We haven't really discussed any wedding details yet, Rebecca," Sarah Ann looked around at her family, excitement and happiness clearly written on every face. "Really everyone, we have made no plans because it's going to be a long engagement," she insisted.

Glancing at Adam with a smile, she said, "But I don't believe it will be a big wedding. What do you think, Adam?"

"Now that you ask me; what do you think about a small, intimate wedding?" Looking around at the group watching them, he added, "Well maybe small won't work with this family."

Sarah Ann groaned. "We haven't made any plans yet but when we do, you will all know. I think you're all ganging up on me; I can see it on everyone's face." Looking at Adam, she said, "Look at them; they're all so anxious to be part of the plans. Have you ever seen such a family?"

"I don't mind if you don't mind, Princess. You've got a great family and I don't mind if they're part of the planning process as long as we have the final say."

"I knew he was great, Sarah Ann. Mom, what do you think about having the wedding here?" Rebecca looped her arm through her mother's.

"Rebecca, you can't expect Mom to have it here. We'll have it at a hall; whenever we decide we're going to have it."

"But when are you going to have it? That's the most important thing to decide. I hope you have it before I have to sit for my exams," Melissa sat down beside her sister.

Sarah Ann shrugged, looking at Adam, she said, "And you want them to be part of the planning process? Come and sit over here beside us, Heather. Since everyone else is part of the planning process, you should be too."

"Why don't we have the wedding in late August? That way we'd still be able to go away for a honeymoon before school went back." Adam smiled at Sarah Ann.

"Yes, that would work for me," Melissa said happily.

"And it's not too long to have to wait, Sarah Ann because I'm so excited that I wouldn't want to have to wait too long," Rebecca leaned down to kiss her sister's cheek.

"And I've already booked my holidays for that time so that works well for me too because I hate having to change them once I've booked," Kathleen half-smiled when she looked in Sarah Ann's and Adam's direction.

"We'll all pitch in to help," Elsa smiled looking around at her daughters. "We want this to be the nicest wedding anyone could possibly imagine."

"And just let us know what Elliott, Martin and I can do and we'll be there." Willie, Sarah Ann noticed, was wearing a very big smile himself. She smiled to herself to see that her brothers were as excited about this event as her sisters were. This would be the first wedding of any of the girls in the family.

"Looking at the calendar, what do you think about August twenty first?" Rebecca placed the calendar on their laps, her finger pointed excitedly to the date.

"Umm, what do you think, Sarah Ann? It might work."

Sarah Ann groaned. "I was thinking of a long engagement. That's not a long engagement."

"It is. It would be almost six months. At least set the date, Sarah Ann," Rebecca pleaded. "Please."

"I think we may have to decide on a date before we leave or they'll never leave us alone for the rest of the day," Adam smiled at her.

"August twenty first," several voices called to them.

Sarah Ann's thoughts were tumbling inside her head. Surely six months would give her time to get her fears under control, she thought. With a sigh, she said, "Okay, the twenty first it is; now are you all satisfied?" She looked around at her family with a mixture of love and exasperation on her face.

"Good, now that's settled," her mother smiled. "Now we can get down to the matter of planning it." Sarah Ann laughed at her now not-so intimidated and quiet mother, thinking briefly that if her father had lived, this would have been a very different scene.

* * * * *

As the weeks sped by, plans were made with Sarah Ann having only momentary feelings of panic when she thought about marriage being forever. Admonishing herself, she would remember that forever was what she wanted with Adam. She knew there were no doubts about her feelings for him and she had no doubts about how he would treat her as a husband. Knowing that her only doubts were because of her commitment issue, she always managed to push the momentary feelings of panic into the background.

The wedding was going to be very much a family affair with all of her sisters standing up for her. Kathleen, when asked, had been a little reluctant, not sure if she wished to be involved in something she didn't wholly believe in. However, she eventually succumbed when Melissa's and Rebecca's excitement became too much for her. Willie was going to give her away and Adam was going to ask Elliott and Martin, along with a long-time friend, to stand up for him.

"It has always been a dream of mine to make my daughters' wedding gowns," Elsa told Sarah Ann as she deftly pinned here and there for the final fitting. "You are going to be the most beautiful bride I have ever seen," she smiled at her daughter with tears in her eyes.

"Thank you, Mom," Sarah Ann was having difficulty controlling her own tears. "I'm taking Heather to get an outfit for the wedding. She said you had asked her to sit with you. I'm glad you did that. She so badly needs a family."

"She has us. Everytime I had a new baby, I was happy because I always knew there was room in my heart for one more and I think that

199

for each of us, our hearts are capable of expanding to be able to love all the new people that come into our lives. We have certainly done it with Adam and we will be able to do it for Heather too."

Sarah Ann threw her arms around her mother. "You are wonderful. You have always had so much love to give, even when you had little else. Thank you for everything, Mom."

"We'll have to stop this business or we'll be a mess when Adam comes to pick you up. We'll make him nervous if he sees tears on our faces. Only one week now! It's hard to believe; the time has gone so quickly. You are happy, aren't you, Sarah Ann?"

Sarah Ann hesitated. "I feel a little panic once in a while and sometimes the feeling of things closing in engulfs me but I suppose that's normal this close to a wedding date. But I do love Adam."

"It is. I don't think you're the only bride who has felt that and I'm sure most grooms also have their moments of panic too, dear."

*   *   *   *   *

Waking up for the last time in her own bed on the morning of her wedding, Sarah Ann experienced panic so severe that it had taken her breath away. *'Could she go through with it, even as much as she loved Adam?'* She lay there willing the fear to go away as she tried to convince herself that marriage was what she wanted. Without a doubt she knew Adam was who she wanted to spend the rest of her life with. She wanted to have his children and wanted to share everything life held with him. *'It's not like I'm agreeing to have my arm amputated and I'm not agreeing to obey.'* They had written their own words for the ceremony – love, honour and cherish was part of them but she would not agree to 'obey'. With an effort she calmed down and climbing out of bed made her way to the kitchen for a much-needed cup of coffee.

When Sarah Ann entered her mother's house later in the morning, she heard the frantic commotion. "Where is she? She's late! You don't think she got cold feet do you, Mom?" Melissa asked.

"You know what Sarah Ann has been like when it comes to marriage." Rebecca's voice rose shrilly above the music from the radio.

"Calm down, Rebecca and Melissa," she heard her mother's calmer, but slightly nervous voice answer. "She loves Adam; she wouldn't leave him in the lurch. If she wasn't going to go through with it, she would have told him, and us, before now."

"She's a runner. She always has been," Kathleen joined the conversation. "My guess is that she isn't going to show up."

"Stop talking nonsense girls; she'll be here," Elsa's voice was stern.

"My bet is she won't. She was pressured into this by everyone in the family. You know she wanted a longer engagement," Kathleen said.

Sarah Ann, feeling slightly guilty about eavesdropping, sat down on a kitchen chair. Clutching her going away outfit to her, she knew that today was the day and there was no turning back now. Reminding herself that feelings of panic were natural for every bride and groom, she walked slowly into the living room, a smile on her face.

"Well I think Sarah Ann and Adam are going to be perfectly happy together and I think it's going to be a lovely wedding. Oh Sarah Ann, we're so happy to see you." Melissa hugged her sister tightly to her.

Sarah Ann heard the sighs of relief around her. "Did you all think I wasn't going to show up?" She smiled at her mother and sisters, feeling suddenly very calm.

"Well, you know…" Rebecca began, then seeing her mother shake her head, didn't continue with what she had been going to say. "We'd better start getting ready."

*   *   *   *   *

Getting out of Willie's car at the church, Sarah Ann glanced at her watch and realized they were almost fifteen minutes late. "Rebecca no, we don't have time to stop at the washroom; we're already late."

Through the slightly open doors she could see Adam, handsome in his black tuxedo, a worried expression on his face as he gazed down the empty aisle. She knew what he must have been thinking; perhaps had been thinking all morning as he had waited and hoped, fearful that her commitment issue had not been completely resolved. Filled with anxiety, he undoubtedly wondered if she would show up at the church. She realized that there had been moments earlier in the day when she had wondered herself but now she knew without any doubt that this was what she wanted to do.

The doors gradually opened and the wedding music filtered to where she stood with her arm linked in Willie's, behind the procession of bridesmaids. Watching Adam, she saw his face slowly transform with a smile she knew she would remember for the rest of her life.

Epilogue

Elsa watched Heather reading with the children. No one would have guessed she was the same frightened and unhappy girl that Sarah Ann had first met. *'Things can and do change,'* she thought remembering the unhappy periods of time in her life. And there were many before Peter drowned those many years ago.

She had never been happier than she was now. All of her children were doing well; even Rebecca, the youngest would be heading off to college soon. *'Yes, they had done well for themselves,'* she smiled to herself.

Elsa thought back to Sarah Ann's wedding almost four years ago when no one in the family was sure whether she'd show up for her own wedding; she'd come a long way since then. With one child already and pregnant with her second, Sarah Ann continued with her private counseling practice and was still as spunky as ever. *'And they're so in love,'* Elsa thought as she watched their son leaf happily through his favorite 'Winnie the Pooh' book.

Heather's gentle voice kept the children's attention; they were always disappointed when the reading came to an end. Elsa clapped her hands together. "We'll just finish up this story children and then we have to clean up. Your parents will be here shortly to pick you up."

"Aw Mrs. Hall, I don't want to go," one little voice called.

Elsa smiled at Heather. At seventeen, she had grown into a lovely, self-assured young woman with plans firmly in place to become a school counselor. She still lived with her mother and siblings but the abusive step-father was gone. He had died of a heart attack three years previously and another, slightly kinder, step-father had taken his place shortly after. Elsa was glad that Heather came almost every day to help with the children – it helped both of them and she was very fond of the girl. Heather had become as much part of the family as any in their fast-growing family.

Driving home she thought about Tony. *'Are you going to marry Tony?'* Sarah Ann had recently asked her. *'You've been seeing him for years – or do you have commitment issues like I used to have?'* her daughter had smiled. *'He's popular with everyone in the family.'*

Elsa liked Tony very much, but was she really free to marry? Peter's body had never been discovered and she periodically wondered if he really was dead. Whenever she mentioned the possibility everyone assured her that he must be – he'd never have remained out of sight for this length of time.

"Hello Tony. I was just coming in the door when I heard the phone ring. What time did you want to get together? Dinner? Well, give me an hour or so; it sounds lovely. Is there a special occasion?"

Sitting across the table from Tony at their favorite restaurant she smiled and watched his gentle smile light up his warm brown eyes. Tall and slim with thick salt and pepper hair, Elsa liked his looks and everything else about him. "What's the occasion?"

"You'll have to wait to find out, my dear," his eyes twinkled. "How was your day?"

"Tony, surely the special occasion isn't to find out how my day went. Out with it – I'm really curious now."

"Since you're being so insistent – there are two reasons really. First of all, remember when I told you that the newspaper might send me away for three months to do a story about what's been happening in Cuba – well they've finally set a timeline."

"Cuba? When?" Elsa's heart stopped beating momentarily when she heard his words.

"Next month. They want the scoop on how the Soviets have been assisting Cuba and a story on the political regime. There's a rumor that the Soviet Union has begun working on a submarine base on the southern coast of Cuba. In 1962 there was a missile crisis so many people are worried about what this means. Raul Castro seems to be the second most powerful figure in the government. The newspaper feels there are several good stories and they want me to get them."

"But Cuba, Tony. It would be such a dangerous place to be," Elsa felt tears prick behind her eyelids.

Tony reached across the table and entwined his fingers with hers. "Elsa, I won't be going to a battlefield. As journalists we have the right of access to information; we are allowed freedom of expression and are legally able to communicate this information within the limits permitted by national law and of particular individual interests. I rather suspect that Castro wants to have his side heard."

"Oh Tony, I would hate for anything to happen to you. It's not a stable country. We still hear terrible stories about what's been happening there."

"That's why the newspaper wants to see what the true story really is. There are legal provisions to protect journalists and I won't be in any physical danger of war – I promise not to put myself in that position."

"But three months....."

"As a journalist I will be given special authorization to go and as such, I will have protection. A civilian is granted protection by the international humanitarian law given to all civilians. And the time will go by quickly. Do you feel any better now?"

"No. I've heard that some visitors to some of these countries have been arrested, or been victims of abuse and some have even disappeared – all done by the authorities in that country. Who will protect you against something like that happening? What if something happens to you and we never see each other again?"

Squeezing her fingers and smiling, Tony said, "Are you trying to tell me something, Elsa?"

Elsa realized how devastated she would be if anything happened to Tony. He had been a constant part of her life for several years and she suddenly realized how much having him in her life meant to her. "I'm afraid I don't feel very hungry anymore, Tony."

"Remember I said there were two reasons. I hope you feel better about the second one because I do assure you that there will be no danger to me. If there is, I promise I'll come home right away."

"I know you well enough to know you wouldn't leave – you're always adamant that the story needs to be told. What is the second reason?" Elsa's heart was pounding with a nervousness she wasn't sure why she was feeling. Could the second reason possibly be worse than the first?

"Well my dear, my love; you know how I feel about you," Tony's loving eyes searched her face.

Elsa nervously nodded her head. "And I feel the same way, Tony. That's why I'm so worried about you going to Cuba."

"We'll talk about Cuba again later, but…Elsa, I would be a very happy man if you would agree to marry me when I return." He took both of her cold hands in his large warm ones. "I would like you to be my wife."

Her heart slammed against her ribcage. *'Was she free? It had been almost sixteen years since Peter had disappeared but was he really dead?'*

"Oh Tony, I would love to be your wife but I have never been sure if Peter is really dead."

"It's been a long time now. He's gone, Elsa. Can I hope that your answer is yes?"

$$* \qquad * \qquad * \qquad * \qquad *$$

"Elsa, how are the plans going for the wedding? I'm sorry I can't be there to help you, dear." Elsa could hear the smile in his voice over the long distance lines.

"The children have all been helping. The hall, the photographer and the flowers are all taken care of, Tony. How are things going there?"

"I'm staying in Havana right now. It's a very interesting place. There have been some black pictures painted of Cuba but from what I've seen, after ten or so years of revolution, there are improvements here in child care, public health and housing. The Cuban Negroes also now have equal status with the whites. There is an embargo on imports so growth has been slow recently but it has helped that they have diplomatic relations with the Soviet Union."

"Do many people speak English?"

"That has made things a little more difficult. I'm glad I have the little bit of Spanish I have plus I never leave home without my dictionary. I've missed you Elsa."

"I've missed you too. When do you think you'll be back?"

"I'm hoping in five or six weeks; six at the most. And two weeks home and then it'll be our big day. You're not nervous, are you?"

"No Tony. Even Sarah Ann with her past commitment phobias and Kathleen who until recently harbored anger against all men are both very excited. My whole family likes you very much so how could I possibly be nervous? I can hardly wait until you get home."

"I'm glad to hear that. Getting access to a phone is very difficult here Elsa but I'll try to get in touch with you again before I leave Cuba. I love you Elsa." Suddenly the phone line went dead.

Savoring her conversation with Tony, Elsa wandered into the kitchen for a cup of coffee. "Mom, I tried calling you but your phone line was busy," Sarah Ann called as she came through the front door. "Could you look after Teddy while I go to the doctor's office? I've been getting some cramping and the nurse said to come in as soon as possible for a check-up."

"Of course dear but I think it would be best if I came with you. It's probably not a good idea to drive in case the cramping gets worse. Just wait until I get my jacket."

*   *   *   *   *

"Braxton Hicks pains again; I'll be glad when the baby is born. This is the third trip to the doctor for them. Do you have any herbal tea in the house, Mom?"

"It shouldn't be too much longer, Sarah Ann. Yes, there's some in the corner cupboard. I'll go check the answering machine; I see the red light is flashing."

Elsa clicked the play button and an eerily familiar but unwelcome voice filled the room. "Hello dear wife. It's been a long time since you've heard my voice. I'm sure you're anxious to welcome your husband back home." His laughter was still echoing in her ears when she swung towards her daughter.

"Sarah Ann, what am I going to do?

207